SELECTED

Brian J. Lynch

Cover design by Colette Sybert

Interior art design by Brian J. Lynch

Editing by CD McKenna

First paperback edition April 2025

Paperback ISBN: 979-8-9987828-0-0

eBook ISBN: 979-8-9987828-1-7

DEDICATION

An indescribable amount of thanks is due to all of my supporters. Without the persistent reminders of your enjoyment from the beginning, I may have lost motivation along the way.

Additional credit is due to Micah Campbell and Chelsea McKenna at Anatolian Press for bringing my story to a larger audience, and to Colette Sybert for the cover design. Seeing the world in my mind come to life is amazing.

Finally, to Karen, this was only possible because of you. I love you.

NOTES

The recommended reading order for these stories, while not in chronological order, is as they appear in this collection. In the ambitious hope that you will want to read about Seb and his friends again, you may find that swapping Part 2 and Part 3 will provide a new view into the minds of the characters.

TABLE OF CONTENTS

PART 1: Zero-Day

PROLOGUE

Sebastian, or Seb as his friends called him, was excited and nervous about what would likely happen this week. If all went as expected, his light would soon be solid. He was down to the last of three. The other two were already solidly lit, and the third had recently started to blink faster, indicating that it was almost time. Once the final light also turned solid, that would be the end of him.

The instant all three lights on his arm were lit, the Global AI would take over. It would run the show from that moment forward, having learned enough about Seb's habits, mannerisms, and overall life to handle things for him. Each day would be the same. Seb would wake up, go to work, sleep, perform the necessary inputs and outputs, and continue repeating this process until his body finally gave out. He would be on autopilot.

Seb was in his thirties now. This was roughly the average age for conversion. His parents made it to their thirties too. He did have friends who were still in full control. However, others had dropped out of school, worked the same job for years, and barely made it to their twenties before being taken over. The more monotonous a person's life, the quicker the Global AI seized control.

The current lifetime record of 101 years is held by a serial hobbyist named Jim. Only one of Jim's three lights turned completely solid before his body gave out on its own. Something about his entirely unpredictable nature kept the Global AI from locking onto him.

Seb was nothing like that. At this point in his life, he did things almost as if he was already following a script: wake up, work at the factory, eat the food needed to maintain his energy, watch some entertainment on the hologram, and sleep.

CHAPTER 1

This day started the same way every day did for Seb. He was lightly nudged awake by the vibrating bed alarm at exactly seven in the morning. He stretched slowly and rubbed his eyes, looking at the faint glimmer of artificial light coming from the display on the wall.

Seb's dwelling was in the middle of a large complex housed in thick recycled concrete. He had no windows, so a screen projecting the concept of the morning sun was his only imagery of the outside world.

Seb hopped out of bed, undressed fully, and meandered to the steam room. He stepped inside, slid the door shut behind him, and pressed the button to activate the steamer, letting out a quiet "Brrr" as the first cool droplets touched him before the warm steam hit. "Why do I always forget to turn this thing on first?" he asked. Seb stood in warm quiet bliss while the steamer cleaned and sanitized his body before automatically shutting off after the allowed five minutes. The warm air dryer started after the steamer shut off, and had Seb completely dry in no time.

He walked to his open closet and began flipping through his clothes looking for something to wear. He had to decide between the blue, the dark blue, or the slightly lighter, but not that much lighter, blue. "Decisions, decisions," he said, as he grabbed a set of blue coveralls and put them on. He ran his fingers through his hair, took a quick glance in the mirror, then headed to the kitchen.

Seb pulled out the drawer where he kept his stash of breakfast protein nutrient bars. "Skim nut butter or cocoa and kelp?" he pondered, his hand wavering over each.

He finally pulled out a skim nut butter package, tore the end off with his teeth, and took a bite. Seb folded the wrapper over the uneaten portion of the breakfast bar and stuck the rest in his pocket as he headed to the front door where his work boots sat. He slid them on his feet and bent down to pull the tightening cord before standing back up to grab the door handle and step into the hallway.

It was quiet in the hall this morning. Seb looked at the other people moving around and found his place in line to get onto the platform lift. No one had anything to say while moving forward in the organized group. *Good, none of these Global AI-controlled people want to interact today*, he thought. *Usually, each one just wants to discuss the weather or scores from the game last night.*

Finally, it was Seb's turn to get onto his platform. Seb was scared of heights, and even though there was a floor underneath his feet, there was still something daunting about stepping onto a platform just large enough for two people with only a small railing to hold on to. The feeling was exacerbated by the platform continuously moving without stopping, especially when doing so from the 21st floor. He rode down while staring blankly at the empty platforms on the other side of the continuous loop going back up. Once he arrived at the ground floor, he quickly stepped off before the platform started its ascent. Seb moved through the complex's lobby and out the main door of the building.

He walked to the sidewalk's edge, carefully sliding through the people walking in both directions. Looking ahead, he saw the hyper taxi coming toward him to his transport stop. *Perfect timing.* That meant he would only need to wait another moment for it to arrive. After the hyper taxi glided to a stop at his pickup spot, Seb and several other riders got on.

The Global AI-controlled driver nodded at each new rider, saying, "Welcome! Thanks for joining us," as the hyper taxi pulled off to head to the next stop.

Seb aimlessly walked toward the seat where he always sat. He almost didn't notice someone else sitting there until he was right next to them. The rider was looking down at their lap, not noticing Seb staring at them while he tried to gather his thoughts. Seb shook off the uneasy feeling and moved to the open seat in front of his usual one. He sat down, scoffing. That was not how he wanted to start his day.

Seb was barely settled when his audiophone made a *chirp* to indicate that he had a call coming in. He looked at a band on his wrist that displayed the text *Mom* and rolled his eyes.

Even after the Global AI took control of one's actions, it still made sure parents called to check in on their children periodically.

"Hi, Sebastian," his mom said. "How are you this morning?"

Seb didn't reply. He knew the beginning of the conversation was always predetermined. It didn't matter what he said, or didn't say, his mother would reply with, "That's good, honey."

Impatient, Seb finally asked, "Was there anything for you to report to me?" It was often that his mom called to tell him to wear a jacket if the weather was below a certain temperature or make sure he was eating foods with the right vitamins.

"No, dear. I just wanted to call and say hi. Can't a mother do that? Have a good day, but watch out for the—"

Beep.

Seb tapped the band on his wrist to end the call as soon as he heard her say, "No." Out of the corner of his eye, he saw the lights on his arm and noticed the last one blinking. He realized he would soon be just like his mother.

He had a few spare moments before the hyper taxi would pull up to the stop at the factory. He removed his Rollascreen from his pocket, uncurled it, and loaded the news for the day. February 12th, 2332. It read:

Sunny today. Rain planned for tomorrow.

Shortages of synthetic beef expected
Explosion at the West Side Plaza leaves one injured

New Global AI additions: 5,362
Global AI removals: 436

"Removals," Seb scoffed. "436 dead people is more like it. No one is *removed* from the Global AI."

Before he could continue reading, the hyper taxi glided to a stop. Seb rolled up his Rollascreen and put it back in his pocket. He stood to depart while staring out the hyper taxi's window at his factory. "Another day, another—" Before he could finish, the rider behind Seb who'd taken his usual spot pushed past so aggressively that Seb fell back into his seat. Seb was dumbfounded and completely shaken. No sooner than he could gather his thoughts and stand back up, the hyper taxi had already closed the doors and started moving. Seb threw his hand up and yelled out to the driver, "Hey, stop! I'm supposed to get off here."

The driver replied, "Welcome! Thanks for joining us. We're on to our next destination." Seb put his hand back down and sat with his mouth agape.

He noticed his protein nutrient bar had fallen out of his pocket and onto the floor. Letting out a loud groan, he picked it up, walked to the front of the hyper taxi, and tossed the rest of his breakfast into the trash. While standing there, Seb looked up at the holographic display above the driver showing the hyper taxi stops. He noticed that the next location would only be a few blocks further. He would be able to walk back, but it was farther than he had ever been in this direction. He always rode directly to the factory. Before turning to go back to his seat, Seb read the time displayed next to the list of stops. He would be late. After years of working at the same place, this would be a first.

As the hyper taxi glided to a stop at the next location, Seb stood up carefully, looking around at all the other passengers before moving. He didn't want to risk any more unwanted bumps and find himself at yet another unknown destination. Finding no evidence that there would be a collision, Seb headed to the doors and stepped onto the sidewalk. He focused on the buildings around him, noticing how foreign they seemed, even though he worked within walking distance of them. He started his way in one direction before realizing it was not the way back to the factory. Stopping, Seb shook his head to clear his thoughts, and turned around. That wasn't like him. He checked the time displayed on his wristband and picked up his pace.

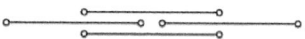

Seb arrived at the entrance of the factory and placed his hand on the door handle, but paused. Forcing a deep breath in, he let it trickle out before opening the door. He looked directly at the eye scanner mounted above the entrance. Next to it, a hologram showed in red text:

Sebastian Cedric
In Time: 8:07 a.m.
LATE

"Arg!" said Seb loudly.

Seb continued walking into the building when a loud alarm suddenly started blaring. *Is this what happens when you're late to work?* he wondered. *That seems unreasonable.*

Inspecting the lobby, Seb noticed several people running in his direction. His friend Danish was in the middle of the pack. He immediately saw Seb, and yelled out, "Seb! There was an explosion! Go!" Seb stopped, stunned. He finally snapped out of it when another worker bumped into him. He turned around and ran out the door, following the crowd of people.

Seb caught up with Danish a short distance away from the building and asked with wide eyes, "What's going on? I stepped inside the building and the alarm started blaring right after I was scanned."

"Seb, my friend, I thought you were inside. There was an explosion in your department. How were you not in there? You're always at your station by now."

Seb stammered, "I—I was late. I missed my stop off the hyper taxi after some rougher knocked me down. I'm not actually sure." He waved off the memory. "I had to walk back from the next stop and got all turned around." Seb stared at the building a little longer before facing Danish. "Any idea what happened?"

Danish replied, "I just assumed you screwed up and tried to blow us all up." He then burst out laughing. "Lucky you weren't in there, Seb. It was loud. I felt it too. I'm not sure anyone is going to make it out of that area in one piece."

Seb took in what Danish was telling him. "That's just—I don't know. That's just crazy. My department? Was anyone in there?" He paused. "So, um, what do we do now? I should be up there working. Are you sure we can't go back in?"

He suddenly felt lost, knowing he should be busy with work by now. He should be running his station in the factory, performing the same repetitive actions until lunch. Then more of the same after eating, until it was time to leave the building to catch the hyper taxi to go home at 4:05 p.m. But now his work area was supposedly gone. He sat down on the sidewalk.

"Seb, are you all right?" asked Danish.

"Uh, yeah, I think so. I just feel uncertain about what to do."

"Are you sure?"

Seb nodded.

"Well, all right, buddy. If you're okay I think I'm going to get out of here. Nothing more to do and I don't think they're letting us back in any time soon."

Seb looked up as Danish started walking away. He caught a glance at Danish's lights. Only one was solid and he was the same age as Seb.

Danish did things a little differently. He showed up to the factory at a different time every day and never went with the flow. He persistently asked Seb to come out with him to the cyber arena, the dance studio, the town center, or wherever Danish's mind decided he wanted to be that day, but Seb always said no. Danish simply walking away from the factory without looking back didn't surprise him. He wondered if he would see his friend again before the Global AI took over.

What should I do? I'm supposed to be here at work. I'm not supposed to be at home yet, and the hyper taxi won't be back this way for a while. He stood, turned toward the direction of his earlier unintended stop, and without fully knowing why, he walked.

CHAPTER 2

As Seb had noticed earlier, everything was different in this part of the city. He'd never been this far. There was never any reason to be here in the past, yet here he was. "All because of some impatient rougher," Seb pointed out. He continued walking onward, taking in the view of the buildings and the people around him.

Chirp.

Seb looked at his wristband. "Mom again? Yaaaay," he said sarcastically. He answered his audiophone. "Yes, Mom?"

"Hi, Sebastian. How are you this morning?"

Seb waited.

"That's good, honey. When are you going to give me grandchildren?"

"Bye, Mo—Wait, what? Mom, ugh. I need a partner before I can give you a grandchild. Never mind. Bye, Mom."

Beep.

"What was that about?" Seb wondered.

Seb knew dating in the Global AI era was complicated. If a person met a partner they matched with, and the match was Global AI-controlled, the only thing the person got out of the pairing was a chance for procreation. This wasn't all bad for some. But if the person wanted any hope of meaningful conversation, and some spontaneity in their lives, they had to find someone before the Global AI took control.

With Seb already being in his thirties, he knew there weren't many options left for him to find a compatible partner that was still under their own control. He began questioning why his mother would call him at a time when he would normally be at work, and why she would be asking for grandchildren. He hated when she gave him these thoughts. It would be easier for him to wait for the Global AI to take over so he would no longer care. *Soon,* he thought. *Soon.*

Seb was so absorbed in thinking about his mother's call that he stopped paying attention to where he was going. He paused and began to get worried. Without having been here before, he wasn't sure where he was or which direction he'd been walking in. He scanned the buildings around him and noticed a café across the street. *Maybe I can wait there until the hyper taxi comes back.*

Seb stepped off the curb and was narrowly missed by a delivery scooter whizzing past. He gasped, looked in all directions, then crossed the street. He moved quickly to avoid another close collision, stepped up onto the curb, and walked to the door of the café.

As he reached for the handle, a young woman came racing out. She smiled, appearing rushed. Seb shouted after her, "Hey, come on now!" He was getting tired of being pushed around.

He braced himself as the woman turned, expecting her to yell back. Instead, she replied with a wide grin, "Hey, yourself!" She stared at him and rubbed her chin. Her face lit up. "Hey, why don't you come with me?"

Seb raised an eyebrow and opened his mouth. He closed it again without saying anything.

"No, really, come on! Let's go!" she said, still smiling.

"Wha—Where?" He was at a loss for words. This woman he'd never seen before, in an area he had never been to, had just invited him to go along with her.

"Does it matter? Are you coming?"

Seb looked toward the café door, then up and down the street, while trying to figure out what to do. He finally said, "Uh, yeah, I—I guess?"

"Good! Come on now." She tilted her head in the direction she had been going, then went right back to walking at a quick pace.

Seb had to jog to catch up to her as she turned down one street, up another, and then down the steps toward the hyper loop station. Seb slowed down, hesitating.

"What's the hold up?" she asked. "We need to keep moving."

Seb faced her. "I don't know about this. I've never been down here. Where does this even go? I don't think I like this."

"Aw. Just trust me. But we gotta get going before we miss this one," she said, taking a step toward the hyper loop train.

Seb confronted her. "Trust you? I don't even know you. Why should I listen to you? I should go back."

"Suit yourself, but you already know what you're going to get if you go back. Don't you want to keep living and not be like them?" She gestured to the people surrounding them, all moving around systematically.

Seb noticed the solid lights on almost everyone's arms. They were all Global AI-controlled. The woman held up her arm to show her first light was still blinking. Seb's eyes widened.

"H—How?" he stammered.

"I'll show you, but we have to go. Now."

Seb wavered, but finally moved forward. They walked to the train and stepped onto the first open shuttle. The doors immediately closed after they entered, and the train started moving.

"Who are you anyway?" asked Seb.

"You can call me Dee," the woman said, introducing herself with a bow.

"Dee, huh. Okay. I'm Sebastian, er Seb. My name is Seb."

"All right, Sebby."

His face twisted, disgusted. "All right, Dee-y, where exactly are we going?"

"We're running."

"Running? From what?" Now he was worried he'd gotten himself in over his head.

Dee looked down at Seb's arm, grabbed it, and lifted it to show Seb his own lights. "This. This is what we're running from."

"And how do we do that? As you see I don't have a lot of time left."

"Well, let's fix that." As the hyper loop train came to a stop, Dee focused on the terminal list highlighting their location. "Been here before, Seb?"

"I haven't."

"Perfect." Dee grabbed Seb's arm again and pulled him off the train.

They walked down the corridor, avoiding other people, until Dee stopped. Seb walked a few more steps before he noticed and turned to look at her.

"I thought we had to keep moving?" he questioned.

"Hit me, Seb," Dee said, ignoring him.

"What? No. I'm definitely *not* going to hit you."

"No really. It's fine. Hit me."

Seb was confused. He made a fist and pulled back. He looked at his balled-up hand, then at Dee, and shook his head. He aimed for Dee's arm, pushed his fist forward, and missed. She had stepped to the side.

"Yeah. You weren't actually going to be able to hit me." She laughed. "I just wanted to see if you were going to be a waste of my time or if you were actually up for trying something different for once in your life. Speaking of, tell me about your life, Seb. What has you down to one light left already? You must be *pretty* boring."

"I'm not . . . boring," Seb trailed off. He started thinking about his life. "I went to school. College even. And I work."

"Uh-huh. Sure. And?"

Seb tilted his eyes downward. "Um. And. And. Uh."

"Ha. Yeah. I thought so. I could tell when I first saw you. Lost in the world like you've never been there before. It's obvious you do the same thing day in and day out. The lights give some wiggle room for new experiences like a job interview, or talking to a girl." She smiled and waved at him. "But if all you do is wake up, eat, and go to work—sound familiar there, Seb?—those lights will eat you alive. I mean, you'll still *be* alive, but will you really want to be?"

"I never put much thought into it. This is just how things work, right? It's been this way for generations. My parents. Their parents. We're born. We get a few years on our own. The Global AI takes over. Then we die."

"Yes. But we can change that. We can live. We can be alive. We can be. We can trick the GAI."

"GAI?" Seb questioned. "The Global AI?"

"Yes, that . . . thing. Whatever it actually is. Some of us think we finally found a way to beat it. Or at least temporarily trick it."

"Wouldn't I have known about that?" asked Seb. "Numbers of new additions and the ages are reported daily."

"They don't report the aberrations, the anomalies. They wouldn't want the general public to know there is a way around their system. If people knew, the GAI would lose most of its recruits, and that would be bad for business."

"Who is *they*? What's the system? What business?" Seb asked in wonder.

"Honestly?"

"Please."

"We have no idea! But it seems like they discover every breakthrough we have, and immediately try to shut it down. The GAI is adaptive. My parents learned from their parents. That's why I am where I am." She held up her arm to show her lights. "But something happened, and one day they both just went full solid. They were in their fifties." Dee stopped suddenly and cleared her throat. "My grandparents too. Maybe they were detected. We don't know. We have learned that you can't cut the lights out of your arm, or you will be immediately converted. The same thing happens if you cut off your arm. It's possible something simultaneously affected their circuitry to cause it. Either way, we're all constantly on the move, just trying to stay ahead of it."

Seb blinked a few times. "Okay. Uh. I don't, I don't know what to say. How do you know all this?"

"We've had generations of trial and error."

"Okay. Um. And who is *we*?"

"Honestly?"

"Let me guess, you have no idea?"

"Wrong! That question I can answer. Come!"

Dee grabbed onto Seb and started walking toward the stairs that led up to the ground level.

It was late morning and Seb was starting to get hungry. "Hey, Dee. Is there anywhere to get food around here? I didn't get to finish my breakfast."

"Hmm. Yeah. There are a couple of places nearby if I remember correctly. Pizza, sushi, burgers? Um—"

"Pizza!"

"Sushi it is. This way," she said, pulling Seb in the direction they should go.

Seb couldn't hide the look of disappointment on his face.

CHAPTER 3

Seb followed Dee for a few blocks until she stopped outside a sushi restaurant. "Here we are!" she said, opening the door and ushering Seb inside. They found a place to sit with a window facing the main sidewalk outside. Seb reached for the menu tablet and started aimlessly swiping through the options while trying to keep his stomach from growling too loudly. "Um, Dee, what's good here?" he asked.

Dee recited several items without looking at the menu, while Seb's eyes glazed over.

"Have you never had sushi?"

Seb shook his head.

"Seriously? Not ever?"

Seb continued to shake his head.

"Wow. Okay. New experiences all around for you."

Dee took the tablet from him, tapped a few items on the display, and put the device down.

"All right! Ordered."

He looked around the restaurant, which was nothing like anywhere he had been before. He couldn't quite decide if he liked it, but there was an uneasy feeling about being here instead of the factory. He stared out the window and began drifting into thoughts of what he would have been doing at work in his much more comfortable and familiar setting. He pictured himself sitting at his desk, setting up the system to run the sequences needed for the day, and taking a break for lunch to talk with Danish about his plans for later.

Dee snapped him out of it, like she'd read his mind, asking, "Seb, what do you do for work? Actually, no. It doesn't matter. Why aren't you *at* work today? You're dressed to be there. Am I really persuasive enough to keep you from going?" She flipped her long hair back.

"There was an explosion. In the section of the factory where I work. Or at least that's what I was told. I would be there otherwise. I'm not sure anyone is persuasive enough to keep me away."

Dee's eyes went wide. "It took an explosion to keep you from going to work?"

"Correct, and I would much rather be there."

Dee scoffed. "Why is that so important? Showing up to work every day. Doing the same thing every day. Everyone is given what we need to survive. You have a dwelling, yes?"

Seb nodded.

"And you have enough to eat?"

Seb nodded again.

"Then why suffer through the same routine all day, every day?"

He shrugged.

Their food was served as Dee questioned, "Really? That's all you have?" She mimicked his shrug. "That's better than this so far?" She gestured around at everything. "Look, let's just eat. Here, try this."

Dee passed a plate to Seb. He hesitantly reached out and took it from her. He looked around for a fork and found none. He picked up a pair of chopsticks, fumbling around with them before stubbornly stabbing at an item on the plate.

"What's this?" he asked.

"That's a dragon roll," she replied. "They're good. I promise."

Seb awkwardly moved a piece to his mouth and took a small bite.

"And?" inquired Dee. "You didn't gag."

"Not bad. It's not bad. It's not pizza, but this is pretty good. I can eat it. But I'm so hungry I think I could eat anything right now, including these chopsticks." Seb continued eating the variety of items in front of him happily.

After they finished everything on their plates, Seb watched as Dee jumped up and immediately headed for the door.

He shouted after her, "Dee! Don't we have to pay? I'm not okay with stealing. If you think breaking the law is *new and different*, then this isn't for me."

Dee laughed. "Seb, calm down. I paid when I ordered. Don't worry, *we* are not breaking any laws today. We're just breaking the norm. Keep in mind that if you do anything illegal and get caught, they can light up another light on you. And in your case, that would be bad news."

"Okay, phew." He was worried he was getting in over his head. He stood and followed Dee to the door.

CHAPTER 4

Seb and Dee walked on the sidewalk outside the sushi restaurant. Dee picked up the pace while he tried to keep up.

"Where are we going now?"

"You'll see. You don't need to know everything in advance. Where would the fun in that be?"

"But—"

"No *but*, keep up. We'll be there soon."

They walked a few more blocks until Dee stopped in front of a tall building. "Seb, have you ever jumped out of an airplane?"

Seb gave Dee a confused look. "What?" He stared at the building. "No. Why? What does that have to do with this?"

Dee narrowed her eyes and laughed. "Seb, can I guess that you haven't even been *on* an airplane?"

Seb continued to stare at the building while wondering what she was talking about.

"Well, have you?" she asked again.

"No. I don't like heights. Planes go high," he said as he pointed up. "Really, really high."

"Yes, they do, but *ohhhh* is this going to be interesting." Dee opened the door and walked in.

Seb followed her inside. He stopped when he noticed large tubes going up to the top of the building, and turned right back toward the door.

Dee grabbed his arm. "Come on. It's not that bad."

He turned back around and noticed the indoor skydivers in the tubes. As he looked up to see how high they went, he started to get dizzy. "Dee, I don't . . . I don't think so."

"Yup. We're doing it," she pressed.

Dee walked to the holographic display near the tubes and moved her finger in front of the two-person button. The display lit up with a depiction of Seb and Dee. Their faces were each highlighted on the image, with a message requesting confirmation of the participants. Dee spoke, "Yes" to the holograph, prompting two skydiving suits to pop out of the locker behind the display. "There you go, Seb. Put that on." He begrudgingly pulled the suit over his coveralls and put the included goggles over his eyes. Dee walked to the platform lift with Seb shuffling his feet slowly behind. They stepped onto the empty platform and took it up to the top.

"Why am I letting you do this to me?" he asked, more to himself.

"Almost there," replied Dee, ignoring his question.

They stepped off the platform and went to the end of the short line. As they waited for their turn, Seb fidgeted nervously.

"It'll be fine, Seb," said Dee, trying to reassure him.

He continued pacing, looking down at his feet.

"You've done this before?" he asked.

"Yup! It's amazing! I'm happy to have someone doing it with me this time."

Seb looked at Dee worriedly.

When it was time for their turn, Dee turned to Seb and asked, "Ready?" He shook his head strongly, and she nudged him through the opening of the tall vertical tube.

Seb screamed as he fell into the tube. With his eyes barely open, he watched Dee jump into the tube next to his.

Seb quickly realized that he needed to extend his arms and legs to allow the air to keep him afloat and stable. He drifted into the sides of the tube a few times before finding a position to put himself in that would keep him centered. His face remained contorted in terror while Dee stared at him with a grin from the other tube. She began spinning around, expertly controlling her speed. Dee added some flips to show off her familiarity with flying in the air.

Seb grew more comfortable in the tube as time went on but he still didn't attempt any of the tricks that Dee was demonstrating. He continued to fly flat in the air until the fans gradually spun down, letting him float slowly to the ground. He stood and sighed with relief. He walked out of his tube, went over to Dee's, and waited impatiently for her to exit. Once she did, Seb half-yelled, "I hate you."

She chuckled. "Do you, though? Was it that bad?"

"I don't think I'm doing that again," Seb replied. "It was fine, I think, but—"

"But what? Outside of your comfort zone?"

"I really don't like heights."

"All right, all right. Let's find something that'll keep you on the ground."

Seb and Dee removed the skydiving outfits and returned them to the lockers. They walked to the exit and stepped out of the building. Dee took a few steps then stopped, looking at the sky in thought. She scratched her chin for a second and then held up a finger.

"Seb!" she said abruptly. "Do you like music?"

"Yes?" he replied after some hesitation.

"Mmm hmm, mmm hmm. Do you play any instruments?"

"Guitar, some. Not the synthesized junk that everyone's using now. A real guitar, with real strings. I can't stand the—"

"Perfect! Onward we go!" said Dee, cutting off Seb as she once again grabbed his arm to lead him.

CHAPTER 5

Weaving in and out among the other people, Dee dragged Seb up one street for several blocks before tackling even more. She stopped in front of a new building. It was painted black with blacked-out windows and had a lit sign that said *Overground*. Dee grabbed the door's handle and pulled it open.

As soon as the seal for the door was broken, Seb heard music coming out through the crack. He had a small grin on his face. "Hey, a show! I think I can enjoy this!"

Dee smirked. "Come on, let's go in. We have to get you signed up."

The smile on Seb's face dropped. "What do you mean?" he asked, as they walked in the entrance. He peered into the room and saw a stage with a person singing while playing a piano. About a dozen people were watching.

"Sign you up to play, obviously," Dee finally replied.

"Whoa, whoa, whoa. Play? Up there? In front of these people. No."

"Yes, and just think, this time you get to stay on the ground!" she said, while walking over to the desk at the entrance where a Global AI-controlled employee sat.

"Here to play?" the employee asked.

"He is!" Dee replied. "Seb. S. E. B." Dee turned to him and asked, "That is correct, yes?"

Seb nodded, looking around, still attempting to comprehend what was happening to him now.

Dee turned back to the employee and asked, "Oh! Guitar. Do you have a guitar he can use?"

"Yes, there is a guitar available," they replied flatly.

"Great! Thanks!" Dee responded.

The Global AI-controlled employee wrote down the information and then faced Seb. "Here to play?"

Seb held up a finger and opened his mouth, but Dee grabbed him and led him to an empty table. They sat and watched the person on stage finish another song.

"Dee, I can't—I haven't really played in a while. I don't even know if I remember any songs anymore," he said worriedly.

"That's not what this is about. You've never come to a place like this and played in front of people, have you?"

Seb's blank stare answered her question.

"And that's why we're here now. It's not about whether you can play. It doesn't matter if you can sing well. Or if you can even remember all the words. Do something new and different, right?"

He scanned the room, anxious.

As they talked, another person was called up to the stage. They picked up a synthesizer guitar and pressed a few keys.

Seb blurted out, "Oh, no. Come on now."

Dee giggled at him. "See, anything you do will be better than that, right?"

"Ugh, I guess."

They sat in silence while watching the person stumble through two songs until a voice came through the speakers calling for "Seeb!"

Dee laughed. "I'm pretty sure that's you, Seb. Get on up there."

Dee nudged him along while he shuffled slowly to the stage and climbed the steps. He walked over to the guitars and picked one up. After plucking a few strings to make sure the guitar was in tune, he finally slung it over his shoulder and nervously walked up to the microphone. "Uh, hi. I'm Seb." He waved awkwardly. "This is the only song I can think of right now." Seb started strumming some chords while trying to remember the order. Once he was happy, he began playing while singing,

"Sunshine in my eyes. Sorrow's left behind.
All can see me here. I won't go away.
Love and more to give. Music in my ears.
Smiles here and there. Care about you all."

Seb finished the song with only minor mistakes, but grinned when he was done as applause came from the room. Dee was standing and clapping the loudest. Seb put the guitar back on the rack and stepped off the stage. He walked over to the table where Dee was sitting and stared at her.

"That was amazing, Seb! Are you sure you've never done that before?"

He blushed.

"Well, nothing like the first time! Do you want to get out of here, or stay and see if the next person will pick up another synth guitar?" she said, laughing.

Seb squinted his eyes, then turned and headed for the door. Dee quickly got up and followed him while laughing harder.

"Would you do that again?" she asked.

"I think I actually would, but I might have to learn another song," he said, smirking.

Dee smiled, asking, "Seb, I've got one more stop for us to make, okay?"

Seb eyed her suspiciously. "Okay."

"Let's go meet some of my friends that I mentioned earlier. Others that are like me."

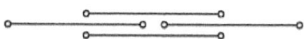

They walked through the streets for several minutes without talking while Seb replayed his small concert in his head. His eyes darted around to the various buildings they were passing, along with the people. Seb was still trying to figure out why he was here with Dee. Finally, she stopped in front of a building that looked very much like the building he lived in.

"This is where my friend Jinuh lives. At least for now. They haven't been here long. We're always on the move, you know," she said.

They walked in the door, and Dee led Seb over to the platform lift. They stepped on and began riding the platform to the top. Dee focused on him.

"So, wait. You keep telling me you don't like heights. Over and over," she said. "This doesn't seem to be bothering you, though. I don't remember it bothering you at the skydiving place either, even though you screamed when I . . . helped you . . . into the tube."

"Helped me, huh?" he snorted. "I'm at least used to this. I ride one of these every day. This is like the building I live in. And it helps when my feet are on the ground. When I'm in a place where I can't control what's around me, or what I can see, that's the problem."

"I think I understand. You like being comfortable." She shrugged. "Here we are."

They stepped off the platform at the second to top floor. Dee started walking toward a door not far from the platform lift, knocking rhythmically when she reached it.

CHAPTER 6

A short, tattoo-covered person with long blue hair on one side, and short red hair on the other opened the door. They shouted, "Dee! Good, you found my new spot!" Dee and Jinuh each held up an arm and waved their hands back and forth in front of the other's. Keeping their hands hardly an inch apart with fingers spaced out completed the greeting.

"Yup, no problems. I think Zell used to be over here a time or two ago." She stopped. "Oh, hey, this is Seb. I picked him up earlier. He was out wandering the other side after missing work because of a fire." Dee faced Seb. "Fire, right?"

"Explosion. I think."

"Hmm." Dee looked back at Jinuh. "Explosion."

Jinuh turned to Seb. "Whoa. Well, come on in. Unless you caused the explosion?"

Seb emphatically responded, "No! I promise."

Jinuh bowed. "*Ma maison* is your house, or however that goes," they said, waving a hand in the air in dismissal.

They walked into the room as Seb looked around. The living area appeared similar to his, including the screen on the wall displaying that it was still daytime. He noticed that Jinuh didn't have any furniture, or anywhere to sit except a few folded blankets on the floor. Dee saw the look on Seb's face and answered, "We don't hold on to much. We make it easy to move from place to place to try to keep the GAI confused. After what happened with my parents, I try not to take any chances, and the rest of the group is pretty much the same." Dee turned to look at Jinuh. "Is anyone else around? Can you get them over here to meet my newest . . . recruit?" Seb faced Dee as she turned and snickered. "Sorry, but I think you're one of us now."

"I'll send out a mass message now," Jinuh replied to Dee as they pulled out their Rollascreen, tapped a few icons, and put it away. They looked over at Seb and said, "Don't listen to Dee. My place is usually a lot more decorated. I just haven't had time to unpack with all these interruptions." Jinuh side-eyed Dee then continued to address Seb. "All right, tell me about you. Dee doesn't usually, or at least not always anyway, show up with someone *I* don't know. She shows up unannounced—All. The. Time!—but, with someone new? That's become rare."

Seb opened his mouth but stopped to think for a second while trying to figure out where to start. He finally began with, "Well, if you asked me yesterday, this would have been much easier to answer. I knew who I was, or at least what I did, and when, and how, and I knew that I didn't have much time left before the Global AI took over." He held up his arm to show his lights. "But today has been something . . . different. I was late to work—I'm never late to work—but since I was, I avoided an explosion, and who knows, I might have died in it, but I didn't, all because I missed my hyper taxi stop. And because my whole schedule was off, I couldn't just take a ride back home." He stared off for a moment. "I just started walking back to an area I had never seen prior. While there, I ran into Dee, or she almost ran into me." Dee giggled. "She has been dragging me all over the place after we took the hyper loop to this area. First, she took me to get sushi, but I still want pizza." He looked at Dee. "Then, she threw me out of a plane."

Jinuh's eyes opened wide. "You did what?"

Dee held up a finger to let Seb continue.

Seb chuckled. "Not an actual plane, but we went to an indoor skydiving place."

Jinuh brushed fake sweat off their forehead.

"After that, and by the way, I really don't like heights, I made the mistake of telling her I like music."

Jinuh covered their mouth and let out a pretend gasp.

"I know, I know," continued Seb. "Dee took me to . . . *Overground?*" Seb looked over to Dee for confirmation. After she provided it, he added, "She signed me up to play, and luckily I still remember one song—"

"Please don't tell me you like that synth guitar junk too, Seb," Jinuh interrupted.

Seb laughed. "No, definitely not. Only real guitars here."

"Phew!" Jinuh exclaimed.

"So, anyway, I went up on stage and played, and, well, it wasn't the worst thing that's happened to me today. But, now I'm here, all because of Dee."

Jinuh nodded for nearly ten long seconds before finally saying, "Okay, cool, cool, but I didn't need your whole life story."

"Sorry," whispered Seb.

"It's good. I enjoyed it. Lots of plot twists. I see why Dee brought you here, though. Most of the people she tells me about run off as soon as they don't get the food they want, or almost *always* at the skydiving place. *Overground* is new though." Jinuh turned to Dee and asked, "First person you found that likes music?"

"First person that's made it this far in a while, and I only just added that place back to my list."

Seb looked between the two of them. "What is this? A test of some sort?"

Before Dee or Jinuh could answer, there was a knock at the door.

"Ah ha, there's the Syndicate," said Jinuh.

"May I?" questioned Dee.

Jinuh motioned for her to go ahead.

Dee turned to the door and slowly opened it, sticking her head out slightly. Seb heard a loud outburst from a group shouting, "Dee!" as she threw the door open the rest of the way to let four others inside. The group went over to Jinuh, holding up their hands as Jinuh held up theirs, each taking a turn waving their hands in front of the other in greeting. After welcomes were complete, Dee said to the group, "Syndicate, this is Seb, I found him today. Seb, here's the *we* I had mentioned. It's not many of us, but so far, we're making it."

Seb raised his hand, waving to the group, before noticing Danish.

Danish eyed Seb curiously. "How are you here? I can't get you to leave work for a minute, and now you're *here*?"

Seb pointed at Dee. "Blame her."

Danish shook his head in disbelief. "All right. Well, hey."

The tallest of the group said, "Welcome Seb, I'm Zell. Has Dee told you what she has you caught up in?"

"I believe so. It's been an interesting day," Seb replied.

"Well, I'm sure you haven't seen anything yet." Zell turned to look toward Dee and Jinuh. "Why are we still just standing here? What's original for today?"

Jinuh shrugged as Dee jumped in with, "Okay, so get this. I was looking for some different things for us to try and came across this from the *before times*." She put *before times* in air quotes. "Everything is always referred to as before times—Anyway, this is before, before times. Apparently from the early 19th century. Have any of you heard of *charades*?" Everyone responded no. She laughed. "Me neither! Good! For this, we don't use any of our devices. No holographs, no audiophones, no Rollascreens, no wristbands." Dee paused, waiting for the groans to stop. "Okay?" She looked around for approval. "First, we have to write some words. Jinuh, do you have any paper and something to write with?"

"Maybe? I can't tell you the last time I needed anything like that. Give me a second, I'll go check."

Jinuh walked out of the room and returned shortly after with a piece of paper and a pen. "Look at that, apparently I do. I guess the last person that lived here left it behind."

"Great. Now we have to come up with a few words. Things or actions. Words like *tree*, or *run*, or . . . *synthesizer guitar*." She looked at Seb and held back a laugh. "We write those words on slips of paper, then we split up into teams. Someone from the first team blindly grabs one. That person can look at what's written on the paper, but they can't show it to the rest of their team or tell them what it is. Then, without speaking, they act out their word to try to help the other members of their team guess it." Dee quickly acted out playing guitar while everyone around her clapped. "Simplistic, right?"

Zell said, "Let's do it. What words do you all got?"

Everyone started shouting at the same time.

"*Ghost!*"

"*Read!*"

"*Doctor!*"

"*Building!*"

"*Hungry!*"

"Who said hungry?" asked Zell.

Jinuh put up their hand.

"Ha, you would."

Zell took the pen and paper from Dee and ripped the paper into small pieces. He wrote down several of the words that were called out.

Dee asked, "All right, what are the teams? Should I take Jinuh and Seb, and Zell, you got the rest?"

"As long as you're not lying about never playing this before, and Seb isn't just your conspirator so you can win this, then yes, that'll work." Everyone laughed. "But we're going first," Zell continued.

Dee nodded, then added, "Okay, everyone, we're supposed to do this with a timer, but do we care? I'm not sure if any one of us knows how to act, let alone figure out what the person up there is thinking."

Everyone emphatically shouted out, "No!"

Zell grabbed a piece of paper from the pile and went over to stand in front of an empty wall. He looked at the word on the paper, and exclaimed, "Oh, yeah! We got this! Ready?" The rest of his team shouted in approval.

While Zell was acting out what appeared to be the word 'hungry', Seb noticed one of the members of the Syndicate had three solid lights on their arm. He stared, wondering what they were doing here.

Dee whispered, "That's Anson. He's been part of the Syndicate for years. We're not sure what happened. We didn't see him for a while, then one day Zell found him sitting on a hyper taxi. We figured out where he's been living, so when we get together, we pick him up and he follows along. He seems to be harmless, and we really did miss him. The conversations are a lot less interesting now, but we're glad to have him around."

Seb looked worried. "So, I guess there's no knowing if everything you've been doing will keep you from the Global AI forever, is there?"

"Unfortunately not. The best we can do is keep on going and keep moving." She stopped, thought briefly, then continued, "You've heard the story about Jim, right? Made it all the way to 101?"

"I have."

"That's the goal. Some of us might make it, but most of us probably won't. The GAI keeps learning, and we have to continue to be more clever." She stopped and watched Zell as he was walking back to his team. "Anyway, it looks like it's our turn. Are you ready?"

"No, but do I really have a choice at this point?"

Dee laughed. "Nope!" She pushed him toward the open wall.

CHAPTER 7

Seb picked up a slip of paper, flipped it over, and saw the word *tree* on it. He wiped his forehead, happy that he chose an easy word, until his team started yelling out guesses.

"*Rain!*"

"*Tired!*"

"*Hot!*"

"*Worried!*"

Seb held his hands up in front of him to try to get his team to stop guessing.

"*Hands!*"

"*Ten!*"

"*Stop!*"

"*Police!*"

A person on the other team started laughing, shouting, "Stop, police!"

Seb finally composed himself. He stood still, put his arms out like tree branches, and started swaying slightly.

"*Wind!*"

"*Dizzy!*"

"*Tree!*"

"Tree!" Seb yelled. He started jumping up and down. Everyone clapped and cheered as he walked back to Dee.

"Not bad!" she said.

Seb smiled. "I still don't like you."

He noticed the display on the wall showed the sun setting. He realized it was getting late, marked by the exhaustion that tugged at him. "Hey, Dee, I know we just started this, but I think it's time for me to go."

"Do you know how to make it back home? Do you need help?" she asked.

"No, but I think I'll be able to figure it out," he replied.

Dee smiled wide. "I think you got it. I'm glad I found you today. Sure, I did a lot of stuff today that I had already done before, but you were something and someone different for *me*. We may never see each other again, but I hope we do. And I hope you see things how I see them now." She paused. "I'm not saying skip work every day to try to do *this*." She gestured around the room. "Quite the opposite. But at least change things up once in a while. Go to bed later. Wake up earlier. Eat different food. Meet new people. Try new things. Live life. Don't just be alive. Be."

"Thanks, Dee," he replied, as he turned toward the door.

"Oh, hey, Seb," she said shyly.

He stopped to face her.

"Kiss me?"

He struggled to hear her, but thought back to an earlier request. "I'm still not going to hit you," he finally replied.

"That's not what I said." She blushed, then leaned over and gave Seb a quick kiss on the cheek. "Good luck, Sebby."

Seb smiled at Dee. He shouted out to the rest of the Syndicate, "I have to get going. It was nice to meet you all. Danish, I'll see you at work." He turned to leave but hesitated. He glanced at the woman who'd changed his life in the span of a day. "Dee, really, thank you." They both smiled at each other without saying another word. Seb turned again and finally started toward the door. He slowly took in his surroundings, knowing it may be the first and last time. He exited the dwelling and walked over to the platform lift. He stepped on the empty platform as it arrived, grabbing tightly onto the railing before loosening his grip, knowing he was safe on the solid floor. He rode it down to the ground floor and made his way through the main door. As he stepped outside, he noticed the sun was setting fast.

Seb walked quickly toward the hyper loop station, passing by the sushi restaurant on the way. He grinned to himself, remembering how that was the first of many things he did that were outside of his norm on this day, all after simply agreeing to follow

Dee. He contemplated stopping for another dragon roll before deciding he should keep moving before it was dark. He arrived at the hyper loop terminal after only one wrong turn, and by taking a quick look at the display, he found the correct tube heading back to his area. He waited briefly for a train to stop at his platform, then stepped on once the doors opened. Seb sat in silence for the short ride back to the terminal in his town, wondering what words Dee and the Syndicate were acting out after he left.

Seb was pleased with himself as he got off at the correct stop. He made his way to the hyper taxi pickup spot—the same spot where his day first turned into one he will never forget.

This was the location that was only one stop after the one that took him to his job at the factory, but that stop would change his outlook on life forever. He looked around at the buildings in the dusk, and even though everything still appeared unfamiliar, he didn't feel as unsure as he had earlier in the day. A hyper taxi glided up to the stop as Seb continued to look around, and once he noticed it there, he got on while nodding to the driver. He walked toward his usual seat. It was empty this time, but he continued going past it and sat in the back.

The ride to his building was quick. The first stop was at the factory. He had somehow forgotten that this was where he normally would have been all day, and he would have been getting on a hyper taxi to go home only a few hours prior. One person got on at the stop in front of the factory. A quick glance made Seb think it was the same person who shoved past him that morning. The person that made him miss this stop and made him late to work. The person that quite possibly saved his life, now in more ways than one. Seb looked at them and said, "Thanks." The new rider gave him a confused look and sat down, looking at their lap while keeping to themselves as the hyper taxi continued. The next stop was finally the one near where Seb lived. He stood as the hyper taxi came to a stop, stepped off, and headed toward his complex.

Seb walked into the building, through the lobby, and onto one of the platforms going up. He watched the empty platforms on the other side of the loop descending and stepped off when he reached his floor. He went to the door of his dwelling and opened it, relieved to be home.

"What a crazy day," he said, thinking briefly about the other people Dee had mentioned. He wondered what made them run off from food they didn't like, or why they were more adamant than he was about not skydiving. Seb thought about how easy it would have been for him to just go home after not being able to work, or after Dee invited him to go with her outside of the café. He wondered why, ultimately, *he* had been selected to be part of her group.

Seb shook off the thought and glanced down at his arm. He noticed something was wrong. His third light was no longer blinking. It was completely dark.

The End

Zero-Day: a vulnerability (as in a computer or computer system) that is discovered and exploited (as by cybercriminals) before it is known to or addressed by the maker or vendor.

-Merriam-Webster

PART 2: 335-Day

PROLOGUE

Seb's audiophone chirped late in the evening. He looked at the band on his wrist, expecting it to display *Mom*. He grinned widely when, instead, he saw it read *Dee*. She'd changed his life eleven months ago.

He'd been days away from becoming another Global AI-controlled drone before Dee came into his life and showed him how to be alive by breaking him out of his monotonous ways. This delayed the Global AI from taking control and caused the third light on Seb's arm to stop blinking and go dark unexpectedly. Had he not met Dee, his last light would have undoubtedly turned solid.

"Dee!" Seb nearly shouted as he answered his audiophone, excited to speak to her for the first time in almost a month. "What's original? How have you been? How's the Syndicate? How's—"

"Sebby! Calm down. Slow down," Dee responded with a chuckle. "I'm good. Everyone is good. We've had some lights light up, but we haven't lost anyone to the GAI yet. I'm glad to hear in your voice that you're still here too. But listen, I do need you for something. I found someone new, but they're fighting me harder than you did." She laughed again. "I'm standing outside of my complex right now, about to go inside to finish packing before I decide where to move tomorrow. So, I'm hoping you can help persuade her to join us and the Syndicate."

"Sure, Dee. Anything for you. You know that. Give me her information and I'll see what I can do. You know I would do anything for you. I'd do anything to keep more people away from the GAI. I'd do anything—"

34

"Sebby! Calm down. Slow down," Dee interrupted, giggling. "I'll send the information to your Rollascreen. Bye, Seb. Thanks."

"Bye, Dee."

Click.

CHAPTER 1

When Seb woke the next morning, he immediately picked up his Rollascreen and uncurled it. He tapped a few icons to bring up the message from Dee containing the information about the new Syndicate recruit. The message began with a picture of a woman with dark curly hair, followed by her details:

Name: Listina Diandre
Age: 28
Work Location: Central Synthetic Meat Processing Co.
Last Known Location: Salazar's Pizzeria
Solid Lights: One. Two expected soon

"According to this, she shouldn't be too far from here right now. But I don't have a lot to go on." Seb scratched his head, thinking. "I'm not doing any good just standing here though. I need to start looking. But where to first?"

Seb looked at a display on a nearby wall, his only imagery of the outside world in his windowless dwelling, showing heavy rain with dark clouds and thunderbolts. As the screen shook slightly with each virtual strike, he was mesmerized. The large, interactive display made him question why he remained in his old complex as long as he had. *The Syndicate has the right idea moving around often if it means upgrades each time.* Seb shook his head to stop his wandering thoughts.

The rain outside made the decision for him. He would go to the closest location first, the synthetic meat plant.

Seb went to the front door, slid on a pair of half-wheeled shoes that were sitting nearby, and stepped out into the lobby. He was thankful to have gotten a dwelling on the ground floor in his new complex. He would no longer have to ride the platform lift each time he wanted to come and go. Seb made his way outside and stopped to stand in the rain. *This feels great*, he thought, as he ran his hand through his hair, realizing he'd been so distracted by Dee's message that he never went into the steam room to get cleaned.

He saw a hyper taxi pulling up. He watched as a crowd of Global AI-controlled people filed onto the vehicle, faintly hearing the driver tell each passenger, "Welcome! Thanks for joining us."

Seb chuckled to himself. He realized that it would normally be time for him to go to work. *I'll get over there at some point today. Maybe.*

He looked toward the synthetic meat plant and then down at his feet. He moved them together so they were side-by-side, allowing the magnets on the half wheels of each shoe to pull together and lock to form two complete wheels. Seb leaned forward and started gliding. He wove in and out of the people on the sidewalk, avoiding puddles while using his hands to shield his eyes from the rain.

Seb arrived at the synthetic meat plant and stopped to stare at the sleek look of the building that was used to create the area's locally-sourced lab-grown beef. *I'm here, but now what?* he wondered. "I always jump at the chance to help Dee, or do anything she asks before I think about *how* I'm going to do it." He snickered briefly at the realization. With over a thousand employees in the building, he questioned how he was going to find Listina, even with having a picture of her. He focused on the people going in and out of the plant, almost all following what Seb noticed to be a predetermined path. He could faintly see three solid lights on the arms of most of the people. "A majority are GAI-controlled. Why would Listina even work here?" The information that Dee had sent him said that Listina only had one light solid of the three. *Something else must be going on.*

Seb stared at the door, thinking. He bent down, pressing a button on his half-wheeled shoes to release the magnets holding them together, and started walking toward the entrance. "Here goes nothing," he said.

The eye scanner above the door flickered to indicate that it finished checking Seb's credentials, then the hologram below displayed the text:

Unknown. Information not available.
Time: 7:47 a.m.
Removal Requested

Seb noticed the words and immediately turned around, pushing past the people behind him.

"Well, that's not going to work." Seb wiped the rain off his face while looking across the street at a bagel shop. His stomach growled at the sight as it registered that he'd left his dwelling without first grabbing breakfast. "I should get some sustenance while I figure out the best way to find this woman." He checked both ways up and down the street, waiting for a hyper taxi to pass before crossing to the other side.

He walked into the shop and looked around before approaching the Global AI-controlled employee behind the counter. He asked, "What's the newest item you have?"

"Sustainable saffron and sage crispy cereal," they replied, locking eyes with Seb.

"Phew, okay, that sounds weird, but that'll do. And a caffeine booster as well, please."

"Please move to the side while you wait for your order. Have a nice day."

A display in front of Seb showed the total cost of his order. He paid by tapping the band on his wrist to the screen, then stepped to the side. He noticed how empty the restaurant was. *Looks like no one else wants sustainable . . . whatever I just ordered.*

As Seb's order slid out onto the counter, he took it and found the closest table to eat at. He pulled his Rollascreen from his pocket and uncurled it, opening the news for the day. An article from a few minutes prior caught Seb's eye while he was flipping through the screens of text.

Update on Area Explosions

He tapped the title of the article while remembering the explosion eleven months ago at the factory where he worked.

The person who set off the recent explosions has been found. They have been immediately converted to full Global AI-control due to the severity of the crimes. Peace can come once again to the area. More details will be provided later.

"It's about time they found that person. They could have killed me at the factory. How many people have suffered because of the damage at the other locations?" He finished eating, put his Rollascreen back in his pocket, and walked toward the front entrance. As he opened the door, a person ran through. Seb watched as they continued, realizing he recognized them. "Zell?" he called out. "What are you doing here? I talked to Dee earlier, I'm helping—"

The person turned to look at Seb and yelled out, "Seb, I can't stop. Something is happening."

Seb eyed Zell as he ran through the shop and out the back door.

What was that about? Is he also doing something for Dee?

Seb left the bagel shop and saw a hyper taxi stop two buildings ahead of him. He ran to the vehicle and got on. He walked past the driver, ignoring their welcome greeting, and headed to the back while carefully looking at each rider, hoping one would be Listina. *Like finding a haystack in the city*, he thought.

As he sat, he pulled out his Rollascreen to review Dee's message that contained Listina's information. He stared at her picture, trying to find any detail that would hint at where he could find her. "It looks like Dee took this picture while Listina was outside of the synthetic meat plant, which is where she should be right now, but I already found out I can't simply walk in there. I could stand around outside the building and wait to see if she comes out, but that seems unproductive." He looked at the rest of her information.

Last Known Location: Salazar's Pizzeria

It's still too early for pizza. Well, not really, I'd eat it. He grinned. "But the pizzeria isn't open yet. Maybe if I have no other leads before then, I'll stop in there and keep an eye out for her. The worst that can happen is I eat too much." He held back an audible chuckle.

Seb turned to look out the window of the hyper taxi and caught a glance of a familiar-looking black building going by. *Overground?* The sign was lit. This early, he couldn't believe they were open already. He looked toward the front of the hyper taxi and up at the holographic display showing the list of stops. The next stop was only a few buildings away. He'd get off there and walk back.

As the hyper taxi glided to a stop, Seb stood and quickly departed. He walked toward *Overground*, and opened the door as he arrived, immediately hearing a familiar, but grating sound. "Oh no. Someone's up there playing a synth guitar. I need to go in there and show them how it's supposed to be done."

Seb entered the building and walked to the table where a Global AI-controlled employee sat. They asked, "Here to play?"

"Yes, Seb. S. E. B." He shuddered at the sound of the synth guitar, then asked, "Can I use a guitar?"

"Yes, you can use a guitar. You are signed in. Thank you."

Seb sat and watched other people go on stage and play several songs before his name was called. He walked up the steps, grabbed a light blue electric guitar from the rack, and quickly checked the tuning before slinging it over his shoulder. He walked to the microphone and introduced himself.

"Hi, all, I'm Seb. I haven't been here in a few months, but I do have a new song to play." He strummed the intro for the song and began singing.

"Need something, to keep me there
Just something, 'cause I don't care
The answer, is plain to see
Just got to, it's time to leave
Goodbye tomorrow, I'm gone."

Seb finished the song and quickly returned the guitar to the rack. He exited the stage and walked out of the building without noticing whether there was a receptive response to his performance.

As the door for *Overground* was closing, he heard another guitar being strummed and smiled. He tapped a spot behind his ear to attempt to chirp Dee while debating which direction to head off to. He waited a while until he realized she wasn't answering. *What else is new?* he questioned. *I'm sure she's still tied up with packing and moving.* He tapped behind his ear again to stop the call attempt and pulled his Rollascreen from his pocket to send her a message.

I just finished at Overground. I played a new song. I thought it went well. I know, I know. That's not what matters, but I did already say it was new, right? Wish you could have seen it. Chirp me.

Seb tucked the Rollascreen back in his pocket. He was unsure of how to continue.

CHAPTER 2

"Decrement!" exclaimed Seb as he caught a glance at his wristband and realized the pizzeria would be open by now. "I need to start heading back. I was in *Overground* longer than I realized and I don't want to miss Listina if she goes there for lunch."

Seb connected his half-wheeled shoes and started gliding toward the pizzeria, carefully looking at the faces of the people he passed, ignoring the ones with three solid lights visible on their arms, hoping one would be Listina.

This is a much more involved task than I expected.

Seb stopped outside of Salazar's Pizzeria and took a deep breath, surprised by the aroma. "That smells *sooo* good," he said out loud.

"It's good," replied two Global AI-controlled people passing by.

Seb chuckled at the responses and entered the restaurant. He looked around, seeing one man sitting at a table eating a slice of pizza, and a Global AI-controlled chef loading ingredients into the industrial pizza maker. Hoping that he hadn't missed Listina, he approached the chef and asked, "Has anyone else been in today?"

"You're in here today."

"Uh, yes, but has anyone else, not me, been here today."

"I'm here."

"Okay, has anyone that's not me, not you, not that person . . ." Seb pointed to the man at the table. ". . . been in here today? Specifically, a woman. She has dark curly hair. She's been in here before. Has she been here *today?*"

"No. But I'm here."

Seb closed his eyes and rubbed them hard before turning and walking away to sit at one of the empty tables. "That was . . . I just . . . Never mind. I need to eat." He picked up the menu tablet and quickly touched several images of individual slices of pizza, before touching the 'Deduct From Balance' button to pay. He held his wristband against the tablet, waited for a green flash to show the payment was accepted, and returned the device to the table.

Seb removed his Rollascreen from his pocket to continue reading the news while waiting for his food.

January 29th, 2333

More details to come regarding the capture and conversion of the individual who caused the city explosions
Dwelling occupancy diminishing
Synthetic Beef BAD for you?

New Global AI additions: 1324
Global AI removals: 2020

"Strange, I haven't seen the number of removals higher than the number of additions before. No one left to recruit? Except me and the Syndicate, of course." He chuckled. With the thought of the Syndicate on his mind, Seb remembered that he wanted to catch up with Danish, but knew that wasn't likely to happen until he went to work himself.

While wondering where his pizza was, Seb looked around and saw a woman standing at the counter. His eyes lit up. He quickly closed the news on his Rollascreen to open the message from Dee. He held up the device to compare the picture of Listina to the woman at the counter. Her hair was down and seemed a bit longer, but the color looked right. *Here goes nothing.*

"Listina!" he shouted.

The woman did not respond or move.

"Listina?" he questioned.

The woman still did not respond.

"Test failed. No luck. It does look a little bit like her. Oh well. I'll have to—"

The chef came out with Seb's pizza and handed it to him.

"Yes, finally."

Seb picked up a slice, but as he was about to take a bite, the woman from the counter walked over and sat at his table. He looked up. "Listina?"

The woman stared at Seb for a few moments before replying, "It's Listy. Who are you and what do you want?"

"I wanted to find you. Dee wanted me to find you. I want to help you. We're trying to——"

"Stop, please stop. Let me start again. Who are you?"

"I'm Seb. I was——"

"Okay, Seb. I don't need any help. I know what you're trying to do." She pointed at the lights on Seb's arm. "I don't know what's taking so long for mine to turn solid. If it wasn't going to break my routine, I'd leave solely to get away from you, but I come here every day for lunch. I have"—she checked the time—"twenty minutes before I go back to the plant. So please, let me keep to my routine. You eat your pizza, I'm going to go over there to eat mine, and in exactly twenty minutes, I'm going to leave, go to the plant, and stay there until I go home to my dwelling."

Seb opened his mouth to respond, but Listina held up a hand to stop him, stood, and went to a different table. He continued to sit with his mouth agape while staring at her. She kept her back to him.

"Well, that was unexpected," he admitted. Dee mentioned to him that Listina was fighting her, but he didn't expect talking to Listina would be the difficult part. Seb thought finding the woman would take much longer.

Seb looked down at his pizza and finally ate his lunch.

Exactly twenty minutes later, Listina got up from her table and walked out of the pizzeria. At just after twelve, and with nothing else to do, Seb decided it was time for him to also go to work.

CHAPTER 3

Seb entered the main door of the factory where he worked and looked at the eye scanner.

Sebastian Cedric
In Time: 12:33 p.m.
LATE

He had become accustomed to seeing the shade of red displayed on the screen. Now that Seb rarely arrived on time for his shift, he almost never saw the green text used to indicate when an employee showed up when they were supposed to.

He walked to the platform lift. His eyes followed it up to the top of the building. Seb was thankful to no longer need to ride one to get to the dwelling in his complex, but he still hated using it in the factory. He found an immediate benefit in showing up late to work when realizing there were no lines for the platform lifts. The anxiety he had when riding one didn't have as much time to build. He stepped onto an empty platform as it arrived and grabbed onto the handrails. He watched as other employees were riding the continuous loop of platforms down to the lobby. A thought that they could be leaving for a lunch break had him wondering if they would be going for some Salazar's pizza. He considered yelling across the way to make an order suggestion, but the blank stares on their faces led him to believe they were Global AI-controlled.

Seb stepped off the platform at the floor of his lab and looked around. Everything seemed to be in its place. He was impressed knowing how much damage had been caused by the explosion eleven months prior.

Seb walked past the entrance of his lab and continued to the next work area on his floor. He stood at the door and peered in the window, seeing Danish standing at his desk. Seb opened the door causing Danish to turn toward the sound.

"Seb! My friend! How unexpected of you to come to work today." Danish chuckled. "Dee has changed you. I used to be able to tell the time by seeing if you were in your lab or not when I walked by. Would it be morning, or time for lunch, or time to go home? Now I have to use this." He held up his arm to show the band on his wrist. "Anyhow, what's original? Are you just arriving, or leaving? Or are you even here?" Danish made a face like he was staring at a ghost.

Seb cracked up laughing. "I'm here. Really. See." He poked himself in the chest to show that his finger didn't pass through. "I did just get here, but I won't be around long. Dee asked me to find someone that she wants for the Syndicate, but this woman, Listina, or Listy, shot me down. I found her, but she didn't want to talk to me. It's like she *wants* to be GAI-controlled."

Danish raised an eyebrow in confusion.

"I mean it. She seemed mad at me for risking breaking her routine. She thinks it is taking too long for the GAI to take over. I don't think I've ever seen anyone that *wanted* to give in to it. Someone that wants to be controlled by the—oh no."

"What, Seb? What's wrong?"

"I think I figured it out. I think she believes there is nothing out there for her, so she's giving up. I have to find her again and see if I can get her to talk to me. The problem is, she should be at the plant where she works."

"Why's that a problem? If you know where she is, you should be able to get to her, right?"

"I tried earlier actually, and their scanner triggered an alert to have me removed. I got out of there quickly. I'll check back at the end of the workday. But since I have nothing to do until then, I'll go run some sequences in my lab. I'll speak later, Danish. Thanks for your help."

"Uh, yes, sure. I'll take credit for that." He smiled. "Another time, Seb."

Seb left Danish's area and went to his own lab. He sat at his desk, ignoring the Global AI-controlled employees moving around in a pattern. He waved his hand in front of the screen facing him to activate the display. It showed several tasks for Seb to choose from. Each had a short description and an estimate for how long the task was expected to take. He knew that he didn't have a lot of time before he needed to return to the synthetic meat plant. The desire to speak with Listina again had him choose the shortest task in the list. Seb wanted to find something that he would actually be able to complete so he could get some extra credits in his account. Now that he was doing more than working, eating, and sleeping, he discovered that the additional income was necessary. The base credits he received covered the necessities, but new food places and upgraded dwellings required more. *So is life. Live, become GAI-controlled, and die.*

Seb used his thumb, pointer finger, and middle finger on one hand to make a pinching motion in front of the display. Aimed at the task with the shortest time estimate, he pulled toward himself to indicate that he was selecting that task. He looked at the list of steps, acknowledged them, then turned in his chair to grab the first couple of pieces he needed from a shelf near his desk. He loaded them into a machine sitting next to the display, read the next step in the instructions, and picked up the next few pieces, also loading them into the machine. He followed additional instructions, repeating the process until he was finished.

Seb pressed a button on the front of the machine and watched as orange lights touched each of the pieces he had loaded, blending the materials together. Four flashes of white lights indicated to Seb the process was complete. He removed the final product from the machine and held it up. He turned it left and right and flipped it end over end to inspect it. "Perfect. I haven't lost my touch." Seb looked at the end of the task's instructions. Seeing that he needed to make four more of the same, he returned the item to the machine and hit the button to duplicate it. He pushed the number four, then the button to start. A wave of blue light covered the item before he saw four flashes of white light. Seb removed the original product, then watched as the machine created an identical one. After four more flashes of white light, he removed the new duplicated item and repeated the process until the next three were finished. He placed the five completed products on a shelf near a wall by the door. "Well, I never know what this stuff is actually used for, but I do a fine job making them."

Seb checked the time. At 3:30 p.m., he was pleased with himself to have completed the work within the time estimate. Seb stepped over to the display on his desk, tapped the 'Complete' button under the task, and held his wristband over the display to collect his credits. Now finished, he knew he had to leave soon to make it to the synthetic meat plant before Listina was gone.

Seb left his lab and quickly stepped onto a platform lift to ride down to the main floor. He looked up at the eye scanner as he walked out the door, and caught a quick glance at the display.

Out Time: 3:35 p.m.
Goodbye, Sebastian Cedric

Seb stepped out and halted. The falling rain hitting him wasn't right. The weather was planned. It had rained in the morning. When that happened, it usually didn't in the afternoon. Rarely did he see rain before and after lunch. "I wonder who didn't show up for their job today." He smiled to himself. "It wasn't me. I did!"

He shielded his eyes from the rain, waiting for a hyper taxi to arrive. He finally saw one in the distance and looked at the band on his wrist. "This is going to be cutting it close. Hopefully there are no interruptions or roughers that keep me from getting to the stop for Listy's lab." Seb chuckled. "Listy's lab, I like that. But I definitely don't want to have to repeat this process again tomorrow."

CHAPTER 4

Seb stepped off the hyper taxi and walked past several buildings until he was in front of the Central Synthetic Meat Processing plant. It was two minutes to four, which meant Listina should be leaving at any time now.

Chirp.

"Mom? Really? Now?" Seb said, frustrated.

"Hello, Mom."

"Hi, Sebastian. How are you this evening?"

"I'm busy. What's the purpose of your call at this time?"

"That's good, honey. Did you hear that the person causing the explosions was caught? We should all be safe now. The conversion was performed immediately and without trial for h—"

Click.

Seb quickly disconnected the call as he watched a crowd of employees file out of the plant and caught a glance of Listina in the middle of the group. "She's even acting like she's GAI-controlled. Walking in unison with all the others. I need to find out what is going on. I hope I can help her before she does something that can't be undone."

Seb walked toward the group and yelled for Listina.

"Hey! Listy!" He waited. "Listy, please."

Listina stopped and stared at him. She rolled her eyes and started walking again, following several other people to a hyper taxi pickup stop. Seb kept close to the group, calling out, "Listy, can I talk to you, please? I think I know what's wrong. Just hear me out."

Finally stopping to address him, Listina said, "I'm getting on that hyper taxi when it arrives." She pointed at a vehicle a few buildings up the street. "What you do is up to you. If you follow me on, so be it. If you leave and go somewhere else, that would be fine, and preferable, but I can't tell you what to do."

Seb went to the back of the line, impatiently waiting for the hyper taxi to arrive.

The group filed on after the vehicle glided to a stop, each Global AI-controlled person and Listina responding to the driver's welcomes. Seb followed, intently watching where Listina was planning to sit. He found an empty seat across from her and turned to speak.

As Seb opened his mouth, Listina faced him and asked, "Why are you here? What do you hope to accomplish? The other woman gave me some nonsense about 'try new things. Meet new people.' Blah blah blah. I don't want to do any of that. I was glad when she backed off and disappeared, but then you showed up. So if you're planning to tell me the same thing, you might as well turn right around, read something on your Rollascreen, and ride this hyper taxi in quiet peace like everyone else."

Seb closed his mouth and turned to face the front of the hyper taxi. He took a moment to put his thoughts in order before turning back to Listina.

"Listy, okay, you're right. I was going to tell you about what you would be missing if you choose the GAI instead of living your life. I was going to tell you how I got time back, and that my last light was blinking so fast that I was all but set to be GAI-controlled. And then after I met Dee and she showed me new things, like how to *be* and live, that—and I still don't completely understand how—my last light went dark."

Seb began to raise his arm to show his lights, but Listina interrupted, "It probably burned out."

He lowered his arm. "You know that's not possible," Seb replied, worried. "I realize now that none of that matters to you. For some reason you *want* to become GAI-controlled. You're not merely going through the normal motions of life knowing there will eventually be an end, you are actively trying to speed up the process. You don't want to be in control anymore. You've given up."

"I have not!" came an immediate defensive response.

"You have." His words were calm, confident. "You have given up. You seem to think you have no purpose."

"That's not true," Listina said, her eyes filling with tears.

"Why do you think you have no purpose? There is plenty out there, plenty to continue for. Joining the GAI as soon as you can is not the way. It's giving up. There has to be something you want to keep going for."

A tear fell from Listina's eye as she wiped at it and sniffled.

"Look, Sa—Su—Si—"

"Seb."

"Seb. I don't have *anyone*. It's only me. My parents were gone before the Global AI could take over. I don't have any siblings, and all of my friends have been converted. I can't seem to do anything right myself. I can't even get converted quickly." Listina tapped the lights on her arm, showing Seb a single solid light, a rapidly blinking light, and a dark light. "I don't exactly want to cut off my arm for immediate conversion, and while I would never go so far as to set explosions around here, I do envy that person now that they were converted."

Seb caught himself staring at her with wide eyes, blinked a few times, and acknowledged her.

"So, Seb, as you can see, I don't want help, or saving, or whatever it is you think you can do."

"Listy, okay, I see now. You believe you have nothing left, but if you let me, I'd like to prove to you that's not true. Can I meet with you later to introduce you to some of my friends and show you the types of things I enjoy? Tomorrow is Monday. Your plant will be taken offline, just like all the other plants and factories around here, to allow the air scrubbers to do their weekly air cleaning. I won't be interrupting work. Will then be okay?"

"I guess."

"Are we heading toward your dwelling?"

"Yes."

"Okay. I'll ride this until we get there, and tomorrow I will meet you outside." Seb looked past Listina and out the hyper taxi window at the falling rain. "I sure hope it isn't raining all day again. But I'll meet you in the morning, if that's okay."

"Sure," Listina responded timidly.

"Great. I'll turn around and ride quietly. I'll stay on at your stop, leave you to yourself, but I'll come by around 9 a.m. tomorrow, okay?"

"Okay."

Seb faced forward in his seat and sighed with relief. *Progress*, he thought. *I still have to figure out how to make her understand that there is something for her, but at least she's talking to me.*

Seb and Listina sat quietly until the hyper taxi arrived at her stop. Seb made a mental note of the location and smiled toward Listina, but she got off without looking back at him. He watched as she entered a building nearby, then he continued riding until stopping at the next location.

He exited the hyper taxi, put his hands over his head as rain started hitting him, and took in his surroundings. It would take him fifteen minutes to return to his complex gliding with his shoes, giving him time to clear his thoughts and make a plan for the following day.

Seb locked his half-wheeled shoes together and started for his dwelling. He began to enjoy the calming patter of the rain, realizing he made some headway with Listina.

CHAPTER 5

Seb was lightly nudged awake by the vibrating bed alarm at exactly seven in the morning.

"Arg! I keep forgetting to turn that off!" he exclaimed. Seb looked at the display on the wall showing the sun rising, with a faint amount of heat radiating from the screen. "No rain! Wonderful," he announced. It was early, so Seb had time to get in the steamer to clean himself and eat something before he needed to leave for Listina's.

Seb got out of bed, walked to the steam room, and reached in to hit the 'Start' button before disrobing and stepping in. He praised himself for remembering to turn it on prior. The steamer stopped once Seb was cleaned and sanitized, and after the air dryer finished drying him, he stepped out and dressed.

Seb walked into the kitchen and, without looking, grabbed a breakfast protein nutrient bar from the food drawer. He took a bite before reading the wrapper. "Hmm, camu camu. This will do. I've got to get my vitamin C." He went to his bedroom to grab his Rollascreen from the stand near his bed then returned to the kitchen to sit down and finish his breakfast. He uncurled the Rollascreen and began creating a message to send to Dee.

Dee! I found her. I found Listina. By the way, she goes by Listy, for when you get to meet her next. Your method would have never worked on her, Dee. She's not like me. She's not just going through life as a bore. (Your words, not mine.) She is trying to speed up the process of being GAI-controlled, but luckily hasn't taken it to any extremes. I think there's a chance I can get through to her. After I meet up with her today, I want to introduce her to the Syndicate. Maybe if we're in her life, she'll feel like there is something to continue for. Hopefully you will be around later, Dee. Chirp me.

Seb finished his breakfast and left his dwelling to head to Listina's.

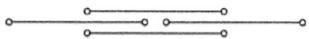

Standing outside of the complex that Listina entered the previous day, Seb was becoming increasingly worried. *9:10. Maybe she's running a little late. She told me she would meet me here at 9, but I'll give her more time.*

Seb focused on the different buildings nearby. *Lots of different food, lots of different things to do. Plenty of places to keep GAI-controlled people working, but I wonder if Listy has even tried any of these, or if she goes out of her way to avoid them.*

Seb looked back at the complex and then checked the time. He had the patience to wait all day for Listina, but was hoping for something a bit more thrilling. A few more minutes wouldn't hurt before he would go looking for her.

From behind, Seb felt a tap on his shoulder. He turned around.

"Seb! It happened! It actually happened!"

Seb gaped at Listina. "What happened? What are you talking about? And where were you? I've been waiting outside your building."

Listina giggled. "I don't live there," she said, pointing to the complex. "I wasn't sure I wanted to see you again, and I knew you were watching me get off the hyper taxi yesterday, so I went into the first complex near the stop. I actually live over there at building 988." Listina pointed across the street.

"Uh. Okay. I can understand that, but at least you're here now. Anyway, what happened? What are you so excited about?"

Listina held up her arm to proudly display two solidly lit lights.

Seb felt his heart sink.

"Keeping to my schedule yesterday helped, Seb! Even your interruptions didn't change anything. Sticking to my times kept the Global AI with me. Only one more to go!"

"Listy . . . What . . . I don't . . . I thought we were doing things today to show you that you don't want to be converted. I . . . I . . . ." Seb had a look of dread on his face that he couldn't hide.

"Seb, this is what I wanted! I'm so happy. I can still follow you around today, but only one more to go! I can't believe it."

Listina was jumping up and down with visible joy, while Seb continued to stand there in a stupor.

"Come on," she said, still hopping. "Where are we going to go? What are we going to do? Who am I going to meet?"

"I . . . I don't know. I think . . . I think I want to go home."

"No way! I'm here. Let's go do something. I want to eat. Let's go eat. There's lots near here. I haven't tried most of it, but I'm sure it's all fine. You pick."

Seb stared at her. "Uh, yeah. Sure. Um." He scanned the area and found a café. "Is that okay?" he asked, directing her attention to it.

"Yeah! Let's go there. I could use a caffeine booster." She giggled. "But let's go see what else they have."

Listina skipped to the café while Seb sluggishly followed. They sat at a table inside and Listina picked up the menu tablet. "What's good here?" she asked.

Seb looked at her. "How should I know?" he asked defensively.

"Whoa, sorry. I figured you've been here before. I got the impression you've been all over."

Seb shook his head no.

"Okay. How about I pick something for each of us? A surprise."

"Yeah, sure, why not," he answered dismissively.

Listina tapped several images on the tablet and put it down. "All right, surprises on their way. So, Seb, what's your problem? You were a lot more enthusiastic to see me yesterday. Today you are . . . sad-faced Seb. You're the one that wanted to meet with me. Here I am now. Amuse me."

"I don't know if there's a reason now. I wanted to show you there was more than just joining the GAI, but you're so excited about your new light that I might as well give up. I already lost you."

"I'm not gone. I'm not lost. I'm right here. I'm yours for the day. You want to get rid of me that easily? It's not happening. So, what are we—oh! Our food is here. Hopefully my surprise picks are good. I feel like this is my last meal. I know, I know.

55

I still have one light left, and it's not even blinking." She stopped and saw Seb's arm. "Oh! I'm like you!"

Seb glared at her.

Listina laughed. "Let's eat."

Seb picked at the items on the plates in front of them while Listina dug in, barely chewing between bites. Seb stopped, his eyes wide. He quickly picked up the tablet, tapped an icon on the display, then held his arm up to touch his wristband to the tablet. He put the tablet back down after the screen blinked green to show that his payment was accepted.

"Nice try," he scoffed.

Listina shrugged in response.

"Not paying so we get caught and they light up our lights? Please don't try to do that again. You've convinced me not to be done with you yet, but even if I never get through to you, I don't want to follow the same path." Seb tapped at the lights on his arm.

"All right, all right. Sorry. I won't. I promise."

After Seb and Listina finished their food, he stood and gestured to her. "Come. I finally have an idea."

She willingly followed him out the door.

CHAPTER 6

"I'm going to take you somewhere," Seb told her. "Somewhere that even I haven't been in a long time. I'd rather not go myself, but I think it's something that you need to see for yourself."

Listina looked at him with a mix of interest and confusion. "Uh, okay. Way to sell me on it. I can't wait," she responded with a hint of sarcasm.

"We're going to take the hyper loop. It's much too far to walk, and the hyper taxi would take longer than I prefer. I always used to take that to drag out the time, but I just want to get this over with today."

They made their way to the hyper loop station and stopped in front of a train. "This place is so cool," she said.

Seb remembered he had a similar thought when Dee first took him to a hyper loop station. "Uh, yeah, I guess it is, isn't it? I haven't noticed that myself in a while. I'm not down here often, but I forget that this place is unique."

They stepped onto the train after the doors slid open, and found empty seats. Seb kept his eyes focused elsewhere, lost in thought.

"Something wrong?" questioned Listina.

"Uh, no. Not really. I don't want to do this, but I need to. We need to. Um, why don't you tell me something about yourself? Distract me."

"What do you want to know? What don't you already know? You found me, so you seem to know something about me."

"Or don't. That's fine too."

"Sad-faced Seb returns! I'll tell you about my job. It's the best. You know I work at the Central Synthetic Meat Processing plant, but what I do is amazing. I get to try out new combinations of ingredients: mixing them, growing them, and then, finally, tasting them! That's the best part. Well, sometimes. Not everything I make actually tastes good. Some of what I make tastes flat-out awful." She stuck out her tongue. "But every once in a while, something I concoct is amazing. So good, so tasty. Yum, yum!"

Seb smiled in response until he realized something about what Listina said.

"Listy, you're the one making and tasting your creations?"

"Yup!"

"Isn't that job for people still in control of themselves? *Not* GAI-controlled employees? You need to actually care about what the product tastes like, rather than just create something that meets the minimum nutritional requirements. Don't the GAI-controlled employees only follow the processes to recreate the things that people like you make? The reason people like us, people still in control, need to go to work is to do the things that the GAI can't do. Taste food, like in your case, or feel, or have emotional responses. If they did all of the jobs, and we did none, only collecting our minimum credits, life for the rest of us would be . . . pointless? We wouldn't need to exist."

Listina's eyes opened wide. "Well . . . I haven't thought of that." She pondered this for a moment. "Oh well! I guess I'll get a new job once this last one lights up." She tapped her arm.

"I saw your face light up while you were talking about your job, but then you brushed it off because you're so obsessed with giving up control."

The hyper loop train glided to a halt and Listina stood up. Seb gestured for her to sit. "Not yet. We still have one more stop to go."

Listina looked at the location of the next stop on the destinations list. "Nullity? Why are we going there? Nothing is there. No one wants to be there."

Seb nodded in agreement. "You're right. But we're going there anyway."

Listina sat down, and she and Seb remained in silence, separately thinking about what was ahead, until the hyper loop train arrived at the next location.

Seb led Listina off the train and made their way up to ground level. They both stopped to take in the uninspiring view of complexes filled with thousands of dwellings on one side of a long street, with factories lining the other side. They watched streams of Global AI-controlled people walking between the complexes to the factories and back, all moving systematically.

"Seb, what is this? Well, I know *what* it is, I've heard about it, but why are we here? This looks . . . I don't know. Boring? Depressing? I was so much happier earlier and this is . . . yuck."

"Yeah, it is, isn't it? Welcome to Nullity." Seb looked ahead. "It even includes a crumbled factory further up that way. They don't bother cleaning it up, or even closing the factories every week for air scrubbing like they do in our area, because only the GAI-controlled live here. I hate coming here, but I feel I need to do it anyway."

Seb and Listina walked along the outside of the complexes, while he read the identification numbers of each, eventually stopping at one labeled *8002738255*. He walked into the building with Listina following closely behind. He continued to the platform lift, stepping on carefully as Listina jumped on it, causing it to bounce. Seb tightly grabbed the handrail and glared at Listina. "System outage! Please don't!"

Listina looked at him, then hopped up and down again. "This?"

Seb held on tighter while the platform continued to bounce.

"Yes!" he shouted. "That! Stop that!"

Listina stilled.

"Thank you," he said, bending down to his knees. "I hate being on these things normally. No one's done that to me before. And hopefully never again."

Listina giggled and apologized through a grin.

Seb breathed deeply to calm his racing heart before realizing they were approaching the floor he was looking for. "This is it, follow me." He stepped off the moving platform and walked to the door of a dwelling on the opposite side of the building. He checked the number near the entrance. "This is it," he whispered.

"Well?" questioned Listina. "What are we doing here? Who lives here? What are we waiting for?"

Seb ignored her questions, knocked on the door, and waited.

The door opened shortly after, revealing an older woman.

"Hi, Sebastian. How are you this morning?" asked the woman.

Seb turned to Listina. "This is my mom."

"That's good, honey," said Seb's mother, oblivious to his comment. "Please come in."

Listina looked at Seb's mother and then back at him. "What are we doing here?"

"I'll show you. Let's go in."

Seb and Listina followed his mother into the dwelling. His mother sat on a seat nearby, waiting for Seb and Listina to do the same. Seb motioned to Listina to sit while he chose a seat next to his mother. As soon as Seb sat, his mother turned to him and said, "Hi, Sebastian. How are you this morning?"

Seb tapped his foot on the ground, impatiently waiting for the next part.

"That's good, honey. The weather today is—" She faced the display on the wall. "Nice. The weather today is nice. Have you—"

Seb stood, causing his mother to stop, and walked out of the room. He called out, "Listy, do you need anything? Something liquid? Or anything else, perhaps?"

Listina responded back in question, "No? I . . . I don't."

Seb returned a moment later and sat next to his mother.

"Hi, Sebastian. How are you this morning?"

"Fine."

"That's good, honey. The weather today is nice. Have you heard about the person they caught that caused the explosions? They said that the wo—"

Seb stood, walked to a wall of the dwelling, and leaned against it.

"Please stop," Listina said with exasperation. "What are you doing to her?"

"What do you mean what am *I* doing to her? I'm not doing anything. That is all because of the GAI. That is what the GAI does to you."

Seb started walking toward his mother again.

"No, really," said Listina, frantic. "Stop. I can't watch this."

He stopped moving. "Maybe after you're converted, I'll come visit your dwelling. Obviously you're too young to live here in Nullity, but we'll see what nonsense you repeat over and over. Or maybe you'll be silent if the GAI doesn't have enough information on our interactions to determine your script." He shrugged. "I guess I'll find out soon enough if you get your way."

Listina got up from her chair and walked out of the dwelling. Seb's mother stared in the direction of the door, remaining silent. Seb followed Listina out of the dwelling, causing his mother to react. "Bye, honey," she called out.

"Bye, Mom," he replied under his breath.

Seb caught up with Listina in the hall, finding her sitting against a wall, wiping tears from her eyes.

"Why did you bring me here?" she said through sobs.

"You said you never got to see your parents become GAI-controlled. I wanted to show you what it looks like. It's nothing. You do nothing. You are no more. I thought I was resigned to it once, resigned to becoming GAI-controlled myself, because I thought that's just how it was. But my eyes were opened, and now I can't even imagine willingly choosing that path. To leave everything. To become"—he pointed toward his mother's dwelling—"*that*. So, come on. We're done *here*, but we're not done yet."

"Nothing else like that, please?" pleaded Listina.

"No. Nothing like that. The opposite. Now, let's get out of this place."

They left the complex and went back to the hyper loop station. Seb pulled out his Rollascreen and sent a message. Almost immediately, the device beeped to indicate that he received a response. He read it and gestured to a train on the other side of the station. "That one. It'll bring us back near your place. It shouldn't take long."

CHAPTER 7

After Seb and Listina returned to her area, he noticed she was visibly happy to be away from Nullity and its Global AI-controlled population.

"Don't worry," he assured her. "I won't take you back to a place like that. Instead, we're going to meet another person, a friend. They're someone who is still in control of themselves."

Seb led Listina to a short building that was long and wide. They stepped inside to see an arena made up of a large open circle with people gliding around on connected half-wheeled shoes. Some were moving in circles, some were twirling, and some were pushing objects back and forth by gliding into them quickly.

"Whoa!" said Listina in amazement. "That's what this building is?"

"I haven't been in anything like this myself." He took in the view around him. "But this is fascinating."

"You've never been here? Then why are we?"

"I'm looking for someone. They said they would meet us here."

Seb continued scanning the arena until he caught sight of a short, tattoo-covered person. "Ah ha. There they are." He turned her focus to a person twirling and gliding in the middle of the arena. Seb put his hand in the air to grab their attention. When the person noticed Seb, they glided over to Seb and Listina, stopping abruptly in front of them.

"Seb, you found it. This place is *increased*, isn't it? It's huge and there's so much room to—" They quickly glided to the middle of the arena, twirled, and came back to Seb and Listina.

"Jinuh!" Seb responded. "Increased is right. Good spot. Thanks for choosing it, and thanks for finding a location nearby."

Jinuh smiled, then looked at Listina and bowed. "I'm Jinuh. Seb has misplaced his manners."

"I was getting to it!" Seb responded, defensively. "Listy, this is Jinuh. They are part of a group I now belong to, the Syndicate. We support each other. We talk when we can, don't talk when we can't or don't want to, and occasionally"—he gestured around the arena—"do things like this."

Jinuh smiled. "That's better."

Seb forcefully kept his mouth shut.

Listina laughed at the interaction between the two. "Hi, Jinuh. It's nice to meet you." She turned to Seb. "This is already better than what you put me through at the last place."

"What did you *do* to her?" Jinuh asked, concerned.

"Nothing! I took her to meet my mom."

"A little early for that, maybe?"

Seb glared. "Not like that. My mom lives, or well, whatever she does, in Nullity."

"Ohhhh. That is something I did not know. But why would you put Listy through that?"

"It's something she needed to see. She—"

"Hey! I'm right here," Listina interjected. "Seb is trying to *saaave* me."

"Huh?" Jinuh asked.

Listina held up her arm and showed her lights.

"Ah. Trying to be like Dee, Seb? By the way, have you heard from her lately? Zell mentioned something's going on with her, but that's nothing new for Dee."

"Nope, nothing from her, but I'd never try to be *like* her. And this is different. But, hey, why don't we all get into the arena and try this out."

Listina looked down at her shoes. "I'll . . . walk?"

Seb chuckled. "It's okay, they have some half-wheels here you can borrow. I noticed them when we walked in. I happened to dress for the occasion." He tapped his heels together. "Let's go get you a pair. Jinuh, we'll be back. Meet you out there?"

Seb led Listina to a screen where she tapped an image of a pair of half-wheeled shoes and watched as a set slid out from behind the display. She took them and put them on, placing her shoes in a storage hole nearby.

"Now what?" she asked.

"Let's get a little closer, then I'll show you."

They walked to the center of the arena where Jinuh was waiting. Seb demonstrated how to connect her shoes, watching as she wavered slightly while learning to keep her balance. The shoes did most of the work for her.

"It's not too difficult," Jinuh said, reaching a hand out to help her steady herself. "Do you mind? I can take you out, help you to get adjusted."

Listina grabbed Jinuh's hand.

"We shall return," Jinuh said to Seb. "Or maybe not. We shall see." Jinuh turned to Listina, giggling. "Shall we?"

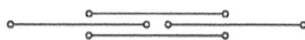

Listina maintained a hold on Jinuh's hand while working out how to start, slow, and stop the half-wheeled shoes, becoming more comfortable over time. She addressed Jinuh. "So, that Seb, huh? Have you known him long?"

"No, actually, not very long. Less than a year, but he's a good one. Seems to figure things out quickly, and wants to help everyone."

Listina waited.

"It's not a bad thing. Our friend Dee found him one day and brought him along."

"I met Dee. I wasn't as receptive," Listina acknowledged.

Jinuh reached out for Listina's hand. After she complied, they spun her around in a circle. Upon stopping, they kept their arms outstretched. Jinuh maintained a hold of her hand and added, "It happens. Sometimes she can be very—"

"Hey, I like your tattoos," interrupted Listina.

Jinuh shook their head, catching up with Listina's statement. "Um, yeah? Thanks. They've gotten me through a lot."

"How's that?"

"I don't usually talk about this, but they help me. Sometimes I feel like everything is very difficult to get through. Sometimes it would be easier to not have to think, or feel, but I look at them to remind me of what I have. Other people use pictures, or memories, but I use these. This one here—" Jinuh pointed to a picture of a small box with words in it. "This one reminds me of messages I exchange with my friends. Ones they send, ones I send. It makes me smile. When I find something else that makes me happy, I add it to myself. It keeps me going. It's hard to remember what I have sometimes, but these are good reminders."

Listina turned her head, hopeful Jinuh didn't see what this meant to her.

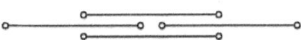

Seb caught up to the duo. He noticed a tear in the corner of Listina's eye. "Uh, what did I miss? Are you okay? Did you fall?"

Listina looked down.

"I guess it was something I said," Jinuh replied.

"No, no. You've both been so good to me, and you don't even know me." Listina noticed the two solid lights on her arm and broke down crying. "What have I done?"

"Seb, I didn't do anything. I was only telling her about my tattoos."

He held up his hand to stop Jinuh. "It's okay. I can fill you in another time. Listy, it's all right. It's okay. You're still here. I'm here with you. We're here with you."

Listina nodded and wiped away her tears. "I think I'd like to go."

"If that's what you want, we can get out of here." Seb faced Jinuh. "Thanks again for meeting us here. Sorry to leave so soon. I'm going to get going with Listy."

"Any time, Seb. Chirp me later. You too, Listy. Feel free to chirp, or message me anytime."

Seb and Jinuh held their hands up in front of each other, waving them back and forth in valediction.

"All right, Listy. Let's get your regular shoes back and get out of here."

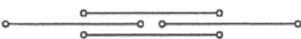

Once they were standing on the sidewalk outside of the arena, Seb asked, "What would you like to do now? I've been the one taking you everywhere."

"Seb, I think I want to go back to my dwelling and be alone," Listina pleaded.

"Is that—are you sure? Is it a good idea to be by yourself right now? I'm sorry I took you to so many upsetting places today. I didn't think coming here would be a problem, really."

"I'm okay. I promise. What you did for me today meant a lot. I do want to go home and be alone right now, though."

"But I don't want you to—"

"I'm not going to do anything. You showed me a lot today. A lot that I think I'd like to keep doing. Jinuh was right about sometimes needing reminders."

Seb cocked his head in confusion.

Listina giggled. "I'm glad I met them. I'm glad I met you. I'm not glad you took me to Nullity, and I don't want to go back there for a long time. I am okay, Seb. Luckily, I have one more opportunity." She tapped her lights. "Most people don't get another chance to think about what they would be missing, but I am relieved that I do. I'm going to go home for now, but I will check in with you later. I would like you to continue to be in my life."

Seb stared at her with his mouth open.

"It's okay, Seb." She turned to walk away.

Finally, Seb spoke. "Listy, that's great. Please do keep in touch. If not with me, then Jinuh will happily talk or meet too. There is always someone who can be there for you."

Listina gave a timid smile and started walking toward her complex.

Seb was relieved that Listina could recognize that there are people in her life who can be supportive, and things that she still wants for herself.

Suddenly rain started falling, coating Seb's face and clothes.

Chirp.

Seb looked at the band on his wrist and saw it read *Dee*.

"Dee!" Seb nearly shouted. "I'm so happy to hear from you. You'll never guess how these last two days went. Did you see my message about *Overground*? And that I found Listy? You were right. She fought pretty hard, but I think I got through to her. And in the process, I tried some new things. I'll have to run them by you and find out what's original for you too. Anyway, how are you? What have you been up to? I guess you've been busy since I'm only just now hearing from you. When can I—"

"Sebby. Calm down. Slow down," Dee responded flatly. "I'm good. Everyone is good. We've had some lights light up, but not enough for conversion. We've recently lost one though. She got away for now. I hear in your voice that you're still in control of yourself. But listen, I do need you for something. I found someone, but they're fighting me hard. I'm hoping you can help persuade him to join us."

Seb opened his mouth to speak, but no words came out. A tear joined the rain on his cheek, causing the two to merge, roll down his face, and drop to the ground.

The End

PART 3: 120-Day

PROLOGUE

Dee was still beside herself with joy. She had met Seb only four months prior, showing him how to break out from his monotonous ways, delaying his conversion. He fought some of the new experiences, particularly indoor skydiving, but eventually Seb tried them all.

For reasons unknown to them both, the last of the three lights on Seb's arm, an indicator of how close a person is to being controlled by the Global AI, had gone dark after almost turning solid. It was a welcome surprise, one that meant Dee could spend more time getting to know the real, in control Seb, continuing to share adventures with him when the other members of her group, the Syndicate, were occupied with different activities.

Dee and Seb spent time together only a few days prior, prompting them to delay meeting for another month to prevent the Global AI from locking on to a pattern. She was eager to see him, but knew that setting plans would help the Global AI determine a script for their conversion. That knowledge did not stop Dee from choosing the next place she wanted to bring Seb to: a restaurant that had been dug three hundred feet underground with a geothermal river running under the transparent floor. After eating, they would collect minerals at the edge of the open portion of the river, being careful to not touch the hot, near boiling, water, while enjoying the cool breeze blowing through the tunnel.

As pleasant and unique as the experience would be, Dee couldn't tell Seb why she wanted to collect the minerals. During her time working in a weather scheduling factory, she had learned how certain minerals could be used to create contained explosions. The minor aerial disruption caused by the blast from the minerals was used to adjust weather patterns, but now she had a new purpose for the knowledge.

Dee's parents had been converted to Global AI-control less than a year ago and she was determined to hinder it from taking control of other people in any way possible. She had already set two small explosions, both at places she believed the Global AI was using to advance and maintain its ability to track non-Global AI-controlled people. The first was at the West Side Plaza, disrupting a minor component factory's power supply after she damaged a solar panel in the plaza. The second was in a factory where a member of the Syndicate worked, after she snuck in using their credentials and damaged a lab that built larger components.

Following the second explosion, Dee quickly raced to a café to hide out until she was sure it was safe to leave. It was then, when running out with a smile on her face thinking of her success, that she nearly collided with Seb and convinced him to join her.

Now that Dee would not see Seb for another month, her focus shifted to selecting a new place to target. One that would slow the Global AI significantly if she were to succeed. She would not let anyone know what she was doing, or ask directly for help, fearing they could be caught and immediately converted.

CHAPTER 1

Dee left her dwelling, beaming while thinking about Seb, and rode the platform lift down to the lobby. She blissfully exited the complex and stood on the sidewalk, taking in her surroundings.

Dee was familiar with the area but had only moved into the building a couple of weeks prior. She believed that one of the many ways to prevent the Global AI from finding a pattern to lock on to was to keep moving and not live in one place for any longer than a year.

She got her bearings and started walking toward the hyper loop station.

While going down the steps, Dee thought, *I'm heading to the last place I want to be, but I need the motivation to find the next target. It needs to be done.*

She glanced at the destinations displayed, found the train going in the direction she needed to go, and plodded toward it.

"Nullity," she said, the smile dropping from her face. "Only one reason to go there, and most that arrive never leave."

Dee boarded and sat in the first empty seat. She pulled her Rollascreen from her pocket, uncurled it, and fidgeted with it nervously, looking for something that would distract her from thoughts of visiting her parents.

She'd only seen her mother and father twice since their sudden conversion by the Global AI. They each had only two lights lit, with the third and final light being completely dark. One day, Dee visited her parents and found them no longer in control of themselves, both with three solidly lit lights. They repeated the same script with her. Because her parents were older than fifty, they were confined to Nullity where aging Global AI-controlled people are encouraged to live. There, the Nullity population continue to work in factories doing jobs not requiring strength and agility until their bodies give out.

Dee still wasn't certain what caused the conversion, but she believed that her parents had been using too many of their credits. They'd both been sick, needing help to become well. While basic services were provided to them with no need to use their credits, services they needed above and beyond the standard care wiped out the remainder of their balance. Her parents had continued working to earn extra credits to pay down their debt, but after a few years, they were unable to catch up. Dee was angry. It was cruel and unfair that they'd been converted because a sickness put them into a debt that they couldn't repay. They were now stuck in the system forever.

Dee finally opened the messages on her Rollascreen and created one to send to Seb.

I'm taking a quick trip. I'm going to visit some people that I haven't seen in a while. It's not really something I want to do, but I need to. It'll help motivate me for my next project. I wish you could join me, for everything, but it's best if I do it on my own. I hope you're not off doing anything boring. I can't wait to see you in a month. Maybe we'll have to make it sooner. Message me, but don't tell me everything. I want some of it to be a surprise.
-Dee

Dee sent the message and placed the Rollascreen face down on her lap. A few moments passed before it beeped and a light shone from underneath. She smiled and quickly flipped the device over to read the text.

Dee! I'm so happy to hear from you. I can't wait to find out what you're doing. And I'm definitely not doing anything boring, I promise. It would be great to see you sooner. Let me know when, and where, and how. But whatever you have to do, you got this. Pleasant journeys.
-Seb

Dee let out a calm breath, put her Rollascreen back in her pocket, and sat in silence.

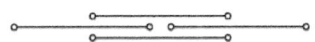

Dee watched the display of stops update as the train was slowing to arrive in Nullity. Her heart rate became more and more rapid as the train finally came to a rest, causing her to hold her breath momentarily before letting it out slowly. She stood and departed, stopping at the bottom of the station's steps and looking up. Dee pepped herself up before proceeding to the ground level, where she paused again to stare at the row of complexes on one side of the street and various factories on the other. Flowing in steady streams between the buildings were Global AI-controlled people moving systematically, coming and going. Dee sighed and started walking along the line of complexes, studying the identification numbers of the buildings to find the correct one. She went past ten nearly identical buildings before stopping at the one that matched the ID number she wanted. She remained focused on it, causing several Global AI-controlled people to step around her to avoid a collision.

Dee exhaled, counting down from four, and walked into the complex. She cut through a line of Global AI-controlled people all moving toward the platform lift and continued to a door at the far end of the building. When she arrived, she knocked and waited impatiently. She looked at the band on her wrist, tapping off several seconds with one finger on the back of her other hand before knocking again.

"Every time. The GAI couldn't at least fix that little nuance? I have to knock twice just to get—"

The door opened to reveal an older man and woman. "Deidra, how nice to see you," they said in unison. Dee pushed past them to go into the dwelling as they turned to watch her walk into the room and sit.

"Deidra, how nice to see you," they said again.

"Hi, Mom. Hi, Dad," Dee finally said. "I guess there's no point in trying to get you to call me Dee anymore." She frowned.

"Deidra, how have you been?" her mother replied, ignoring the request. "We haven't seen you in—" She paused, briefly looking off in the distance. "Quite some time."

"I know, Mom. I'm sorry. I don't like seeing you and Dad like this. After all the time I had with you, to just have you both taken away so suddenly." She stood and started walking around. "You've both taught me so much, and I've been able to share that with others, but it's still not fair. Just because being sick put you both in a debt

73

that you weren't able to come back from, they took you from me." She raised her voice. "This is all the GAI's fault. I just—I want your approval for what I want to do. What I need to do. I have to try to shut this all down. Make it all go away. I want you to come back. But you can't tell me anything new. You can't laugh. You can't cry. You can't tell me yes or no unless we've already had this conversation before." She looked at her parents, waiting for a response. Exasperated, she turned and yelled, "I'll take anything as an 'okay' from you." She looked at them again. After receiving no response, she sat down defeated.

"Deidra, how nice to see you."

Dee let out a groan. "Good enough." She stood again, walked to her parents and gave them each a hug. "I'll come see you another time." She went to the door, turned back to her mother and father one last time, then left the dwelling.

"Goodbye, Deidra. Thanks for the visit," she heard faintly.

Dee left the complex and stopped to face the line of factories on the other side of the street. She watched the streams of Global AI-controlled people coming and going from the buildings. "Drones. All of them. Their only purpose is to make what's needed to get us to spend credits, or to make more of themselves. If only those buildings were gone. Then the Global AI wouldn't need us. If only there was a way to remove them, to take them offline, to—that's it!" She looked up and down the endless row of factories and nodded to herself. "This is my target."

Dee quickly ran toward the hyper loop station. She sprinted down the steps and entered a train to ride back to her complex, grinning as she sat.

CHAPTER 2

Dee arrived at her dwelling and started digging through the few large boxes of possessions she'd brought to her new complex.

"Come on. Where is it? There's not much here and it's not that small." She moved from one box to the next until finally dumping the contents on the floor and sifting through the items. "Ah ha! Here it is." She picked up a tube the length of her forearm, placed it on the ground in front of her, and pressed a single button on the end of it. She watched as the tube unrolled itself and a light started glowing from the bottom. "Oops. Upside down." She giggled and flipped the flattened item over to reveal a lit display showing a welcome screen. "That's better!" She held her hand above the display, making an 'Okay' sign, being sure to keep her fingers separated while the view changed to show several icons.

"Maps and Cams, Maps and Cams. Where is that icon?" Dee scanned the options, looking closely at each. She stopped and touched an icon on the display depicting an eye. "I see you!"

The display changed again, prompting Dee to choose a location. She quickly entered 'Nullity' and watched as the screen began building a layered view of the place she had just visited. She could see the spacing between the complexes and factories lining the street. "I need a current view. Where's the Cam overlay option?" She tapped an icon that caused the buildings to flatten. "Not that one." She tapped it again, pleased when the buildings appeared to pop back up. Continuing her search, she found an image of a bird and tapped it. The display changed, adding a view of people walking between the buildings. "That's better. Strange icon image, though. There are definitely no birds in Nullity."

Dee stared at the display, watching the image of Global AI-controlled people walking in a synchronized pattern between the buildings. "Some of these factories are going to be used for making parts for the hyper taxis or hyper loop trains, or even parts for the Rollascreens and audiophones, but some must be used for the GAI's own goals. There has to be a pattern somewhere. Something to indicate what these buildings might be used for. None of them are named. They just have IDs. Each GAI person gets synced to their corresponding location." She moved her hand over one of the buildings, pinched it, and twisted her hand, causing the view to rotate so she could see a more direct link between the people and buildings.

"Where is my parents' complex?" She touched an icon on the display showing a number sign that placed the IDs of each building on the tops of their roofs. She read the numbers while sliding the view of the buildings until she found the ID of her parents' complex. She focused on the factory across from the complex and noticed people both going in, and then back out toward the street. She looked at the other factories nearby and paused. "Okay, that's strange. This one here is just like the factory my parents would be assigned to. GAI-controlled people are walking in, and some are walking out. But this other one on the other side only has people walking in. No one is coming back out." She watched as a hyper taxi stopped at the complex immediately across the street from the suspicious factory. Global AI-controlled people filed off the taxi and immediately into the complex.

"That's it! This factory has to be designed specifically for the GAI. Where people under its control go in but never leave. Replacements are shuttled to the complex and stay there until they're needed at the factory. But once they leave the complex, they never return. Their tasking never ends. The GAI uses them to their full potential." Dee was solemn about that revelation but a grin stretched across her face. "This is my target."

She grabbed the factory shown on the screen and pulled her hand close to her body, causing the display to bring the factory into closer view. She moved her hand around to make the building spin left and right, while she focused on the entrance and different corners of the factory. "I can't see any way to get in here without walking through the front door. And the only people going in are the GAI-controlled employees." Dee paused and slapped the palm of her hand against her forehead. She repeated, "The only people going in are the GAI-controlled employees. And they never come back out. Meaning, anything they take into that factory with them will stay in there."

Dee closed the Map and Cam display and tapped a new icon that brought up a three-dimensional floating picture of a black cube. "All right, this one is a little big as-is. It worked out the first two times I needed a *boom*, but I'm going to have to scale it down and make more of them. I'll distribute them out to as many of those GAI people as I can. That should help spread out the damage. Maybe I can take the entire building offline, instead of individual rooms like the previous places."

Dee used both of her hands to pull in on the black cube. The display changed to show what was inside. "I think I can cut back on some of this. I'll still need the timer." She tapped a piece inside the cube and then touched an image of a lock next to it. "I can scale down the rest of this stuff. I don't need one big bang this time. Just lots of little ones." She tapped an image of a mound of pebbles to bring it to the foreground, then placed both hands around it and pushed them together, causing the image to shrink. "Less minerals needed in each of these. I have to see what I still have on hand from the last two times, but I know I will need that trip with Seb before I do this."

She tapped several more images within the cube and shrank them down to the same size as the pebbles. "That's pretty good. Now I can make the entire cube smaller and maybe even sneak these into the pockets of those GAIers without them knowing."

Dee tapped on the outside edge of the display and then lifted both hands, causing the image to change to show the outside of the black cube. She put her hands on each side of the cube, moving them toward each other, to shrink it down. When the cube would no longer get any smaller around the interior pieces, she stopped. "That will do. Now I just need to make . . . a dozen of these? That should be enough. Then I need to get them over to Nullity and into the pockets of those GAI-controlled people. Easy? Hmm." She grinned. "Yeah. Easy."

She closed the image on the screen and scanned the icons shown. Deciding that she was done, Dee pushed a button on the side of the display, causing it to roll up. She picked the tube up off the floor and placed it back in the box it came from. She continued cleaning up the other items on the floor and returning them to the boxes when she came across a necklace.

Dee picked up the jewelry and laid a charm hanging from it in the palm of her hand. She pushed in a gem on the front of the charm, and watched as a hologram of her parents appeared and slowly spun. She stared at the rotating image, taking in all the details. "This is for you, Mom and Dad." Dee pushed the gem again, causing the hologram to fade away, and placed the necklace carefully in the box.

CHAPTER 3

I'm going to need a little help, Dee thought. *But who? And who will let me keep them in the dark, but still follow through?* She stopped, listing off names in her head, but disapproving each until her face finally lit up. "Zell! Obviously." She recalled the previous times she had used him to acquire various parts and gain access to the duplicators she needed. He didn't seem to care then, so she assumed he wouldn't care now.

Dee tapped a spot behind her ear and heard a short beep. "Zell," she said, and then waited.

"Dee? What's the pleasure of this call?"

"Hey, Zell. Can I make a request? Do you have the throughput?"

"You know me." He paused. "Nope!" Zell laughed deeply. "Of course you can ask, and I can say yes or I can say no."

"Helpful. When's the next time you're going to your factory? I could use some of those pieces that I don't have access to at mine for a new project that I'm working on."

"Let's see. Today is . . . it doesn't matter, and tomorrow is . . . it also doesn't matter. I'll let you know the next time I need some extra credits and will be going," Zell chided.

"You're a GAI light, you know that? A big, bright, GAI light. Maybe I should just chirp Anson. At least he can't come up with the nonsense that you do."

"Whoa. You didn't have to take it that far. Give me two or three days, okay? What's the rush anyway? Our lights shouldn't be lighting up anytime soon. I'll let you know?"

"Yes, thank you. I value your time. But I still stand by what I said. GAI light." Dee tapped the band on her wrist to end the call. "All right, that's one step forward."

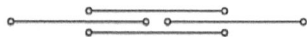

Chirp.

Dee looked at the band on her wrist. *About time*, she thought. She answered the call. "Zell? It's been five days. What happened to two or three?"

"I'm sorry. I must have the wrong person. I'm looking for the Dee that wants to use me for access to my factory, not the Dee that wants to complain about how long it takes for me to chirp her. So, complainer-Dee, can you get the other Dee for me? If she's around that is. If not, I can chirp back another time. Maybe in . . . five more days?"

Dee held back an audible scream. "Sorry, Zell. Hello, thanks for calling. Can I come meet with you?" she said through clenched teeth.

"Oh, hey, Dee!" Zell snorted. "Yes, you may come meet with me. Do you know where I'm at?"

"Still the same place I met you before?"

"Indeed. Gotta let the GAI think it might have a chance with me someday, right?"

Zell's comment broke through Dee's frustration and made her laugh loudly. "Right. That's right, Zell. I do thank you."

"And I do accept your thanks. I need to grab a few things at home, but then I'll see you soon?"

"Of course. I'll get my bag, then head over."

Beep.

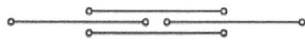

Dee arrived outside of Zell's factory to find him waiting for her.

"I've been here long enough today, so I'll get you in, but then I'm going to leave," Zell announced.

Dee looked at the time. "It's only 9:30 in the morning. What do you mean you've been here long enough today?" She scoffed.

"What can I say? Work hard or hardly work. I'll always go for the latter. Anyway, let's get you in. And in case you've forgotten, my spot is on the third floor. Take the platform lift up, then go two doors to your left."

Dee nodded in acknowledgment.

"Now, get close behind me and shield your eyes. After I've been scanned, break off toward the platform lift while I walk back out. When you leave, well, good luck."

"I followed you out the previous times."

"Just find a GAI guy and follow them out the same way. Or run. Whatever suits you. You'll be fine."

Dee chuckled nervously. She stood behind Zell, staying close, and put a hand over her eyes to shield them. They slowly walked into the building and Zell faced the scanner. Displayed immediately below read the text:

Zell BaDell
In Time: 9:32 a.m.
Welcome back

Dee peeked between her fingers and saw the text. "Zell BaDell," she sang. "I don't get to use your full name often."

"Hush or I will push you right back out of here."

Dee covered her mouth. They stepped into the lobby of the factory and separated. "This is where I leave you," Zell said. "Don't make a mess of my station, all right?"

"I won't. I should only need a few different pieces. Thanks, Zell."

Zell bowed and walked back out, looking at the updated display near the door.

Out Time: 9:33 a.m.
Goodbye, Zell BaDell

Dee walked quickly to the platform lift, stepped on an empty platform, and rode it to the third floor. She stepped off and stopped dead. "I've always blindly followed him." Looking in both directions, Dee continued, "Um, left. He said it was left. Two doors." She went to the correct door and quickly moved out of the way when it swung open. A GAI-controlled employee walked out, silently acknowledged Dee, and continued. Dee let out a breath and walked through the opening. She took in her surroundings and went over to a disorganized desk with no one sitting at it. "Oh, Zell. Leaving his desk in disarray. It makes sense after he told me *not* to make a mess of it."

Dee sat at the desk, causing the display sitting on top to light up.

Welcome, Zell

"Correct desk, but this won't do me any good. I won't be able to use it. Luckily I brought my own." Dee pushed the display on the desk back and pulled the bag she was wearing around to her front. She slid out a tube, put it on the desk, and pressed a button on the side to make it unroll. She opened the picture of the black cube on her display, looked through the list of parts needed, then turned to a shelf next to her. "Perfect!" she said, loud enough to cause two Global AI-controlled employees in the room to turn and look at her. "Uh. It worked?" she called out. They returned to their tasks.

Dee took a few pieces from the shelf and laid them out in front of her. She looked over at a large machine sitting on the desk. "Let's see what this can do." She selected a few buttons on the machine, causing the screen to flicker, and watched as the device flashed several times before presenting a tiny black cube. "Too small. What did I do wrong?" she questioned. "No reason to put this one to waste though. I just won't be able to fit a timer in it." She put the small cube in her bag before turning back to the machine. This time she tried a few different buttons, then waited for the flashing to stop before she pulled out a larger black cube. "Yes!"

The two Global AI-controlled employees turned to look at her again.

"This is all very exciting." She grinned.

Again, the employees returned to their tasks.

Dee picked up the cube and opened the top of it. She carefully placed the components she had previously laid out on the desk inside the cube. "Enough room left for the minerals. This will do nicely."

She went back to the machine and entered the number eleven. "A dozen should be enough to put a small dent in the GAI's operations."

While Dee waited for the machine to finish making an additional eleven black cubes, she turned to the shelf and took eleven more of each of the components she needed, carefully laying them on the desk. She spied a small, empty box on a shelf above Zell's desk, took it down, and started loading the parts into it. As she finished, the machine producing the black cubes flashed to alert Dee that it had completed. She put the cubes in her bag along with the small box of parts.

It's time to get out of here before anyone realizes I'm not really Zell. She shuddered at the thought.

Dee pushed a button on the side of her display, causing the picture of the cube to disappear and the screen to automatically roll up. She picked up the tube from the desk and held it under her arm. "I better make sure I leave Zell's desk how I found it." She pulled Zell's display back to where she had found it. "Organized disorder, I guess."

Getting up from the desk and quickly leaving the room, she stepped on the first empty platform lift going down. She got off when she arrived at the lobby, found a Global AI-controlled employee walking toward the exit, and ducked closely behind them. She followed them out the door while she shielded her eyes.

"Phew. Okay. Made it out!" With parts in hand, Dee decided that she would contact Seb to see if he would be willing to push up their next meeting.

She pulled out her Rollascreen and began creating a message.

Seb, is there any way you would be able to get together with me earlier than next month? I miss seeing you.

Dee paused while she thought. *I don't want to lie to him about why I want to move up our plans, so it's not complete dishonesty.* She continued.

Please let me know, and I look forward to hearing from you.

Dee put the Rollascreen back in her pocket and made her way to her dwelling.

CHAPTER 4

The next morning, Dee paced her room impatiently. "Why haven't I heard from Seb yet? I hope he's okay. I'm sure he's okay. He wouldn't be ignoring me, right? He knows why I want to go there, doesn't he? He figured it out. He won't ever want to talk to me again." She shook off the thought. "No. That can't be. He's probably just busy. Or maybe still sleeping. What time is it anyway?" She looked at the time displayed on the screen on the wall in her dwelling showing that it was still dark out. "Five in the morning? Yeah, he's still sleeping. I'm too excited and nervous to do any more of that."

Dee sat on the edge of her bed and played out possible scenarios in her head of how her meal with Seb could go.

"Hi, Seb. What? No, I'm not collecting these minerals because they're nice and shiny. I'm trying to single-handedly take down the GAI, one building at a time. And after, maybe a little indoor skydiving?"

She chuckled.

"Hello there, Seb. How's your meal? What's that? You hate the GAI and want to destroy a couple of their buildings to keep them from recruiting more people. Just like they did to my parents without any warning? What a coincidence!"

"If only it was that easy. It would be nice to not do this alone."

Dee got up from her bed and walked into her kitchen. She began pulling out the drawers, one by one, finding most to be empty until she found a piece of paper and pen. She laid the paper on the counter and used the pen to draw two lines of cubes spaced evenly apart. She detailed each cube, shading the dark side, and adding shadows under each. On one line, all of the cubes were identical. On the other, she left one cube missing, placing only the shadow of where it would be. After she was happy that each detail was perfect, she picked up the paper, crumpled it, and dropped it on the counter.

"In time," she said. "Once I'm done, that's how Nullity will look."

Beep.

Dee excitedly removed her Rollascreen from her pocket.

Weekly credits applied to your account.

She frowned.

Beep.

With disappointment, she looked at the device again.

From: Seb
Time: 7:01 a.m.

She opened the message as quickly as she could touch the screen.

Of course I'll meet you earlier. How about now? Now is a little early, isn't it? How about 12? Same place that we agreed on?
-Seb

Dee grinned to herself and quickly typed a reply.

Yes! Same place. See you there at 12.
-Dee

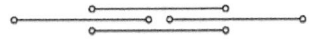

Dee walked to the location where she was meeting Seb to find him already there, facing a stand with a single Global AI-controlled employee. She ran up behind him, wrapped both arms around him tightly, and gave him a quick kiss on the cheek.

Seb turned, blushed, and gave her a hug. "Dee, so good to see you. I'm sure moving this up is a good trick on the GAI. You really know how to keep everyone guessing."

Dee chuckled nervously. "Um, yeah. It's good to keep the surprises coming. Anyway, I'm really happy to see you too. Ready to go down?"

"You know it! I'm always ready to eat." Seb gestured for her to lead the way.

She approached the stand with the Global AI-controlled employee. "We would like the full experience, please. The meal and minerals?"

"There must be two to partake in the two functions. Are there two?" replied the employee.

"Yes! There are two." Dee gestured back and forth between Seb and herself. "Us two."

Seb was confused. He asked, "Two people need to be here for this? Why? I can't just come here by myself sometime? That seems strange."

"The meal you can have by yourself, but for the other part, looking for minerals, you need two people. I think it's a safety thing," she said, not too sure of her own answer.

"But you've done this before, right? Who did you come with?"

"Yes, I've been here before," she replied, trying to hide her annoyance at the questions.

"But with who?" Seb persisted.

"Anson, all right? With Anson. I've told you about how we miss him at times. I brought him here. Is that okay? Are you going to leave now, knowing you're not the first?" Dee immediately regretted what she said, knowing she didn't want him to leave. Not only would she miss him if he did, but she needed him to get to the minerals.

"What? No! I don't want to leave. I was just curious. Anson? Okay. I know he was a good friend. Anyway, I'm hungry. Can we go in?"

Dee was relieved. "Yes! Let's."

They followed the Global AI-controlled employee to a platform lift behind the stand.

"Watch your step and enjoy your meal," the host said.

Dee and Seb carefully stepped onto the moving platform going down.

"Thanks again for coming, Seb."

"Of course. You say it like you had to twist my lights, but you know that all you have to do is say my name and I'll be there."

"Yeah, and that worries me too," she mumbled.

"What was that?"

"I said, I know," Dee fibbed.

They stepped off the platform as it arrived at the bottom of the long shaft, and onto a transparent floor where they could see a river flowing underneath.

"You brought Anson here before me?" Seb joked.

Dee scoffed. "I didn't even know you yet. Nice try."

He grinned. "Want to go find a table? The view looks great from anywhere."

They chose a table in the center and sat. A waitress immediately approached and greeted them. Dee said, "Hello." The casualness prompted Seb to look up at their interaction. She noticed and laughed. "Seb, other than the person at ground level, everyone here is in control of themselves."

The employee grinned and held up her arm, displaying a single solid light.

"Show off." He smiled. "Hello."

"Hello to you both. I'll be back with your food shortly. Please enjoy yourselves. And since there are two of you, don't forget to visit the mineral site after your meal. It's near the uncovered part of the geothermal river over that way." The waitress gestured to the side of the area.

Once the employee walked away, Seb inquired, "Did she say she's going to get our food? We didn't order anything. Did you pick ahead of time?"

"Nope! It's all surprises here. The employees pick for us. And I wouldn't expect it to be pizza either." She glared at him.

"Hey now. I eat different things! Not *always*, but usually, thanks to you."

Dee laughed. "Glad to hear that. So, what's original, Seb? Have you been doing anything different? Have you learned any new songs for *Overground* yet?"

"I'm working on one." He grinned. "I haven't been there since I went with you, but I'll let you know when I do. What about you?"

She thought for a moment. "Mostly the same, of not doing the same things." She shrugged. "I'm just happy to be here with you."

As Seb nodded, the waitress returned carrying four plates containing a variety of foods.

"Here we are," she announced. "We have all five available fruits on this plate, biryani here, dolma on this plate, and lastly, we have tabbouleh. I hope you enjoy."

Their eyes widened at the sight of the food in front of them.

Dee winked at Seb. "You said you were hungry. Dig in!"

Seb's face lit up. "Gladly!"

They took turns sampling the different items on the plates, while looking around at the spacious, open area, rock walls, and jagged rock ceiling.

Seb finished a bite in his mouth before offering, "The river flowing under us has to be the best part. The food is really good, there's no question about that, but watching the river move is very calming. It's making for a perfect day."

"I hoped you would enjoy this. We're not done yet, though. Just wait till you see the mineral cave. We can even take some with us. I like, uh, collecting them. Maybe you can help me? I want some for a, uh, project I'm working on."

"Wow. We can take them? Of course I'll help you. Maybe you can show me your project when you're done? But aren't they dangerous? I thought there was something that could be done with them, but I can't remember what."

Dee looked around nervously, trying to decide what to tell Seb. "Um. Dangerous? Hmm. I don't—dangerous? Not that I know of. Um. I'll be careful with them. But I still need to get them. Um. I promise?"

Seb laughed. "Maybe I'm wrong. Maybe it was something else." He put another bite in his mouth. "Let's finish our food—mmm, such good food—and go get a look at these dangerous, or not dangerous, minerals you've been so excited about."

"Excited? I'm not—" Dee calmed herself. "Yes, let's finish up. I can't believe how good the tabbouleh is. And that I've never had it before. The food was completely different when I came here last. But being here and sharing the experience with you is making it so much better." She blushed, happy to see that Seb was not looking directly at her to notice.

Dee took another bite while Seb pushed away from the table.

"I actually can't eat anymore." He puffed out his cheeks.

Dee swallowed the food in her mouth, nearly choking on a laugh. "Let me pay, then we can head to the cavern."

"You pay? No way."

"Yes. You're doing me a favor."

Seb raised an eyebrow.

"I mean that I invited you, so I will pay."

"I'm not winning this, am I? So, thank you."

Dee huffed in victory then waved toward their waitress.

The employee walked over to their table and asked, "Are you both finished? Did you enjoy the selection?"

Dee and Seb responded in unison, "Yes! So good, but so full." They laughed at the synchronous response.

"Wonderful!" The employee presented them with a display showing the cost.

Dee tapped her wristband to the screen to pay.

As the waitress walked away, Seb stood. "Let's go get you some minerals."

She smiled and followed Seb toward the entrance to the cave.

CHAPTER 5

Dee and Seb walked through a narrow corridor that led them to an expansive cavern. From one wall flowed the river that they had been looking down on through the transparent floor while eating. They could feel the heat of the uncovered portion of the water as it dissipated into the cool air around them.

"This sensation is amazing," Seb blissfully announced. "The warmth below and the cool air above, all mixing, wow."

Dee smiled as she watched him take in the sights and sensations. She found herself getting lost in his enjoyment until she remembered why she needed to be in there. Dee looked toward the flowing river and caught sight of a glimmer of the minerals she was seeking along the edge.

"Seb, feel free to stay where you are," she called over her shoulder. "I'm going to go down and start looking through the rocks over there."

Seb, still elated, faced Dee. "I'll be over in a few."

"Don't rush, I'll be fine." Dee walked toward the spot along the river where she saw the shimmering minerals. She headed closer to the edge, feeling the heat rising up the steep hill, and stopped at a pile of stones. She moved them around with her foot, brushing off the settled dust.

Dee mentally calculated how much of the mineral she needed for the twelve cubes. "It shouldn't be too much. I'll be able to carry it all myself. And I always bring a bag with me. I just need to get—"

"Dee, what are you thinking about over there?" Seb yelled, trying to be heard over the sound of the river.

The sudden question broke Dee's concentration and startled her, causing her to slip and begin sliding toward the river.

"Seb!" she called out.

He ran over and grabbed her hand, yanking her up. "I guess this is why they want two people in here. I really don't think you want to go swimming in there. It's probably a little too warm to be enjoyable." Seb winked.

"I'm glad you can find this funny," Dee said behind a grin. She brushed herself off. "Thanks for saving me."

"I always will. Anyway, do you need some help? Did you find what you were looking for?"

"I did. I was just trying to figure out how much I needed for my project before you nearly made me jump into the river." She glared at him.

Seb frowned, shaking his head. "I didn't mean to!"

Dee laughed. "I think I only need enough to fill my bag. If you want to help, just grab what you can and put it in here." She set the empty bag on the ground between them.

They both crouched down and started sifting through the various rocks, dust, and minerals on the ground, separating the shiny minerals and placing them in the bag.

"Whatever you're doing with these will probably look really nice. Bright and shiny."

"Yeah," Dee said nervously. *Probably bright*, she thought. *If I do it correctly*.

They continued loading Dee's bag until it was nearly full of minerals, then they both stood to stretch.

"Is there anything else you need, Dee?"

"I think that's it. Do you want to stay a little bit longer, or are you ready to go?"

"I am a bit hot now after being so close to the river, so maybe we should head somewhere cooler."

Dee picked up her bag and started walking toward the corridor, while Seb followed closely behind. They entered the main eating area, and waved goodbye to their waitress as they continued to the platform lift.

They arrived at ground level after the short ride up.

"Thanks again for joining me, Seb," Dee said as they departed. She began to walk away.

"Yeah, sure, but aren't we going to do anything else?" Seb called out. "You usually drag me around all over the place."

Dee stopped and laughed. "Not today. How's that for a change? I have to go do my own thing."

"All right." Seb smirked. "Well, thanks again for bringing me. I don't know what I liked best. The food, watching the river while we ate, or the cavern."

"Why do you need a favorite? Just remember it all as one experience."

Seb smiled.

Dee hugged him. "Bye, Sebby. Chirp me later?"

"You know it."

She watched as Seb left, then turned to go to her complex, clutching the bag of minerals tight.

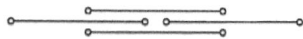

Dee entered her dwelling and tossed the bag on the ground. The loud thud caused her to jump. "Luckily you need a little more than a thump to make those go off, or I'd have just leveled this entire building."

She went into another room and picked up a different bag, returning to the main entry and placing it next to the one with the minerals. She sat down and started pulling cubes from the new bag, opening the tops of each, and lining them up side by side. Dee reached into the bag of minerals and removed enough to layer her palm. She poured some of the minerals into the first cube to cover the bottom, then deposited the remaining minerals in her hand into a second cube.

Dee continued filling the bottom of each open cube with the minerals until they all contained an even amount.

I have a lot of leftover minerals. I'll hold on to the rest of these for another project. Maybe I'll actually make something nice for Seb. She grinned at the thought.

From the bag that contained the cubes, Dee pulled out a box of components and emptied it, lining up one of each item behind the open cubes. She went down the line again, carefully placing each component into the cube, attaching wires at connection points, and realigning as needed. Finally, she added the timers, placing one inside each cube and connecting the final wiring. She carefully looked over every cube, making sure they all appeared identical with no leftover pieces, and closed the lids. She pulled the too-small cube out of the bag and placed it to the side. "I don't have plans for this one yet, but I will definitely be keeping it around." She picked up the twelve identical cubes one at a time and carefully placed them in the bag she had previously emptied.

Dee grabbed the small, unused cube along with the bag of extra minerals, and took them into the kitchen, placing them on the counter. She walked back to the main room, picked up the bag of assembled cubes, and placed it near the door to her dwelling.

"Tomorrow will be the day. Back to Nullity much too soon." Dee yawned. "But sleep now. Fun later."

She went to her bedroom, flopped onto the bed, and quickly fell asleep.

CHAPTER 6

Dee woke with a start and looked all around the room. She patted at her arms, body, and face. A quick glance reassured her that she was alone.

"That was unsettling. I could have sworn someone was in here. What a crazy dream." Dee checked the time. *6 a.m.* It was too early to start her day, but she didn't think she'd be able to get any more sleep. *I wish Seb was awake, but I'll see him after my, hopefully quick, trip to Nullity today.* She decided the best way to kill some time was to read the latest news.

Dee picked up her Rollascreen from beside the bed, uncurled it, and opened the morning report.

June 26th, 2332
Sunny today. Sunny tomorrow.

Head synthetic meat designer brings new flavors.
Explosions being investigated. Leads welcome.

New Global AI additions: 2231
Global AI removals: 2047

"Huh, I wonder if I know anyone who could help investigate those explosions." Dee rubbed her chin. "I wonder, I wonder. Hmm, nope. No one at all." She grinned and opened the article about the synthetic meat designer.

Listina Diandre, age 28, is a designer at the Central Synthetic Meat Processing Co. She has been working in the same position for a number of years, but provides us with a wide range of flavors that no other could achieve. When asked how she does it, she responded by saying, "Sometimes it's good, and sometimes it's not." We look forward to the next good flavor.

Dee passed by the synthetic meat plant often. While they may have never crossed paths directly, Dee expected that Listina would make a good candidate to join the Syndicate. Anyone that had a job that required them to think for themselves would.

Dee looked at the time. "It's almost late enough now. Transports will be running soon. I'll get a quick breakfast and get ready to go."

She walked into the kitchen and took a protein nutrient bar from a nearby drawer. She opened it, pulled back the wrapper, and took a bite. She gagged, wondering how anyone in control could possibly eat them. They contained the necessary nutrition needed, but every one tasted the same to her, regardless of what the packaging said. *At least they are provided to us and I don't have to waste my credits on them.*

Dee finished eating, walked to the door of her dwelling, and after sliding on a pair of shoes, left. She immediately turned around and walked back in, picking up the bag she forgot by the door. "This trip would have been for nothing had I forgotten this." The unwelcome wake-up in the morning had rattled her more than she realized. She shook her head and left the dwelling again.

She rode the platform lift down to the lobby of the complex and exited the building. She began walking in the direction of the hyper loop station, noticing how few people were on the sidewalk early in the morning.

At the hyper loop station, she quickly headed to the train going to Nullity. She stood with a group of Global AI-controlled people waiting for the doors to open, watching them nod over and over to each other. Dee rolled her eyes at the sight. *I hope I can put a small damper on the GAI. This is awful to see. Nod, nod, nod. No other interaction. Just waiting for the next trigger to continue their script.*

The doors opened and Dee sighed as the Global AI-controlled people filed on. She found a seat and sat, carefully placing her bag on her lap and holding it tight. As the train began to move, she started picturing in her head the steps to carry out her plan. She would first set the timers on each of the cubes, then sneak them into the jacket pockets of the Global AI-controlled people walking into the factory where no employee ever left. Finally, she would visit with her parents until she was sure her plan went off without a hitch.

Before Dee could run through the steps in her head again, the train came to a stop and displayed *Nullity* as its current location. Dee breathed in deep. She understood that this visit had a different goal than the previous trip and nervousness was taking over. She exhaled slowly as she stood, then departed the train.

Dee walked toward her parents' complex. She entered the building and didn't stop until she was knocking on her parents' door. After counting off several seconds, she knocked again. Dee's mother opened the door.

"Deidra, how nice to see you," both greeted. "We've seen you recently."

"Yes. I have something to do. Something for you both. I'm stopping in quickly now, but I'll be back in a little bit to stay for a while longer."

Dee walked into the dwelling and directly to the kitchen. She unloaded the cubes from her bag and opened the lid of each. She began setting the twelve timers. When Dee was halfway through the process, her father walked into the room. Startled, she shut the lid of the cube in her hand and stood to block the view of her collection. She eyed her father as he went to the chiller, removed a container, and walked back out of the room. After releasing a breath, Dee continued her task. Once completed, she closed the tops and placed the cubes in her bag. She returned to the room where she had left her parents, finding her father sipping out of a glass bottle. She approached them and gave each a hug.

"I'll be back. It shouldn't be long," she said. "I'll see you soon."

Dee walked out the door of the dwelling and heard her mother call out, "Goodbye, Deidra. Thanks for the visit."

She quickly made her way through the lobby and out of the complex. She scanned the factories lining the other side of the street, focusing on the one where people were entering but not leaving. Dee looked up at the top of the building, seeing billowing black smoke coming from it. "It must be time to clean out the GAI removals. I wonder how often they need to free up the space." Frowning, she walked to the complex directly across from the target factory, put down her bag, and opened it. She took out a cube and waited.

A Global AI-controlled person walked out of the complex, heading in the direction of the factory. Dee followed them, muttering, "Replacement time across the street. Thank you for your sacrifice. Signed, the GAI." She slid the cube into the pocket of the Global AI-controlled person and watched as they crossed the street and went into the factory. "One down, eleven to go."

Dee glanced behind her and saw no one else leaving the complex to go to the factory. She was afraid she miscalculated how long it would take a dozen new GAI-controlled people to arrive and replace the current ones in the building. A brief moment of concern washed over her when thinking about the timers she set on the cubes. She peered at the bag on the ground and then checked her wristband. "I should be okay."

She looked up as another Global AI-controlled person walked out of the complex, followed by two more. "Okay," she chuckled. "I'm the one that needs to keep up now." She went back to her bag, pulled out three more cubes, and quickly approached the people. She dropped a cube into each of their jacket pockets.

The process continued until all twelve cubes had been placed in pockets of Global AI-controlled people, and all had made it into the factory directly across the street. Dee took a moment to stare in that direction.

BOOM.

Dee quickly dropped, then looked ahead of her.

"Oh no. No, no, no." She checked her wristband. "That one was too early. Did someone find it and change something? No, no, no. They were all supposed to all go off at once."

She picked up her bag and ran into her parents' complex. She stepped into the lobby and tried to catch her breath. "If the other ones don't go off now, this may have been a waste. What went wrong? What if it gets traced back to me, or Zell, or Seb for that matter? Oh no."

Dee hurried to the door of her parents' dwelling and knocked. As she looked at her wristband and began bouncing impatiently to count off the time, the door was opened by her father.

"Deidra, how nice to see you."

There was an uneasy feeling that she shoved off before pushing her way inside. She went into the kitchen and leaned over the counter, trying to take several deep breaths, but all that came were short, shallow gasps. She thought for a moment before looking around the kitchen. She opened a nearby drawer and pulled out several pieces of paper and a pen. She began writing, letting words flow easily across the page. On the last page, she sketched a rough drawing, then organized and straightened the papers. Dee took them and ran to her parents' bedroom. She crawled under the bed and shoved the papers into a band attached to the bottom of the frame.

Just in case, she thought before leaving the bedroom.

Finding her parents in the entry room, she took a seat.

"Deidra, how nice to see you. How have you been? We've seen you recently."

"Yes, I know. Very recently, but I must go soon. I won't be able to sta—"

BOOM.
BOOM. BOOM. BOOM.

BOOM. BOOM.
BOOM.

Dee's eyes widened at the sounds. She leaned forward in a mixture of relief and worry. Her parents showed no reaction and continued to look at her.

She couldn't be sure that every cube had detonated, but there were enough muffled blasts to give her hope. She looked up. "Mom, Dad, I have to go. That wasn't the plan, but I don't think I can stay. It will probably be a while before I see you again." She stood, went over to her parents, and gave each a long hug. "I'm sorry." She grabbed her bag, walked out of the dwelling, and picked up her pace. Nearly jogging, she hurried through the lobby before exiting the complex.

Across the street, there was a new, lighter shade of smoke coming from different spots of the targeted factory. She grinned and started walking quickly to the hyper loop station.

Dee rode the hyper loop train back to where she lived, heading directly to her dwelling. She tossed her empty bag aside and went to her steam room. She disrobed, stepped into the steamer, and turned it on. Staring at her feet, she stood in silence.

After she was clean and dry, she got dressed in new clothes and returned to her entry room.

Sliding on her shoes, she announced with a newfound grin, "Time to finally start my day."

CHAPTER 7

Dee left her complex, unsure of where she wanted to go. She boarded the first hyper taxi she could find, pulled her Rollascreen from her pocket, and opened the news. At the top read:

Explosion in Nullity

"That was fast. Not that I should expect anything less from the GAI."
She opened the article.

An early morning explosion in Nullity eliminated a building that was part of the maintenance of the Global AI network. A minor disruption is expected, however other factories nearby can be converted to replace the damaged building. An investigation is on-going, but it is suspected that the explosion was deliberate. By whom, and how, is currently unknown, and may take time. Removals from the Global AI as a result: 129.

"Of course they're just going to bring another building online." She was hopeful that she had made a difference by taking one building offline, but wondered how she would be able to repeat her latest accomplishment without risking her friends. She sighed deeply. 129 removals from the Global AI seemed unlikely. She anticipated that the employees entering the building would have removed their jackets, placing them in storage, and would not have been directly impacted by the explosions. Any other removals would have been from other, more natural causes. *Not much I could have done about that. I can't clear a whole building on my own.*

Dee looked ahead, rubbed her tired eyes, and smiled. "That's done and I won't be going back to Nullity in the near future. Let's have some fun."

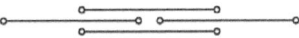

Dee spent the next several months enjoying time with Seb and the Syndicate. They found more original activities to do and places to explore.

She would periodically go to work to earn additional credits to pay for food and new experiences. While at her factory, she would see minerals that were used for her job controlling weather patterns, thinking back to the things she had accomplished with them.

Global AI additions had decreased slightly, and while Dee was not sure if she was the reason, she was happy, nonetheless.

One day, Dee arrived at her factory and entered her lab to find it empty.

"Huh. It looks like I won't be earning any credits today." She wondered if everything had been removed for cleaning or if there was a reorganization. She decided to come back another week in hopes that everything would be back in place by then.

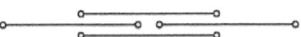

Dee shot straight up in her bed. The skin around her lights prickled as if someone was running their fingers over them. Heaving for air, she focused on her arm. It was the second time this week she'd awoken feeling watched. Maybe she was falling into the same routine that she preached so hard to avoid. *Good thing today is my last day in this dwelling.* She looked at the display on her wall. In the lower corner read *9 a.m. January 28th, 2333.* "That's the latest I've been able to sleep in a while. Maybe that's a good sign." She stretched and got out of bed.

"What am I going to do today? What's my credit count look like?" She tapped the band on her wrist to change the display from the time to her credits. "Not great. I'm running low. Maybe a trip to my lab needs to happen. I hope it's up and running."

Dee changed her clothes and left the complex to go to her factory. She entered her lab and found it filled with new equipment. "Back to, well, not normal, but it's no longer empty. There sure are a lot of GAI-controlled people in here now. There weren't so many before. Do I still have a desk?" She looked around and found an open desk near where hers used to be. She sat, causing the display to light up.

Welcome, Deidra

"My stuff is here. What are my tasks now? Has that changed?" She waved her hand in front of the display, keeping the tips of her fingers facing the screen. A list of tasks was shown to her. "Ugh, how repetitive. Doing these every day would be sure to light up my lights. But I really need some credits, so I'll do a few. I'm not sure I'll be back here again. It might be time to find a new factory."

Dee opened several of the tasks, completing each as quickly as she could. Once each one was finished, she held her wristband in front of the screen to claim her credits.

After a few hours passed, she yawned loudly. "All right, it's almost lunchtime and I have enough credits to get me by for a little while."

Dee pushed away from her desk and stood. Every one of the Global AI-controlled employees in the room turned to look at her. "Okay . . . I'm just gonna—" She quickly left the lab and exited the factory, stopping on the sidewalk.

"What to eat today?" She picked a direction and started walking until she saw a pizza place. "Salazar's Pizzeria. That will do! Seb would be so happy to know this is what I chose."

Dee walked in, noticing a single customer sitting alone in the pizzeria. She ordered a slice of pizza, took it, and sat. "Not many people in here, I'm not sure what Seb sees in pizza anyway. It's soft in some spots and crispy in others. I guess it does taste okay though."

She finished eating and went to the entrance of the restaurant. As she opened the door, a young woman walked through, quietly thanking Dee while continuing. Dee's eyes followed the woman. *There's something about her.* Dee went back to her table and sat, watching the woman order a slice of pizza and sit by herself to eat. She noticed the women had one solid light, and a second light blinking rapidly. Dee opened her Rollascreen, holding it in front of her to hide that she was observing the woman.

When the woman finished eating and began to leave, Dee got up and followed. She caught up with the young woman just outside the door and called out.

"Hey!"

The woman stopped and turned.

"Why don't you come with me?"

"What? No," the woman replied.

Dee blinked several times. "No? Uh, I noticed your lights. I can show you new and different things. I can help keep you from losing control to the GAI. Don't you want to—"

The woman held up her hand to stop Dee. "No thanks. I have to go back to work."

She stood with her mouth agape as the woman began to walk away. Dee followed her from a distance, watching her enter a nearby factory. She picked up her pace to see the information on the display below the eye scanner after the woman walked in.

Listina Diandre
In Time: 12:00 p.m.
Welcome back

Dee backed away from the factory, pausing to think. "Listina? The one from the news article? I wonder why she didn't want to talk to me. I might need Seb's help with her. He didn't fight me like that."

She headed back to her complex, stopping just outside. She called Seb and explained that she needed his help with a possible new Syndicate recruit. "I'll send the information to your Rollascreen. Bye, Seb. Thanks." She began walking to the door of the complex, but stopped. "I need to send this info to Seb now, or I might forget."

Dee created a message, including a picture of Listina, her work information, and the last place she'd seen her. She sent it to Seb.

"Now to get to my dwelling and finish packing it up. I've moved most of the important items to the new place, but I've been living at this one long enough."

Dee walked into the complex and took the platform lift to her floor. She went to her dwelling and found the door open. She quietly crept inside and peered into the kitchen to find a person standing at the counter, opening a crumpled piece of paper. Already sitting on the counter were minerals dumped out of Dee's bag.

The person looked up. "Hello, Deidra. We've been excitedly waiting for you to join us."

They turned the piece of paper around to show her. "This drawing will certainly speed up the process of your conversion. You did particularly well on the shading."

Two other people stepped out and grabbed Dee by the arms. The group led her out of her dwelling.

"We hope you found your new work setup to your liking. You will be helping our cause from there for quite some time."

The End

PART 4: 365-Day

PROLOGUE

A primal scream escaped Seb. His face contorted in emotional pain.

Using both hands to wipe the rain and tears from his face, he fell to his knees. He remained on the ground, pants soaking up the water around him, until he slowly stood, composing himself.

"Okay, okay. Don't panic," he said calmly, trying to reassure himself.

"How can I not panic? No one escapes from the Global AI," he countered.

Seb felt a flood of emotions flow through him as he thought about the call from Dee. "She had no passion in her voice. No warmth. None of her giggles. None of her assuredness or shyness. She was . . . not Dee."

"Maybe it wasn't Dee? Hopefully it wasn't Dee."

"But she knew my name. She said all the things she always tells me. How did the GAI get her? And who was she talking about? 'She got away.' Listy? She left minutes ago. How would Dee, or the GAI, know that? And who are they trying to get to join them? A member of the Syndicate? Someone else? Me?"

Seb slowed his thoughts and looked at the lights on his arm. He poked at each of the two solid lights and one dark light, knowing that when all three were lit it would be over.

"Why me? Why would the GAI want me? I know it will eventually get everyone, but if Dee was talking about me—'I'm hoping you can help me persuade him'—then I must have done something, or know something, that I shouldn't."

"Is this because of Listy? I stopped her from intentionally joining the GAI. Are they mad about that? Is that why they took Dee?"

Seb replayed the conversation from Dee that was stored on his audiophone, making sure he was not overlooking, or missing, anything.

"Sebby. Calm down. Slow down. I'm good. Everyone is good. We've had some lights light up, but not enough for conversion. We've recently lost one though. She got away for now. I hear in your voice that you're still in control of yourself. But listen, I do need you for something. I found someone, but they're fighting me pretty hard. I'm hoping you can help persuade him to join us."

Tears welled in Seb's eyes.

"I have to be correct. They're after me with what I did. What can be done about it? Dee is gone. Do I hide forever? Can I keep going about my life without her, and stay away from the GAI? Should I resign myself to what's to come, no matter what I do?"

Seb continued wiping at the rain on his face.

"There has to be something I can do. Dee knows too many people—she's friends with too many people—I'm just the newest. Who is there? Zell? Jinuh? Anson? Anyone and everyone else in the Syndicate?

Seb looked up and down the street from where he was standing.

"I think the people in the Syndicate are the only ones who can help me." He thought briefly of Anson, the only Global AI-converted member of the Syndicate. Seb knew he wouldn't be any help. "I've barely known her for a year, but everyone else has been in her life much longer."

Seb looked around again, trying to find answers.

"I need to meet with everyone. Maybe they know something that I don't. Maybe I know something they don't."

Seb bent over to pick up his Rollascreen after noticing it had fallen from his pocket when he dropped to his knees. He wiped off the device and began composing a message to Zell.

Zell,

Dee has been converted. I don't know how. I don't know when. But we need to get her back. I don't care if I have to be given up to the GAI to do it. Please help. I don't know what to do.

-Seb

CHAPTER 1

"I know."

The voice came from Seb's audiophone. He looked at his wristband, realizing he answered the chirp before checking who it was.

"You know? Zell? What do you mean 'you know'?"

"I know about Dee."

"How do you know? I just talked to her. The GAI-converted her. She was still in control when I talked to her only a few days ago."

"I was there."

"You were there? What do you mean you were there? Zell! This is your fault? You did this? Where are you? I'm going to rip out your lights."

"Seb. Seb. I was outside of her complex. I saw a few people leading her away. I didn't know who they were—if they were in control or part of the GAI system—but Dee did not look like she wanted to be with them."

"Why were you at her complex? Where did they take her? What are we going to do? We have to get her back." Emotions began to overtake Seb.

"We can't get her back. There's nothing we can do."

"That's not true! Where did they take her? Tell me!"

"Seb, they loaded her into a personal transport. I don't know where they took her. I tried to follow it. That's—that's when I saw you. In the café nearby. Why were you there, Seb? Near her complex."

"That's not—what? You mean she was right—where is she, Zell?"

"I don't know. I lost them."

"Then we can find her."

"Be logical about this, Seb. She's gone. And even if we found her, what are we going to do? Join her?"

Seb closed his eyes hard to think. "I don't know how, but we have to try. Please. We have to."

Seb heard Zell sigh.

"Please," pleaded Seb.

"Okay. Okay. I don't know how, but let's get everyone together. It's going to take more than you and I to figure this out. Meet me at my complex. I'll send you the location."

"Don't I already have it?"

"Not this one. This one nobody knows."

"Uh. All right. Thanks, Zell."

"Sure."

Beep.

Seb immediately heard a sound come from his Rollascreen. *At least he was quick about it.*

He pulled the device from his pocket and opened the message. He looked at the location displayed and cocked his head, raising an eyebrow.

"That can't be right. This location is in Nullity."

Seb quickly sent a reply.

Did you send the correct location? Maybe you chose the wrong thing?

Almost immediately, Seb's Rollascreen lit up with a response.

It's correct.

"Great. As if I haven't been there recently enough, I already get to go back. I'm sure there's a reason Zell's there, but I'm also sure I'll never find out why."

Seb felt his stomach growl. He checked the band on his wrist. Seeing that it was after 2 p.m., he knew he needed to meet up with Zell, but had to find something to eat first. *I could risk waiting until I get to Zell's, but I don't expect him to be hospitable.* 'Hey.

Thanks for having me to your place, in this really strange location for someone with only one light lit up. Can I have some food?' The idea momentarily broke Seb's depressed mood. He opted to look for a quick grab and go option.

"There has to be something. Anything."

Seb stopped searching and stared at one particular building.

"Oat milk ice cream? Maybe I can load it up with some extra protein, though synthetic beef in ice cream doesn't sound appetizing."

He again looked at the surrounding buildings.

"Pizza? No, I don't even want that right now." He continued scanning his options, muttering *no* to himself.

"Ah ha. Synthetic beef, but in a much more appetizing burger form." Seb walked several buildings ahead and stepped inside a restaurant. He went to the counter where a Global AI-controlled employee was standing and staring at the ceiling. Seb moved his eyes up to the same spot. Confused, he turned back to the employee to place his order.

"A synthetic beef burger, with all of the toppings, please," Seb requested.

"Okay," responded the Global AI-controlled employee. They continued to stare at the ceiling.

That's weird. He tapped his wristband to the screen to pay. At the end of the counter, he watched as his meal slid out through a window from the kitchen. He walked over, picked up his food, and headed toward the door to leave. He looked back at the employee, who was still staring intently at the ceiling. Seb started to speak, saying, "That was grab and g——" when the employee changed their focus from the ceiling and locked eyes with Seb.

"Ahh!" Seb exclaimed, startled. He quickly turned around and left the building.

He took a bite from his burger and grinned. "If this is one of Listy's creations where she works, I'm really glad she's still in control. Maybe she has some other flavors she's working on."

Seb finished eating while walking toward the hyper loop station. He was finding it hard to fathom that he was making another trip to Nullity in such a short period of time. After taking Listina, he now needed to go back because Zell intentionally lived there. *How is that even possible? He is definitely not GAI-controlled, I hope.* "But I never thought Dee would be!"

He arrived at the steps of the hyper loop station and quickly descended. When he got to the bottom, he scanned the area. His eyes went wide.

"Where are all of the hyper loop trains? There's not a single one down here. What is going on?"

Seb noticed the commuters in the station, all Global AI-controlled, walk to one platform, look at the empty track, then walk to another.

"I've never seen this before. There has always been a train, multiple trains, here to ride. Where have they all gone?"

Seb looked at the board on the wall, finding the usual list of hyper loop destinations blank.

"That's not promising. Looks like it's back to taking the hyper taxi. Between stopping for food, and now this, Zell is going to lose his patience waiting for me to get to his dwelling."

Seb removed his Rollascreen from his pocket and created a short message to Zell.

I'm coming. I'll make it to you as fast as I can.

Seb's Rollascreen lit up with a response.

Please do.

Seb placed the device in his pocket and ran up the station steps back to ground level. He watched a hyper taxi stop a few buildings ahead and began jogging toward it. He broke stride as he noticed the direction it was going. "Nothing is easy today. No hyper loops, and now this hyper taxi is going in the wrong direction. None of this would even be important if it wasn't for losing Dee."

As the taxi began to pull away, Seb saw another on the opposite side of the street that had already stopped. He quickly darted across the road, narrowly avoiding a collision with the other moving transportation vehicles. He ran in front of the second hyper taxi as its doors were beginning to close. Seb swung himself around and stuck his arm in the opening. The doors continued to close, covering the second lit light on his arm. They automatically reopened, and Seb embarked.

"Welcome, thanks for—"

"Please stop," he interrupted.

Seb slumped down in an available seat. He focused on the other riders, noticing each had three solid lights on their arms. This was the right taxi.

He spent the remainder of the ride trying to work out how Dee got converted, how to get her back, and what he would do assuming he could not. He knew that she would likely end up like Anson—a member of the Syndicate with no free will, and no free thinking, but only around for the nostalgia of a former friendship.

Seb closed his eyes, prepared for the long ride.

CHAPTER 2

Seb was standing on a sidewalk with Dee by his side.

"What are we going to do next?" he asked. A huge grin stretched across his face.

"It's your choice, Sebby. I picked the place. It's your turn." She smiled back.

Seb examined the surrounding buildings. He started to speak, turning to Dee. "Oh, I know. How about we—Dee? Dee? Where are you?"

He looked between the two buildings to see her walking away with another person.

"Dee! Wait up!"

Seb began running to catch up to them.

"Please, Dee. Stop. Don't leave. I want to go with you."

As he caught up, he focused on their arms. Both had three lights solidly lit. He grabbed Dee's arm, causing both her and the other person to spin around and look at him. Lights took the place of their pupils, matching the brightness of the illumination on their arms.

"Dee? What's wrong?" he choked out. "Answer me, Dee. Dee?"

Seb felt a thump on the back of his head. He turned to look and saw no one near him. He turned back to find Dee and the person with her continued walking ahead.

He felt another thump. And then another.

Seb opened his eyes and noticed himself slouching into the aisleway of the hyper taxi. A disembarking passenger ran into the back of his head.

"Ouch!"

He rubbed his eyes.

"Dee?"

He scanned the inside of the vehicle.

That was—what was that? I could have sworn Dee was right here.

Seb read the hyper taxi stop list and saw the next destination was Nullity. He shook his head, trying to clear his thoughts.

"Nullity?"

He shook his head harder.

Oh. Oh! I need to get off soon. Did I—was I asleep? That seemed so real. Until Dee's eyes. What—why were they lit like that? Who was she with?

Seb rubbed his eyes again.

It was just a dream. A great dream. Then a horribly wrong dream.

The hyper taxi slowed as the display above the driver showed they were arriving in Nullity.

Seb stood and stepped into the aisle of the hyper taxi. A Global AI-controlled passenger bumped into him from behind, but Seb held his footing.

"Not today. I'm not staying on here any longer."

He departed and stopped, removing his Rollascreen from his pocket and loading the message containing Zell's location.

"I still don't understand why Zell would be here. And voluntarily? For someone with just one light lit, he's awfully close to the GAI. Hiding in plain sight maybe?"

Seb looked at the IDs of the complexes surrounding him, and then the ID provided by Zell. "He's near the far edge. Almost as deep in as he can get."

Seb peered down at his feet. He was thankful to be wearing his half-wheeled shoes. Without them, it would take another fifteen minutes to walk to Zell's, and Seb was sure the fellow Syndicate member was growing impatient from the waiting.

Seb moved his feet together side-by-side to allow the magnets on each shoe to connect to form two complete wheels. He leaned forward and began gliding toward Zell's complex. He dodged the Global AI-controlled people crossing between the complexes and the factories on the other side of the road. He almost crashed into one person as they stopped suddenly in front of him.

"Arg!" Seb cried out, turning to watch as he went around them. Avoiding the GAI-controlled crowd was difficult enough when they were moving, but when they stopped, they created a new set of obstacles.

That one must be broken. He continued to inspect the IDs of the nearby complexes. He still had another dozen or two buildings to go, but he was making progress.

Seb arrived at Zell's complex, stopping in front and double-checking the ID against the one in Zell's message.

What I'm getting into with this, he thought as he walked toward the door.

Seb stepped into the complex to a loud commotion. He scanned the lobby as his eyes slowly got wider.

"There's—there are—little ones in here. A lot of little ones."

A small boy bumped into Seb and yelled out an apology as he continued running. Seb's mouth dropped as he turned his head to watch where the boy went.

Seb slowly worked his way through the lobby, avoiding additional collisions, to get to the platform lift. He stepped on an ascending platform while staring intently at the chaos he was rising from.

"Why are there little ones here?"

Seb looked at the floor he was moving toward.

"I need to have Zell explain this."

Seb stepped off the platform as it arrived at Zell's floor. He studied the numbers on the surrounding doors, and walked toward the one matching the number sent to him. Seb knocked cautiously and waited a moment for the door to open.

"Seb. Welcome."

"Zell, thanks—"

Two little ones ran out the door, squeezing past Seb. He focused on them as they raced to a platform going down.

"Please, come in," Zell announced, breaking Seb's engrossment.

"Uh, yeah. Zell, thanks for letting me come—"

"In, please?" Zell gestured inside.

He walked into Zell's dwelling while peering over his shoulder at the little ones riding the platform lift down.

"What are those?" Seb asked. "Well, not what, but why, or how, or . . . Why here? I thought Nullity was . . . Isn't Nullity just . . . ."

"They are mine."

"They're yours? How are they yours? What are you doing with them?"

Zell gave Seb a stern look.

"Sorry. I'm very . . . Yours?" He looked back and forth between Zell and the doorway.

Zell reached past Seb and shut the door.

"What do you need, Seb?"

Seb's jaw dropped. "Don't you . . . I thought you knew? Dee——"

"What about Dee? Huh? She got herself into this. Why should I risk myself for her? For you. You see what you walked into here. I have a lot more to risk than she did, or you do."

"Please——"

"Really, Seb. What? I let you come here, come to a place where almost no one else has been, so you can see what I have to lose. It's a lot. Not only a couple lights on an arm. It's much more than that." Zell trailed off, looking away. "Did you notice the smoke-stained building on the way here?"

"I did."

"That was all Dee. She did that and that's why the GAI has her. She did it to herself. She has no one to blame but herself."

Seb's eyes widened as the gears in his head ground to a halt.

"So, Seb. Tell me. What do you think I can do?"

He remained quiet.

"Hmm?"

"Dee didn't do that," he finally replied. Zell was growing visibly impatient.

He huffed. "Seb, think. Do you really believe that? Haven't you seen the news? Do you know what Dee does with all of her time? How sometimes she's unreachable? Unavailable?"

Seb let the gears start moving. "She—it can't—but—" He slumped his shoulders. "I know."

"Yes, you know. Now, back to my question. What do you think *I* can do?"

Seb composed himself. He knew he needed Zell's help if he was going to be able to find Dee and get her back. Zell was well-versed in how the Global AI worked, as evidenced by him living openly in the area where the Global AI held a vast majority of its people. People that continued its goal, whatever that may be.

Seb finally addressed Zell, "Can we sit?"

"Uh, y—yeah, sure," Zell stuttered, surprised.

They walked away from the entryway and sat in the main area of Zell's dwelling. Seb quickly glanced at the information display on the wall, one similar to what he had in his previous dwelling, and saw the depiction of the sun setting. He sighed. He turned to face the man before him.

"I know this is impossible. No one comes back from the GAI. But it's Dee. Without her, I don't have anything. If it wasn't for her, I wouldn't be here."

Seb looked at the lights on his arm and started picking nervously at the dark light. He faced Zell and continued.

"Please. I can't do this on my own. I need help. Please, Zell. Will you help?"

"Yes."

He was preparing to beg, to continue providing arguments for why they needed to try to rescue Dee, when Zell's response finally registered.

"But—wait. Yes?"

"Yes."

"Why—but I—yes?"

"Yes. Of course, yes. I've already been trying to come up with a plan, but I wasn't sure if you were going to be a part of it yet. I still don't know you, Seb. I've been trying to decide if I can trust you. I still don't know that either, but it's obvious you're invested. Plus, it would be better to have you working with me rather than have you in the way."

Seb slumped forward in his chair, dropped his chin in the palms of his hands, and looked Zell in the eyes. "Thank you."

Zell nodded.

"What's first?" Seb asked.

"First, we get over to Dee's place and see what we can find."

He stood.

"Whoa. Not right now. I have to get my little ones settled. Tomorrow we can start. I'll figure out who else can meet us there. Hopefully most of the Syndicate. We're going to need as many of us as possible. Go back to your dwelling and rest up. We'll reconvene in the morning, outside of Dee's complex. Do *not* go in until I get there, understand?"

Seb raised an eyebrow in confusion.

"We don't know what, or who is in there. If they take you too, don't think I'm coming for you. Understand?"

"Yes."

"Good. Now you can go."

Seb gestured toward the entry door and got a pointed glare in response from Zell.

"Thank you," Seb said as he turned to walk away.

"Hmph," Zell responded in dismissal. "We haven't done anything yet."

Seb left the dwelling and was overwhelmed by the sounds of the little ones playing in the lobby below him. He grinned at the discovery of Zell's life. "So he does have feelings. Who knew?"

He exited the complex and waited for a hyper taxi to return to his area.

After arriving at his own building, he entered his dwelling and slumped down in his bed. He was physically and mentally exhausted from the events of the past days.

Tomorrow, he would rejoin Zell and try to get Dee back.

CHAPTER 3

"Dee, don't leave!"

Seb sat straight up in his bed and wiped sweat off the back of his neck. His breathing was heavy as he looked around his room expecting to find someone there. Seeing Dee was part of another dream. When he realized he was alone, he reached over to the table beside his bed, grabbed a mineral from when he collected them with Dee, and threw it against the wall as hard as he could in frustration. A small spark lit up the room as the mineral made contact, causing Seb to squint his eyes and shake off a fleeting thought.

"Weird. Must be something wrong with the wall."

Seb was awake before the vibrating bed alarm went off. He reached down and flipped a switch on the side of his bed, finally remembering to turn it off.

He stretched and leaned over to the bedside table, feeling around for his Rollascreen. Once it was in his hands, he uncurled it and created a message for Zell.

I'm awake. When can we get started? The dreams I've been having about all of this need to stop. I feel like I'm not getting any rest.

Seb placed the device on his bed, leaned forward, and closed his eyes.

Dee, come back! Who are you with? Where are you going?

Beep. Beep. Beep.

Seb's eyes popped open at the constant sound.

"Defects! My dreams are full of nothing but defects."

He looked around for the source of the beeping, finally noticing the Rollascreen sitting face down on his bed. He flipped it over to find a list of messages from Zell.

"Oh no. How long was I out for?"

He opened the first message.

I have little ones, I never sleep.

Seb chuckled and read through the rest of the messages.

We'll start at 9 a.m.

I don't care about your dreams.

I said 9 a.m. I thought you were awake.

I'm going with or without you.

"Yikes. He sent each of these a minute apart. I was only out for ten minutes. He is impatient. Is that what little ones do to you?"

Seb composed a new message for Zell.

Yes. 9 a.m. I'll be there.

Seb was mid-blink when he was interrupted by his Rollascreen beeping again. He looked down to see the message.

Good.

He glanced at the clock. "Plenty of time to get cleaned up and grab some breakfast. Maybe something near Dee's place so I can keep an eye out for Zell. I wouldn't want to be late."

Seb slinked out of his bed and shuffled to the steam room. "Yesterday took a lot out of me. It's hard to get moving." He pushed the button in the steamer to get it started while he disrobed. He stepped in and slouched as the steam slowly loosened his muscles. When the steamer stopped after the allotted five minutes, Seb pushed the button to start it again. After nothing happened, he pushed it again, and again. He groaned while waiting for the heated air dryer to finish blowing the remaining moisture off of him. Once done, he stepped out of the steamer and dressed in a set of clean clothes.

Walking to the bed, he picked up his Rollascreen, curling it up in the process, and stuck it in his pocket. He went to the entry door and checked out his selection of shoes. Risking falling into a routine by wearing the same article of clothing over and over, he decided to take the half-wheel shoes anyway, knowing it would help him move quicker. After sliding on the shoes and tightening the straps, he walked out the door to the lobby of his complex. Seb noticed the people in the open area moving in a streamlined manner, until he caught someone staring at him. He peered behind himself, seeing nothing that the person would be focusing on. After turning back, he could no longer find the one staring. He scanned the area briefly before giving up and heading to the exit.

Seb looked out toward the street, trying to spot a hyper taxi. He stood, looking both directions for what felt like an eternity until he finally spotted one. A brief worry that he would have a repeat of the situation with the missing hyper loop trains quickly washed over him. He walked to the edge of the sidewalk and stood with several other people while he waited for the hyper taxi to arrive. After it glided to a stop and opened its doors, Seb boarded, along with the rest of the passengers. He mouthed the driver's welcome simultaneously.

"Welcome, thanks for joining."

Seb sat and stared straight ahead. He was concerned to visit Zell on his own, afraid that he would experience a new barrage of insults. Listina was involved now because of Dee, so he hoped she would join him. Seb created a message to send to her.

Listy, I hope you had a good evening and yesterday wasn't too much for you. If you're available, I'm meeting with someone from the group in an hour. We lost someone important and we're trying to figure out how it happened before putting together a plan to get her back. The more of us the better, but I understand if you need time to yourself. Let me know. Thanks, Seb.

Seb closed his messages and opened the news on the device.

Area in relief after bomber caught and converted.

Seb's eyes twitched as he frowned. "Maybe the news isn't the best idea right now." He returned his focus to the screen.

Citizens elated at the conversion.

"Yep. Nothing today."

Seb's audiophone chirped. He read the text on his wristband cautiously, expecting it to show *Zell*. "I'm sure I did something wrong already." He made a sound that was a mix of relief and surprise when he saw Listina's name displayed. "Not one to send a message in response?" he wondered before answering.

"Listy, hi. Did you get my message?"

"I did, I did. Um, I'm at work right now."

Seb chuckled loud enough for her to hear.

"Hey, look, I still need some credits, but I did plan to leave early. You know, break out of my routine, or whatever you told me, but if you don't want my help, and want to laugh at me, I can stay here."

Seb abruptly stopped the sound. "I'm sorry! I'd be appreciative of your help, if you're available. Can you make it by nine? I know that's not a lot of time. Let me send you the location."

He sent Listina a message containing the spot where he was headed. He heard her chuff. "What? Something interesting about that?"

"Yeah, actually. If I had a window to look out, I could probably see that building. I can make nine."

"That's great, thank you."

"Hmm."

"What? Why, hmm?" Seb questioned.

"I'm not sure why I'm helping you already, but I guess I'll find out how this goes."

Seb snorted. "Either way, I appreciate it. See you in a byte."

Click.

"Wow. Not even a bye?" Seb watched out the window of the hyper taxi as it began to slow. He looked up at the display of stops above the driver. This was where he needed to be. It was time to find some food before the day got too old.

Seb disembarked. He surveyed the nearby buildings and saw Dee's complex a short walk ahead.

He began walking forward, noting the food places he passed. Seb spotted a sushi restaurant with a line of sight to the front of Dee's complex. He walked inside and sat at a table with a view out the window. He picked up the menu tablet and flipped through the pages of options. Seb paused and held back a soft sob. Seeing dragon rolls on the menu had him question his choice of location. The food item was one of the first new experiences Dee had used to break him from his habits. It led to the chain of events that prevented his third light from lighting up. But now Dee was part of the GAI, and he was left with nothing but thoughts of her.

Seb slapped his forehead hard, causing a loud sound that made the other patrons turn and stare. He looked around briefly before turning his attention back to the menu tablet. "I don't have time to find another place. I'll have to suck it up." Seb tapped a few items, making sure to choose those that were not part of the first meal he'd shared with Dee, then placed his wristband against the tablet to deduct his credits.

He gazed out the window of the restaurant, watching the people walking along the sidewalk, coming and going from Dee's complex. He made sure Zell was not outside waiting. His meal was delivered as his mind wandered, hoping he would see Dee walk out of her complex, and into the restaurant. Seb looked down at his food, then picked up a pair of chopsticks, carefully holding them how Dee showed him. As he grabbed a bite, he glanced out the window. His eyes lit up. "Listy's here already? It's early." Seb pulled out his Rollascreen.

Listy, I'm in the sushi place behind you. Turn around and come in.

Seb watched as Listina pulled out her Rollascreen, looked at it, and then scanned the buildings behind her. He saw her place the device back in her pocket and cross the road.

"Listy!" he yelled as she opened the door. He waved her over, standing to greet her while she took a seat at his table.

"Hi," she said.

"Thanks for coming out. If you're hungry, help yourself." Seb waved a hand over the plates in front of him. "I always order too much."

Listina looked down and curled up her top lip. "That? No, I'm okay."

"Hey, you can't always eat pizza."

"No, but I can try."

"Really, at least take a bite. I was skeptical at first too, but it surprised me."

"A bite. Just one. I also already had breakfast. And why is this your breakfast?"

Seb picked at the items on the plates. "I needed food, and this is where I ended up."

He watched as Listina grabbed a piece of nigiri and popped it in her mouth.

"No hesitation. You're braver than I."

"It's only food. Good or bad, I still need it to live," she said between chews.

"Acknowledged. But *was* it good?"

"It's fine. Maybe I'll eat more another time. So, what are we doing here anyway?"

"I'm eating."

Listina stood up.

"Wait, sorry. Sit." Seb laughed. "Do you remember Dee?"

Listina bobbed her head.

"She's a friend. She was converted by the GAI. We don't know why. Eh, well, we do know. Everyone knows. It's in the news. But we're not sure how it got her, and if there's anything we can do about it."

"Why am I invited? I didn't exactly give her a warm welcome when I saw her."

"Mostly, it's for me. Who I need to meet with, I don't want to do alone. Also, I wanted to see how you were doing. You seemed okay when we split yesterday, and I wanted to make sure that was still the case."

"You're checking up on me? I told you I'm fine." Listina scoffed.

"I still wanted to make sure. Anyway, do you want more of this before I finish it?"

"No, thanks."

Seb placed the last few bites of food in his mouth. "Mmmm," Seb hummed through a grin.

She laughed, turning away from Seb.

He looked at the time. "Zell, uh, who we're meeting, should be here soon. Let's go out and wait for him."

Seb and Listina stood, pushed in their chairs, and left the restaurant.

CHAPTER 4

"Jinuh!" Listina shouted, jumping up and down, causing Seb to quickly turn his head.

"Oh, wow! Yeah, that's definitely them," Seb replied in surprise. "You can spot their tattoos clear across the area. I wasn't sure who else Zell had coming."

They watched as Jinuh spotted Listina jumping, cocked their head, and then ran over to greet them. Seb and Jinuh each held a hand in front of the other, moving them back and forth in greeting.

"Well, isn't this a shock," Jinuh said, startled. "Listy, so nice to see you again already. No more visits with Seb's mother, I hope."

Seb pursed his lips, thinking of a retort before Listina responded.

"Ugh, no, sushi instead. I'm not sure which is worse."

"Hey, now!" replied Seb and Jinuh in unison, causing each to face the other and giggle.

"So, Dee, huh?" Jinuh changed the subject. "Who would have guessed we'd lose her? But if she did do what's in the news, then I can't be surprised."

Seb scowled at Jinuh.

"I'm not saying I'm on the GAI's side, but there are just some things you can't do. And certainly nothing that high profile without someone coming to get you."

Seb sighed in defeat.

"Hey, look. I'm here, all right? I want her back too. All I'm saying is maybe we don't blow up a couple buildings in the process."

Listina's eyes opened wide. "She what? Dee? The woman I met before you, Seb?"

Seb stared down at his feet.

"Hello, all!" came a voice from behind them.

Seb's head popped up as Danish walked toward them. "You too?" he called out.

"Uh, hi, my friend. Nice to see you as well," Danish responded, confused.

"Apologies. I didn't know we were all going to be here." Seb looked at the band on his wrist to see the time said 9 a.m. "Well, almost all of us. No Zell yet." He scanned the group standing in front of him. "Before I'm told my manners have been lost, Danish, this is Listy. Dee found her just a few days ago, and I spent time with her yesterday. She was nice enough to come today when I thought it would just be me waiting for Zell's arrival."

"Listy, hello. How kind of you to keep my friend, Seb, company." Danish bowed. She smiled shyly at Danish.

"Seb, what's the plan? Or Jinuh? Or anyone? Do we have one?" Danish asked.

"Not yet," Seb replied. "Zell said to meet here, but he's the one missing."

"Any thoughts on how they got her?" Jinuh inquired.

"I'm not sure. Wasn't the last explosion months ago? I have no idea how they found her. I'm trying to remember the date when that was, but it's not coming to me. I'm too distracted." Seb drifted off in thought, coming up empty. "But I guess that's why we're all here. To look around Dee's place and see what we can find. To get an idea of where she is, and who got to her. But where is Zell? You don't think he went in already, do you? He was sure to tell me not to go by myself. Maybe we should go check?"

"I don't know, Seb," Danish answered. "Should we? Should we not? Do we know what to expect? If Zell went in by himself, then maybe we should let him."

"What do you all think?" Seb faced Listina and Jinuh.

They stared at each other before turning to Seb and shrugging.

"All right, I'm going to go check. We could be out here forever if he's already in there."

Seb began walking toward the door to the complex, and reached for the handle before hearing someone yell out.

"Sebastian!"

He stopped in his tracks and spun around, guilty. He glared when he saw who the voice had come from.

"Seb, I told you not to go in there by yourself. You don't know what you'll be walking into," Zell scolded.

"We've all been waiting here for you, so we figured you must be inside already."

"We?" Jinuh snickered. "Not we."

"Fine. *I* thought you already went in since it's past nine. I've been in the area for the last hour." Seb scoffed. "Little ones slow you down?"

"Don't mention them!" Zell yelled. "There were no hyper loop trains. I had to take the hyper taxi, if you must know."

"Still?" Seb questioned.

"Still? What do you mean *still*?"

"There weren't any yesterday when I tried to get to your location. That's why I was—"

"Why didn't you tell me there weren't any, Seb? If you would have told me, I could have planned to leave sooner and been here promptly. This is all your—"

"How could I know they'd still be missing," Seb interrupted. "I'd never seen that before, and I had other things—people—I'm worried about. Who cares about a couple missing trains?"

"I do!" Zell screamed back. "I care about—"

"Hey! Stop it!" Jinuh jumped in. "This isn't about missing trains, and whose fault it is. We're here because of Dee. Stop arguing and let's come up with a plan."

Seb and Zell both crossed their arms and faced Jinuh.

"Better. Now, uh—" Jinuh scratched their head. "What's the plan?"

Zell glared and huffed at Seb before he turned his focus to the group. "Here's what I know. Dee was preparing to move out of this complex." He waved his hand past the building in front of them. "I was here, outside, to see if she wanted help."

"You? Help? Do you mean help the GAI get her?" Seb scoffed.

Zell ground his teeth and took a step toward Seb before Jinuh stepped between them. Seb and Zell stared each other up and down.

"As I was saying," Zell continued. "I arrived here to help Dee move out of this complex when I saw her being hurried out the door. Two people were holding her arms while a third was following close behind. They all got into a personal transport vehicle."

"A personal transport vehicle? Who has one of those," Listina pondered aloud.

"Only the GAI," answered Zell. "Um, and who are you?" He looked at the others. "Who is this?"

Listina blushed.

Jinuh answered, "This is Listy."

"Uh huh. Why's she here?"

"She was one of Dee's latest, or last, recruits," Seb continued. "Dee had me help."

"You? Ha."

"Yeah! Me!"

"Gentlemen!"

Seb and Zell turned to look toward Jinuh's outburst.

"She's here. She wants to help," Seb pleaded.

"Fine. But only because Jinuh is vouching for her."

Frustrated, he said, "Can you continue, please?"

"Fine. They all got in the personal transport vehicle, that only the GAI have, with Dee riding in the back. I tried to chase after it on foot but lost it. At the same time, I saw Seb nearby." Zell faced Seb. "I still think you had something to do with it."

"Then why am I here?"

"Probably to make sure we don't find Dee, but at least now I can keep an eye on you."

Seb covered his ears with his hands and mouthed words without actually saying anything, an attempt to ignore the comment.

Zell scowled.

"Okay. So now what then?" Danish asked. "We know Dee was here. Someone, or someones, took her and drove off. Can we find her?"

"Maybe," Zell responded.

"Maybe?" Jinuh questioned.

"Yeah, maybe. She was moving her belongings to a new complex. Hopefully there's still something in this one to give us a clue, though I'm not hopeful."

"Then shall we go in?" Jinuh continued.

"Let's."

The group entered the complex. After walking to the platform lift, they paired up to ride the platforms to Dee's floor. Seb rode with Listina.

"Sorry about that," he said to her. "Zell has a strong personality. He's not all bad, but we're all high-strung right now with what happened to Dee."

"I understand. It's out of your control. Hopefully I'm not just in the way and can help."

"I'm sure we'll need everyone we can get." Seb turned to look ahead. "This is the floor."

They stepped off the platform lift and joined the rest of the group waiting outside the door to Dee's dwelling.

"The door is already wide open," Zell announced. "Let's be careful going in." He snuck through the door, looking around as he proceeded, while the other four followed closely behind. "I don't see or hear anyone or anything. Let's break out into separate rooms. See what we can find and try to get out of here quickly. I'll take the main area. Jinuh and Danish look in Dee's bedroom. Seb and Listy, take the kitchen. Seb, don't mess this up."

Seb covered his ears again and led Listina to the kitchen.

When they got into the room, Seb put his hands down and looked at Listina. "Ah, quiet."

She laughed. "What are we looking for? Anything in particular?"

"I'm not actually sure. I doubt that whoever took Dee is going to leave instructions on how to get her back, but maybe we can get an idea about how they got to her in the first place."

Seb studied the countertop and felt his heart sink seeing what was on it. "I can't —"

"What? What is it?"

"These." Seb picked up a mineral from the counter and turned to face Listina. "These are—I—Dee and I got these together. She took me to get food, and afterward, we visited an underground cavern to collect these minerals. I should have—had I known—she said she was using them for a project, but she was being a little secretive about it. I thought that was her being her. I didn't think she was hiding anything this big from me." He leaned back, reaching behind himself, and knocked something off the counter. He heard the item hit the floor and went looking for it. Seb bent over and picked up a small black cube. "I wonder what this is for."

"Hey, Seb, I found something. This was on the floor in the corner." Listina walked over to Seb and handed him a crumpled piece of paper.

He looked at the cube in one hand, then the paper in the other. He sat the two items down on the countertop, then smoothed out the paper to get a better look. He stared at the drawing on the paper. It was a sketch of several cubes lined up in two rows, with a blank spot where one was expected to be. Seb grabbed the small black cube and held it above the paper.

"Hmm."

"Seb, we got nothing," came a voice from the other room.

Jinuh, Danish, and Zell walked into the kitchen.

"We are empty-handed," Danish started before looking at Seb. "What do you have?"

"I'm not sure yet." Seb held up the black cube. Using his free hand, he grabbed some minerals, holding them up next to the cube.

"Let me see those better," Zell asked, squinting.

Seb held them out further for everyone to look at.

"Well, it appears that Dee knew what she was doing," Zell added.

"Why do you say that?" Seb asked.

"Think about it. What would you do with minerals like that, and a cube to enclose them?"

"Huh? Oh. Oh!" Seb bowed his head.

"And what's this?" Listina interjected, holding up the paper with the sketch on it.

Zell grabbed the paper for a closer look. "This looks like Nullity's layout. See how everything is identical?" He pointed at the spot of the missing cube on the paper. "And this must be the building that Dee took out. If whoever got Dee saw this stuff, there's no question as to why they grabbed her. Why would she leave this all out?"

"Maybe she was in the process of packing it, and left it out. You said you were here to help her move, yes?" Seb queried.

"I guess, but it was still careless of her. Did anyone find anything else?"

The group looked around at each other and shook their heads.

"Just as well. I think we're done here."

"But now what?" Seb spoke up.

"I'm going back to my dwelling. I need to think about this."

Seb blinked several times.

"Is that okay, Seb?" Zell continued.

"Sure. I guess we're on our own."

Seb watched as Zell left the kitchen, then heard the dwelling door shut soon after.

"Well, it's the four of us."

"Sorry, Seb. I have to leave now too," Danish apologized.

"And me as well," Jinuh added. "But I will reach back out later."

"And you?" Seb faced Listina.

"Nope. I'm invested now. This got interesting."

Seb laughed. "All right, let's get out of here." He tossed the minerals up and down. "I have somewhere I want to go, and I need another person. Jinuh, Danish, I'll chirp soon."

The pair bowed as they headed out the door. Seb and Listina followed, riding a platform down to exit the complex.

"Where to now?" Listina asked.

"I'll show you."

CHAPTER 5

Seb and Listina boarded a hyper taxi outside of Dee's complex. They found a pair of seats where they could sit side-by-side, and took them. After Seb settled, he looked down at his open hand, the mineral staring back up.

"You didn't finish saying what that was," Listina said. "It looks nice, but you were very concerned when you found it. And the cube. And the paper. Zell said Dee took out a building? Those aren't part of a—"

Seb nodded slowly without taking his eyes off his hand.

"But how did she learn to do that?"

"I don't know."

"She took out a whole building?"

Seb hung his head low before looking up at Listina. "Dee seemed really angry at the GAI for converting her parents. I don't know how she learned to do this. I do know that I was aware that these"—he held up the mineral—"could be dangerous, but I never guessed that Dee would have done something like that." He stopped and looked off in thought, then rubbed his forehead. "She was doing this before I met her. I remember reading about an explosion the day I met her. And . . . hold on, I have to look up something real quick. Can you hold this?" Seb handed the mineral to her. She leaned back, away from Seb. "It can't hurt you like this. It needs an additional trigger. Something else would have to be inside the black cube, causing the two to react."

"Are you sure?"

"If you throw it hard enough, it might spark, but that's it."

Listina took the mineral. "How do you know this?" She gave him a suspicious look. "I read a lot."

"Uh huh."

"No, really. It's one of those things I learned, then forgot. You do need to be careful with these, but you can't do much more than make them spark without an additional trigger. When I was with Dee, when she was collecting these, I thought I had gotten my information confused with something else. But after seeing all of the puzzle pieces at her place coming together, I finally remembered."

Seb reached into his pocket and pulled out his Rollascreen. He uncurled it and opened the news. After a brief pause to think, he looked down at the screen and chose a date range.

February 1st 2332 - February 29th 2332

Seb flipped through the stories until he found the one he was looking for.

Explosion at the West Side Plaza leaves one injured

"Here it is. The date of the article is the day I met Dee. And . . ." He stopped and let out a loud scream, causing the other passengers to turn and look. Listina covered her ears.

"What was that about?" she whimpered.

Seb stared at her for a moment before finally speaking. "Dee set off an explosion in my factory. In my lab. Why didn't—I was late that day. I would have been there when it happened, but I wasn't."

"You just remembered an explosion happened where you work?"

"I never forgot it. It set off a whole chain of events that led me to Dee. But some of it was because of her in the first place. I was so happy when I heard they caught the person who set the explosions. But now that I know who it was, and why, I don't know what to think. I don't know what to do."

"Seb, sorry to interrupt, but the hyper taxi is stopping, and I don't know where we're going."

Seb glanced at the list of stops above the driver and quickly stood. "Here! This is where we're going." He rolled up his Rollascreen, stuck it in his pocket, then took the mineral back from Listina and held it up. "I'm going to show you where these came from."

Seb started walking to get off and looked back to see Listina still standing. He gestured for her to follow.

"I don't know about this."

"Don't know about what?"

"This sounds dangerous."

"It's not. I promise. I hope. And there's food?"

Listina gave a thin smile and joined him. They both deboarded and started their way up the street.

After a short distance, Seb stopped at a stand with a Global AI-controlled employee standing behind it.

"We're here for the meal and minerals," Seb said to the employee.

"Only meal," the employee responded.

"Meal and minerals. There are two of us," Seb added.

"Yes. Meal. This way." The employee gestured toward a platform lift.

Seb opened his mouth, but looked back at Listina, confused.

They walked over to the moving platforms and stepped on one going down. Seb saw Listina staring at him, grinning.

"Um. What's that look for?" he asked.

"I was thinking about the first time I got on one of these with you. I want to bounce."

Seb grabbed the railing.

"I won't. I promised I wouldn't do it again. I know you don't like heights. The thought just made me laugh in my head a little."

Seb let go of the railing and grabbed at his heart. "Okay. Phew. Thank you."

They stepped off when it arrived at the bottom. Listina gazed around, taking in the view of solid rock overhead and tables sitting on top of a transparent floor with a river running under it. "What exactly are we here for? This looks fancy."

Seb held out the mineral.

"Uh, Seb." Listina tapped him on the shoulder quickly. "You might want to put that away."

"What? Why?" Seb noticed all the employees had stopped what they were doing and turned to look at him. Seb slowly stuck his hand in his pocket, gesturing with the other for Listina to follow him to an empty table. They sat, watching suspiciously as an employee walked over to them.

"Hello, welcome. I will get you your food."

"Get what food? We just got here," Listina said.

"They pick for you, but—" Seb peeked at the arm of the employee as they were walking away. "The last time I was here, the employees were all in control. Except for the one up on the ground level. This one is definitely controlled by the GAI, and by the reactions of the others when I pulled out the mineral to show you, it seems like all of the rest are too." Seb stopped, thinking about their options. "Maybe we should at least eat some of whatever food they bring out to us."

"Do you only think about food?"

"No. Well . . . no. Just, right now I think it would be better for us to blend in before we go running off. But I can eat while we're here." He winked at Listina.

Listina snickered in response. "Sure."

The employee arrived at the table with a stack of plates, dropped them off, and left.

"Uh, thanks?" Listina scoffed. "Very friendly."

"Strange," Seb added. "This is a lot different than last time. Hardly any interaction with the employees, and . . . what is this food they brought out?" Seb examined the plates and scrunched up his nose. He reached out, picked up a small solid square, and studied it. "Is this . . . They just broke up some protein nutrient bars and put them on plates. They didn't even arrange them nicely."

Listina reached out, picked up a square, and popped it in her mouth. "Oh. Yum! Chocolate kelp."

"Yum?"

"Yeah! I do actually like these. I'm not responsible for this flavor, but my work at the synthetic meat plant has given me an appreciation for how hard it is to make something taste good while fulfilling your nutritional needs."

"I can see that. I always just looked at it as food. With it being provided to everyone, I guess I took it for granted." Seb popped the square of protein bar he was holding into his mouth and chewed with a smile on his face. "Okay, you're right. When I actually stop to taste it, it's not bad at all."

Listina grinned.

"Let me eat a few more of these and then we can go look at what we came for," Seb added.

He stuck a few more squares in his month, then puckered his face. "Mix and match might not have been the best idea."

"Only if you don't do it right." Listina eyed the contents of the plates carefully, picked up two specific squares, and reached out to Seb. "Try these together."

Seb looked at her suspiciously.

"No, really. Here, look." She put the pieces in her mouth and picked out two more identical ones, handing them over.

He cautiously took them and bit into both. He chewed for a moment before his eyes lit up.

"Why don't they make a protein bar in this flavor?" he said with food in his mouth.

"Life can't be easy and enjoyable at the same time, can it?"

Seb chuckled. "No. It certainly doesn't seem to be that way." He tapped at the two solid lights and one dark light on his arm, gazing at Listina's matching set. "Definitely not easy," he mumbled. "Let's go see what we can find in the area with the minerals."

He stood, waiting for Listina to do the same. She hesitated, but rose and followed as Seb walked toward a cavern entrance. Seb felt a tug at his shirt and turned to look at Listina.

"They're all staring at us again," she said in a hushed tone.

Seb huffed. "We're not doing anything wrong. We can keep going."

They continued through the narrow corridor and into an expansive cavern.

"Whoa," Listina said in excitement. "I know we're here to try to help your friend, but . . . whoa. I'm glad I came along. You're still showing me new things when I know that's not your focus right now."

"I particularly liked the cool air while the heat from the geothermal river hits your skin at the same time."

Seb looked down at the water and saw several people nearby. They were dressed the same as the restaurant servers, each holding a large container. He watched them sifting through the dust and picking up a few remaining minerals, placing them in the containers.

Seb pulled Listina closer to him and whispered in her ear. "I think they know where Dee got the minerals she used. They must be clearing this place out. I don't know how they found it, but it makes sense now. All of the in-control employees have been replaced by GAI-controlled people. They're removing all of the minerals so no one can replicate what Dee did. They must be preventing anyone else from collecting them. That's why they all stared at me when I pulled out the mineral earlier. There must be other sources though, so I can't imagine how they'll fully control a natural substance."

Seb noticed an employee near the river looking up toward him and Listina.

"And that's why it's so beautiful here," Seb spoke loudly, his voice echoing in the open area. "Just look at the river out there, and how, uh, nicely it flows from there, to there." He lowered his voice. "Maybe it's time to go."

She nodded.

They walked through the cavern, peering over their shoulders at the employees by the river, and continued back to the restaurant through the narrow corridor. They proceeded to the platform lift and rode it up to ground level. Seb walked directly to the employee at the stand, noticing Listina's look of confusion.

"I need to pay." Seb turned to the employee and repeated, "I need to pay."

"After you yelled at me about trying to leave without paying yesterday, you risked *my* last light by almost forgetting?"

Seb looked back at Listina mouthing, "Sorry." He glanced at the tablet being presented by the employee and touched his wristband to it. The tablet lit up green, indicating acceptance of his credit deduction.

"Done. Happy?" Seb winked at her. "Let me check in with the rest of the group and then I have a different place to stop." Seb removed his Rollascreen from his pocket and created a message for Zell, Danish, and Jinuh.

I stopped in the place where Dee got the minerals. It's being cleared out. They knew she had been there. Everything has been changed, probably to keep a repeat from happening. I'm going to Overground next. I'm curious about something. I need to know how they were tracking her and found her. If any of you find anything else, let me know in the flip of a bit.

"All right, we can go," Seb said.

They boarded a nearby hyper taxi. Seb stared out the window, watching the restaurant go by.

"What is going on here?" he pondered.

CHAPTER 6

The hyper taxi began to slow while going past a completely black building, with blacked-out windows. It glided to a stop.

"Here we are," Seb said.

The pair got off the hyper taxi and Listina followed Seb to the door of the building.

She stared at the sign on the building. "*Overground*? What's this?"

"It's a place to play music." Seb grinned. "You like music, right?"

"No. Not really."

Seb eyed Listina. "No? Not really? What do you mean?"

"I don't listen to much music."

"I take it you don't play an instrument or sing either?"

She chuckled. "No. Definitely not. Never needed to learn. Never had any interest. And I don't like my voice."

"Uh. Okay then. Well, maybe you'll enjoy this. Just listen."

Seb cracked open the door to *Overground*, holding his ear to it.

"To what?" Listina asked. "Was I supposed to hear something?"

Seb closed the door and reopened it. He still heard nothing. "Well, maybe they're just in between songs. We'll check it out."

After opening the door the rest of the way, he gestured for Listina to go through, then followed.

Seb walked up to a table by the entrance with an employee sitting behind it.

"Here to dance?" the employee asked.

"Yes, I'm here to—what?" Seb answered quizzically.

"Here to dance?" the employee repeated.

Seb turned to Listina. "Maybe this GAI employee is stationed in the wrong place today. Repeating their script for dancing instead of playing."

"I don't think so." Listina pointed toward the inside of the building.

Seb saw a dozen people partnered up, slowly dancing, in near silence.

She faced the employee and enthusiastically said, "We'll dance!"

Seb spun around and gaped at Listina with concern. "We'll what?"

Listina turned to him and grinned. "We'll dance. Come. Looks like it's my turn to show you something." She held out her hand, waiting for Seb to grab it. She moved her fingers slowly to get his attention, and when he finally noticed, he grabbed on nervously. Listina walked Seb out to the floor with the other people, stopped, then put her hands on his shoulders. "Ready?" she asked.

Seb shook his head and let out a long questioning, "Nooo?"

Listina laughed. She grabbed Seb's hands and put them on her shoulders. Her hands went back on his. "Follow me and do exactly like I do."

She moved a foot forward, lightly nudging Seb's, forcing him to shift his. She moved her foot back, prompting him to do the same. Leaning back, she pulled Seb with her, then stood straight again. Listina stepped slowly to her left side, and continued to take small steps, turning the two of them in a circle. She then started moving to the right, completing another full circle. Finally, she leaned forward, tipping Seb back, then stood up straight.

"Good! Again!" Listina said, grinning.

"How did you learn to do this?" Seb asked.

"My parents taught me when I was younger. Before they were gone." Listina frowned. "It's one of the good memories I have. One that I probably would have lost if I had let all of these light up." She motioned at her arm.

Seb gave Listina a light smile and tightened his hands on her shoulders. "Again."

They repeated the dance motions, ignoring the other people around them, locked in each other's gaze.

"So, what were you going to show me here? Or why were we coming here anyway?" Listina said, breaking the silence.

Seb stopped and let go of Listina. "This was another place Dee brought me. The stage over there was used for people to play some songs. There were instruments available to use too. I came once with Dee, and once by myself. I played a different song each time. I don't understand why it changed."

"Dee brought you here before?"

Seb cocked his head. "Yes?"

"And she took you to the meal and minerals place we were just at?"

"Also yes. Why?"

"And both of them have changed or are now crawling in, what do you call them? GAI?"

"Yes. Global AI." Seb's eyes lit up. "Is the GAI going through every place Dee has been and cleaning them out? But I still don't know how they would know that." He stopped to think. "Is it only places I've been to with her, or is it everywhere she's been? Am I in trouble too?"

Listina smirked. "Too early to tell?"

Seb frowned. "Not funny. I think we should get out of here. I need to talk to the others. Maybe they've come across something similar."

Listina put her hands firmly on Seb's shoulders. "Again?"

Seb looked at her curiously.

"I don't get to do this often, and we're already here. Just one more time?"

Seb gave in. "Sure, but then we really should go."

They followed the steps for the dance an additional time, enjoying the peace, before Seb led her outside of the black building.

He focused on the sign. "Maybe they should change the name."

"Why? And ruin the surprise when people walk in and hear silence, like you did?"

Seb rolled his eyes.

Chirp.

Listina looked at Seb. "I don't think that was me. My audiophone chirp is less sing-songy."

He chuckled at her description while looking at his wristband. He answered his audiophone, allowing Listina to hear.

"Zell, I was about to chirp you and the others."

"That's wonderful," Zell replied sarcastically. "I'm at my factory. Well, possibly not my factory anymore."

141

"What do you mean by that?" Seb asked.

"If you would let me talk, I'd tell you."

Seb took a deep breath and closed his eyes, waiting for Zell to continue.

"I got your message about the place with the minerals while I was walking past my factory. I didn't plan to go in today, and maybe I shouldn't have, because . . . it's not right."

"What's not right about it?" Listina inquired.

"Listy's there too? Thanks for telling me, Seb."

Seb ignored the snide remark.

"Hi, Zell," Listina replied. "What's not right?"

"Well, to begin with, I almost couldn't get in. When I went into the building, the display near the eye scanner said I was unknown. Like I was undefined. Deleted out of the system. Me. I've worked at this factory for a long time. It said *removal requested*."

"I thought you said you were in there now?" Seb queried.

"I am."

"How did you get past without being removed?"

"I walked out, and then followed someone else in. Of course."

"Of course?"

"Yeah. Of course. How do you think I got Dee in here?"

"Dee's been in there?" Seb asked loudly.

"Why do you keep repeating everything I say? GAI got your tongue? Yes, she's been here. Yes, I'm in here now. I'm staring at my lab, or what used to be my lab. All of the tables are cleared off. The parts are gone. The replicators are gone. It's like they wiped this spot and are rebuilding it."

"But Dee has been in there?"

"Yes, Seb. Yes. Why do I have to say it again?"

"That's another place that Dee's visited that is being changed."

Seb heard silence.

"Zell? Are you still there?"

"What do you mean another?" Zell finally responded. "The minerals, and my factory?"

"And *Overground*."

"*Overground?*"

"Yeah. I'm standing outside of it with Listy. We had just left when you chirped. All of the music equipment is gone. It's only people dancing in silence now. So yes, another. That's your factory, the minerals, and *Overground*. All places Dee has visited, at least since I've known her."

"Hmm."

"Hmm? Do you have any idea why this would be happening to the places she is associated with?"

"Hmm."

Seb sighed. "What was Dee doing in your factory anyway?"

"I'm not sure. I got her inside, then left."

"You let her in without seeing what she was doing?"

"Yeah. She probably made those black cubes here. It looked like parts you can make in my lab. The replicator could have easily created several for her. But I don't know. Maybe she needed to check her messages."

"Zell, if you had watched her, maybe you could have stopped her from making those," he accused. "She never would have set the explosions, and never would have been caught."

"Don't blame me for this. Even if I stopped her from going in, or did stand and watch, she still would have found a way to do what she wanted to do, and you know it."

Exasperated, Seb replied, "Yes, I do know it. Is there anything else Dee could have been doing there?"

"Unlikely. We also have timers, and any of the internals she may have wanted to put inside those black cubes. She definitely picked the right spot to get what she wanted."

"What do you do there that requires those kinds of parts?"

"I make toys."

Listina laughed. "You make what? I think I heard you wrong."

"Toys. I make toys."

"All right," Seb conceded. "Dee was definitely using your lab incorrectly."

"That she was. And now it's empty. I should stop doing favors for people. Anyway, it sounds like someone is trying to get in here. I better disappear."

"Right. Let me know if you find anything else. If I do, I'll chirp you," Seb said.

"Hmm."

Click.

Seb and Listina looked at each other before she broke the silence. "He's helpful."

"Sarcasm aside, he actually is. That's why we need his help. He has a bit more insight into the GAI than I do, and certainly has known Dee longer. If there's anyone who might be able to find a way to get her back, it's unfortunately going to be him. So, as much as he twists my lights, I need to stay on his good side."

"If you say so. I've known him for a day, and all he's done so far is complain. Like he has more important things to do than help someone who's supposedly his friend."

Seb laughed. "Complaining is right. Though he does have little ones. They're probably the most important thing to him, but he's still here."

"Okay. Yeah, okay. Now what?"

"I think I need to go back to my dwelling and regroup. Go through everything we've found so far, see if there are any other connections I'm missing, and figure out the next steps."

"Should I come with you?"

"No. That shouldn't be necessary," Seb replied, staring off in the distance.

Seb turned to Listina after she didn't reply, finding her looking rejected.

"What? What's wrong?" he said with concern.

"I just . . ."

"What?"

"I've been with you all day, and now you don't need me? I thought I was being helpful."

"You are! You are. I thought you might want a break. From me. From all of this. You were stuck with me yesterday, which was all my fault, and you've been stuck with me today—and I do appreciate that—so I thought you'd finally want to go off on your own."

"I don't. I want to help. I want to help you. I want to help Dee. I want to help your friends. I'm not leaving unless you make me."

"No, I'm not making you. If you still want to help, then I can use your help."

"Good!" she said, stomping her foot, crossing her arms, and grinning widely.

Seb laughed at Listina's actions. "All you had to do was ask. Let's find a hyper taxi and get out of here." He looked up the road, hoping to see one in view. "Did we just miss one? We've been standing out here a while now. I haven't seen one. Have you?"

"I haven't."

"But there's no one else out waiting for one either."

"Should we start walking?"

Seb peered down at his half-wheel shoes, then at Listina's feet. "Walking it is."

She caught his gaze. "Sorry, no half-wheels for me."

"That's okay. This will give us more time to share information, but we should start moving before it gets dark."

"Or before you get hungry."

"That too," Seb chuckled.

CHAPTER 7

Listina exhaled slowly.

"That is amazing." Seb was spellbound by her story. "And that's how you got your job at the meat processing plant?" He stood with his mouth agape before adding, "Phew. What a great story. And you just—"

Listina interrupted, "Yup. I've never actually told the whole story to anyone, but that's how I ended up working there."

"No one else knows that?"

Listina blushed. "No."

"But it's an amazing story! And it has a happy ending."

"Yeah, I guess." Listina looked down, focusing much more on her feet than the direction she was walking.

"Well, I enjoyed it. And it made the walk go really fast. But now, here we are. Right as it's getting dark." Seb gestured at the front of his complex. "Home, for now."

"It did help, didn't it," Listina agreed. "And not a single hyper taxi along the way."

"No, not one. First the hyper loop trains, and now the hyper taxis. What's next?"

"I don't know that I want to find out."

"Me neither. Anyway, let's go in." Seb walked into the complex, leading Listina across the lobby, and to his dwelling. He opened the door, walked in, and waited a moment for the lights to turn on. "Welcome," he said, spreading his arms wide. "Are you hungry?"

Listina laughed. "No. I'm not. But thank you."

"Same." Seb smiled. "But I figured I would ask. Feel free to sit." He gestured toward some chairs in the main area.

She took a seat while Seb continued over to the display on his wall.

"I know this has a few features beyond showing the weather, but I've never needed them." Seb touched a few places on the screen, finally bringing up a map. "Okay, so first we went to the meal and minerals location right—"

"Whoa, so we're getting right into this?"

Seb stopped and turned to Listina. "Huh?"

"I don't know. We just got here, and you're already jumping right into reviewing our day."

He shook his head quickly. "Huh?"

"Nothing. I thought maybe we'd talk about something else, or do something else." She patted the seat next to her. "But never mind, go on."

Seb returned to the display. After taking a moment to remember what he was doing, he used his finger to draw a circle around the spot on the map. "The meal and minerals location is right here." He zoomed out on the map, then moved his finger slowly in front of the screen, up and down between the buildings before stopping. "Ah. *Overground* is here." He drew a circle around *Overground* on the map. "And last . . . hmm, hmm, hmm. Okay. Around this area is Zell's factory." A third circle was drawn around a group of buildings. "These are the spots that Dee has been that we know have been changed."

Seb turned to look at her, but found her chair empty.

"Listy?"

After a quick scan, he found her lying down on the longer bench in the room with her eyes closed.

"Listy?" he whispered.

She didn't move.

Seb checked the time in the corner of the wall display. "I guess it *is* getting late."

He walked into his bedroom, grabbed the cover from his bed, and brought it out to carefully lay over Listina. He then sat in the empty chair and leaned back while running his hands down his face.

I don't know that I can sleep yet, he thought as he closed his eyes.

Seb was sitting in a hyper taxi looking down at the news on his Rollascreen.

February 12th, 2332
Sunny today. Rain planned for tomorrow.

Shortages of synthetic beef expected
Explosion at the West Side Plaza leaves one injured

"Huh? Another explosion? I thought they already caught that person and converted them." Seb glanced at the date again. "That's not right. It's 2333. I must have opened old news."

Seb tapped a few spots on his Rollascreen to bring up the current news for the day. "All right, today's news. February 12th, 2332. Huh? This thing isn't working right."

Seb began hitting the device against the palm of his hand until he saw a flickering light out of the corner of his eye. He looked at the lights on his arm. "Two solid lights, and one blinking. Just like it—"

Suddenly the two solid lights went out, and the third light turned solid.

"What is—"

Seb closed his eyes tight. When he opened them again, all three lights were solid. His eyes widened before he looked up and around the hyper taxi. Everyone was staring at him. He focused on the face of the person next to him and squinted.

"Dee?" He leaned forward. "Dee, you have to help!" Seb held up his arm to show her. "We have to find a way to make the light go out again."

"Welcome," came a voice from behind.

He turned toward the sound and mouthed, "Dee?" Seb looked at the person next to him, still seeing his friend's face.

"So nice of you to join us," said several voices in unison. "Thank you for giving in."

He surveyed each person, seeing Dee's face on every one. Slouching back, he wanted to get away.

"We've been waiting, but now it's finally ready," said the person closest to Seb.

"Wha—what's ready?" he stuttered.

She touched the lights on Seb's arm. "Your plan. It's complete. We know what to do with you now."

"No. No! I'm not ready. I'm supposed to help you. I need to get to you. I'm not—I don't want—no!"

"Seb! Seb! Wake up," Listina shouted. "Wake up. You're yelling."

Seb cracked his eyelids. "What—no. No!"

"Seb, hey!" Listina grabbed his shoulder and shook it.

He opened his eyes more. "What? Dee?" He blinked, focusing on the person in front of him. "Listy? Where are we?"

"What do you mean where are we? Um, this is your dwelling. I must have fallen asleep, but you woke me up with whatever you're yelling about."

Seb's eyes darted around while he got his bearings. "Huh?"

"We're. In. Your. Dwelling," she said, drawing out each word. "Where did you think you were?"

"Uh. I was in a hyper taxi."

"You were? How did you find one of those?"

Seb sat up. "I guess I was dreaming that I was in a hyper taxi. I was reading the news, last year's news. All of my lights started flickering and then went solid." He tapped his arm, running his fingers across each light, paying extra attention to the dark one. "Then everyone on the hyper taxi was Dee, welcoming me to the GAI."

"Um. What?" Listina's lip curled up.

"I don't know. It was last year. February. And before I would have even met Dee. The news said something about a . . . synthetic beef shortage."

Listina cocked her head. "Uh, yeah. I remember that. We couldn't source one of the ingredients for our main product at the plant. That's when I designed the current recipe to replace it with something more sustainable. I *am* pretty good at what I do." She held up her hand, blew on the nails, then brushed them across her shirt several times. "Anyway, how do you remember a news article from that long ago?"

Seb opened his mouth slightly and shook his head, indicating that he wasn't sure himself.

"Any other news you remember?"

"The weather was normal. Sun, then rain." He suddenly opened his eyes wide.

"What? What is it?"

"Explosion at the West Side Plaza leaves one injured."

"Huh?"

"Explosion! That must have been one of the first, if not *the* first, places Dee targeted. And when the GAI started watching her closely."

"Okay. So, where's the West Side Plaza?"

Seb stood and walked to the display. He touched the screen showing a depiction of a moon hidden behind moving clouds, causing it to fade away and reveal the map with the circles he added.

"It's uh . . ." He kept moving the map around. "Uh . . . Where in the stack heap is it? It used to be right around . . . here." Seb drew a large circle around an area covered in tall buildings.

"I thought the plazas around here were nothing but grass and walking paths. They're arranged around those high-energy solar panels," Listina pondered.

"They are. But I don't see anything like that in this area on the west side of the city."

"Are you sure you have the right spot?" Listina walked over to the display and started moving the map around. "What about here? This looks right."

"It *is* one of the plazas, but that's the east one." Seb zoomed in on the map, allowing the name 'East Side Plaza' to show. He zoomed out again. "Here's the north—" He pointed to the top plaza. "And the south—" He moved his finger to the lower plaza.

Listina punched him in the arm.

"Ouch!" Seb glared at her. "What was that for?" he asked, rubbing his arm.

"I know my directions."

"Ow," Seb said, still rubbing the sore spot.

"So, where did the West Side Plaza go?"

Seb cowered, concerned that he would get hit again.

"Don't look at me like that. I won't hit you again. Sorry. But really, how does an open area just disappear? The map can't be wrong, can it?"

"Only with a major glitch, but these maps are updated several times a day. There's always something overhead looking down." Seb thought for a moment. "If Dee was at the West Side Plaza, maybe the GAI covered up any destruction she caused. Like, actually covered it." Seb stopped again.

"What? What idea did you just have?"

"The GAI is finding all the places Dee has been and is replacing them."

"Right. But are we sure the West Side Plaza is actually gone?"

"No. But I'm sure this is correct." He tapped the map. "Though there's only one way to know for sure."

"Are we going there?" Listina asked dryly.

"Yes. We're going there."

"How?"

"Huh?"

"How are we getting there? We're here." Listina touched a blue dot on the map. "That's where we are, right?"

"Yes. We're there."

"And we have to get way . . . over . . . here." Listina slid her finger to the expected location of the West Side Plaza.

Seb cocked his head in confusion.

"With what transport? If the hyper taxis are still off the grid, how will we ever make it from here to there?"

Seb slumped his head forward.

"We've done a lot of walking lately, but I don't think we want to do that much more."

"No, you're right. I expect to have everything I need. There's always a hyper taxi in sight. What would we do if our food stopped showing up too?"

"Let's not think about it. Maybe it was a blip, and we'll find one the next time we go out, but let's be prepared in case that doesn't happen."

"All right."

"Hmm. Seb?"

"Yeah?"

"I'll be right back." Listina ran out the door of Seb's dwelling.

He barely knew what happened before she came running back through the door.

"There still aren't any hyper taxis near here. Who do you have nearby that you can walk to? Jinuh? Or, that other one? Not Zell."

"Danish?"

"Yeah, Danish. Are either close?" asked Listina.

"Both. Why?"

"Ask them if there are hyper taxis running near them. Maybe we have to go find one, and not wait for them to come to us."

"Hmm. Okay." Seb read the time on the display. "Hmm."

"What?"

"Danish is probably still asleep."

"What? What time is it?"

"Really early."

Listina looked at the display too. "Ugh. You woke me this early?"

"Sorry."

"So what about Jinuh? Would they be awake yet?"

"Awake or still awake." Seb pulled out his Rollascreen and created a message.

Are you awake? Can you chirp?

Seb addressed Listina. "Okay, sen—"

Chirp.

Seb and Listina both laughed.

"That's a yes," he said. He answered the call so both he and Listina could hear. "Jinuh, hi. I hope I didn't wake you."

"Never. It's easier to not sleep. Though, why are you awake?" Jinuh responded.

"I'm at my dwelling with Listy, and—"

"That's why you need to talk? I can't help." Jinuh laughed.

Seb started again, ignoring Jinuh. "There are no hyper taxis near my dwelling. Are there any by yours?"

"Maybe? I could be out half-wheeling. Or perhaps I'm getting another tattoo. Who says I'm at my dwelling?"

"I can hear you laughing while trying to say that, Jinuh," Listina interjected.

"Hi, Listy!"

"Hi, Jinuh!"

"Yes, I'm at my dwelling. I'm already riding a platform down to go check for you. Let me have some fun. Sheesh."

"I'll let you have some, all right," Listina declared. "Just ask Seb what happens when I do."

"You don't want that, Jinuh. My arm still hurts," Seb interjected.

"I am sure it does, but I'll pass. Anyway, I'm outside, and I see . . . a hyper taxi."

"You do?" he questioned, surprised.

"And another coming."

"Okay, great! They're running again."

"But wait. That's odd," Jinuh added.

"What? What's odd?"

"The ones headed in your direction are turning around and coming back."

"So they're not coming my way?" Seb asked.

"It doesn't look like it. No. They all keep coming right back," Jinuh added.

"Did the drivers' scripts get rewritten to keep them from coming to me?" Seb wondered aloud. "We're coming to you."

"Oh? You are?" Jinuh asked with delight.

"We are. We'll be there soon."

"I can't wait!"

Click.

Seb and Listina looked at each other with confusion.

"We found them, but why aren't they coming here?" Seb questioned.

Listina shook her head. "Why is the sky blue?"

"Because the air scrubbers just ran yesterday, so the sky is clear again for the remainder of the week."

Listina balled up her fist and pulled back.

"No, please don't," Seb said, laughing, covering his arm.

CHAPTER 8

Seb and Listina arrived at Jinuh's complex to find Jinuh waiting for them.

"So, where are we going?" Jinuh asked excitedly.

"You're coming with us?" Seb questioned.

Jinuh nodded enthusiastically.

"But you don't even know why," Listina added.

"Somewhere fun again, right?"

Seb puckered his face. "Probably not? We're going to the West Side Plaza."

Jinuh cocked their head. "Why there? What's there? Meaning, what's actually there? Aren't the plazas just full of little ones playing or people exercising? Or I guess sometimes the GAI workers handling maintenance for the power grid. Are you looking for a new job, Seb?" Jinuh grabbed his arm, putting their face close to his lights. "You still have one to go."

Seb pulled his arm back, beginning to laugh before switching to a more serious expression. "We're going because of Dee. That may have been the first place she set off an explosion."

Jinuh looked back and forth between the pair, blinking rapidly. "So, why am I going with you?"

He chuckled. "Who said you were? We just want your hyper taxis."

Jinuh stuck out their bottom lip pouting. "You're not here for me? Regardless, I'm coming. Here comes a hyper taxi now. Once we get on, you can tell me why I'm going with you."

The vehicle stopped nearby and opened its doors. Seb stepped on first and faced the driver, waiting for the typical welcome greeting. The driver looked at Seb without saying a word.

"Um, hi to you too?" He continued walking, looking back as Jinuh and Listina boarded, overhearing the driver greet them.

"Welcome. Thanks for joining us. We're on to our next destination."

Seb stopped and held up his arms in confusion while mouthing, "What?" to the other two.

"What was that?" Seb whispered after taking a seat. "I've never had a driver not give me a welcome."

"Do you always acknowledge them?" Jinuh asked.

"No. Of course not. Do you?" Seb huffed.

"Sure! Why not?" Jinuh grinned and added, "No. It gets exhausting."

"I do," Listina said timidly.

"Huh?" The other two questioned.

"I do," she said louder. "I say hi every time."

"But they don't react if you do or don't. They don't have feelings. They're full GAI," Seb insisted.

"We don't know that. They could still have some of their old self in there," Listina pushed.

"It's true. They could," Jinuh added. "We have to hope it's true if we're going to get Dee back."

Seb conceded. "You're right." He yelled toward the front of the hyper taxi, "Good morning, driver!"

Jinuh and Listina both covered their faces in embarrassment.

"So, now, what's at the West Side Plaza?" Jinuh asked through their hands.

"Hopefully nothing," Seb responded, turning to face the others.

Jinuh stood suddenly. "Well, this is my stop. Good luck." They sat back down. "No, really. What's there?"

"I remembered an article I read around the time the explosions started, last year. Long before we knew Dee was involved. It was about the West Side Plaza. I think that may have been Dee's first target. But when Listy and I checked the maps earlier, it looked like the plaza had been replaced by a new building. Everywhere Dee went has now been cleaned out or changed. So like I said, we're hoping we find nothing. We hope the maps are wrong, and it's still an empty plaza. But the only way to know is to go see for ourselves."

"Onward to nothing it is." Jinuh held their fist up in the air. "Wait, what other places have changed? You mentioned something about minerals and . . . mushrooms? Food and fluorite? Pizza and pleochroism?"

Seb laughed. "What? No. It's meal and minerals. Though now it's being cleared of all minerals."

"So meals only. Got it. They should change their name," Jinuh joked.

"That's not the only place that needs a name change."

Listina interrupted. "You already said that once. It wasn't funny then either."

"Huh?" Jinuh questioned.

Seb stuck his tongue out at her, then answered Jinuh. "*Overground* has changed. No more music. No musical instruments. It's a dance place now."

Jinuh stood. "Well, this is my stop. Time for some dancing. Who's coming?"

Listina raised her hand.

Seb ignored them and continued, "I talked with Zell after we went to *Overground* and he said his factory lab had been cleared out."

Jinuh sat. "Why there?"

"Zell said he snuck Dee in, and he suspects that's where she was able to make the black cubes she used in the Nullity explosion."

"And now you're going to the plaza to see if it's changed or gone?"

"Yes. Now we're going to the plaza. Hopefully there's a hint as to what Dee was trying to accomplish. Or something there related to how the GAI found her."

"Exciting."

"I hope not." Seb read the list of hyper taxi stops displayed above the driver. "We'll find out in a minute. We're almost there."

The vehicle stopped and the group stood to deboard. They walked off with Seb at the end. As he passed the driver, he looked at them and said, "Bye."

The driver turned to him. "Soon," they replied.

Seb's eyes widened as he stumbled out of the hyper taxi. He tripped and landed on his chest, almost knocking into Jinuh and Listina.

"Did your shoes get stuck together?" Listina asked, looking down at Seb on the ground.

"Ouch." Seb rolled over onto his back and pointed at the hyper taxi as it was pulling away.

"They spoke to me."

"They speak to everyone. Well, usually. When not ignored." Jinuh chuckled.

Listina reached out an arm to help Seb get up. "What did they say? No one else was getting on the hyper taxi to welcome."

"Soon. All they said was soon."

"Maybe they think you'll be getting back on board soon," Listina suggested. "Maybe they'll be back soon, to pick us up."

"I don't know, but it was unexpected and I tripped. Nothing, and no one, seems to be doing what I expect them to and now the driver said something I've never heard them say before—"

"Sorry to interrupt, but I see a whole lot of somethings, and not enough nothings here," Jinuh said, looking around at the surrounding buildings.

"We do have to walk a little ways," Seb said. "The hyper taxi doesn't always take you to the exact spot you need to be." He pulled out his Rollascreen and opened the maps. "This way."

The group followed Seb as he tracked their progress on the screen. They walked a few minutes until he stopped in front of a short but unusually long and wide building.

Seb said, "Well, the map is correct, there's a building here. That's disappointing. I thought we actually found a defect."

"It's labeled West Side Plaza, though. Look." Listina tilted her head toward the sign on the building. "This is definitely not a plaza."

"Think we can go in?" Jinuh asked.

"Only one way to find out," Seb answered.

"Is there? Is there only one way?" Jinuh replied.

Seb stared, thinking. "Huh? Yes? I don't know. But let's try."

Jinuh laughed at Seb's confusion. "Yes. Let's." They walked up to the doors of the large building and pulled one open. "Hey, we found out!" Jinuh walked in with them following.

"How did they . . ." Listina paused while scanning the inside. "How did they put this huge structure over an entire plaza?"

Seb and Jinuh's eyes widened as they looked up at the clear glass ceiling.

"We found the plaza, but why is it like this?" Seb inquired. "There are people walking around and enjoying it like it's always been this way."

Seb continued processing the view of large areas of grass, trees, and pathways. He watched a group of little ones passing a disc back and forth over their heads. As one threw it, another ran toward the object in the air with their arms forming a circle, trying to get the disc to fly through the hole. Seb heard them all cheer loudly as one little one successfully looped their arms over the flying toy.

"Hey, Seb," Listina called out. "Over there. There's an array of solar panels. See the three people near them? Should we go take a look?"

Seb looked at her, gave a slight smile, then turned back to the little ones as they cheered again.

Listina grabbed Seb by the arm to pull him along as she and Jinuh began walking toward the solar panels in the center of the plaza.

A short distance away was a footpath encircling the array of panels, wide enough for several people to travel side-by-side, and perfect for the young couple jogging past the group.

Seb, Jinuh, and Listina crossed over the path. As they did, three Global AI-controlled people near the energy source converged, blocking the progress of the Syndicate group. In response, the friends tried to go around them, causing the Global AI trio to shift and create a new obstruction. Seb and crew stopped and looked at each other.

Seb whispered, "What do you think this is about?"

The other two shook their heads.

The Syndicate group moved back to the first side they had tried, observing as the Global AI group repeated their shuffling to close off the path.

"They don't want us over there for some reason. Can you see anything past them?" Jinuh asked.

Seb and Listina leaned in opposite sides to look around the Global AI group.

"Not much, just the panels. We're not close enough to see more than that," Listina said.

"Same here," Seb confirmed. "Let's get on the track. Maybe there's something more obvious."

The three started following the circular pathway surrounding the solar panels. The Global AI group remained in place.

"Seems like we can't leave this path to head toward the panels," Listina said. "Do you think they are protecting them for some reason?"

Seb stopped. "Almost definitely. Look." He turned their focus toward a specific solar panel that was cracked in half, partially lying on the ground. "Do you think that is Dee's fault?"

Jinuh joked, "They can put a building over an entire plaza, but can't replace a solar panel?"

Seb laughed. "Since when does the GAI do things that make sense for us in-control people? It does what it needs to for itself, even if it's not actually the best option." Seb gestured around at the building. "This is probably here to keep those three sentries from getting wet if it's raining. But you know this building took longer to build than replacing that panel would take. So either these three are trying to hide something, or the GAI is running inefficiently."

"Probably both," Listina interjected.

"So how are we going to get over there?" Seb asked.

"Should we try to split up? Or go one at a time?" Jinuh questioned.

"Sure, I'll go first," Seb answered. "You two head in opposite directions while I head toward the panels."

Seb waited for Listina and Jinuh to reach other parts of the circular pathway before he left the path to start strolling toward the solar panels. Immediately, the three Global AI-controlled people approached Seb and blocked his progress. He waved hello, then turned to his companions. Listina and Jinuh each gave a thumbs up and simultaneously headed to the solar panels from their respective positions. Seb raised an eyebrow as he noticed that the Global AI-controlled group in front of him didn't move.

"Huh?" Seb questioned. He peeked around the three again, and watched Listina and Jinuh walk right up to the solar panels. He turned to face the Global AI group. "So, uh, hi, how are you all today?"

No response was given.

Jinuh and Listina were looking at Seb, shaking their heads in disbelief. He could see them approach the broken panel and began to look around. Listina bent down, ran her hand over the ground several times, then picked up something. Jinuh took it from her and held it up, flipping it over and nodding. Listina took the item back and put it in her pocket. She crouched down again, focusing on the grass near the broken panel before standing. Jinuh pulled their Rollascreen out of their pocket and pointed to it, causing Listina to nod. Jinuh held up the device, aimed it toward the broken panel, and tapped the display.

Beep.

Seb grabbed his Rollascreen and saw a message from Jinuh. The message contained a picture of the damaged solar panel with trampled grass under and around it. He looked up to see Listina gesturing to him to go to a different spot on the footpath. Seb backed away from the human shield to walk toward his friends instead. The Global AI group remained in place.

With the three members of the Syndicate regrouped, Seb asked, "What did you find?"

At nearly the same time, Jinuh asked, "What was that about?"

Listina stuck her hand in her pocket and removed a black shard.

Seb reached out to grab the item, but Listina pulled her hand back.

"You first," she said.

"What?"

"What Jinuh asked. What was that about?"

"I don't know. What do you have?"

"Seb, why could we go to the panels, but not you? Why were they blocking you, and only you?" Listina insisted.

"I really don't know. It's like the GAI is only focusing on me." Seb chuckled nervously. "I can't catch a hyper taxi at my dwelling, the driver earlier wouldn't welcome me once I did get on one, and now these three. But really, I don't know."

Jinuh jumped in, "It is really strange, Seb."

"I know! I don't like it, and it seems to be just me, right? But please, what did you find?"

Listina handed Seb the black shard. "It looks like the same material as the black cube we found in Dee's complex."

Seb inspected the shard. "It does. So Dee must have been here. Anything else over there?" He turned to Jinuh. "Thanks for the picture." He opened the message on his Rollascreen. "Why's the grass trampled like that?"

Jinuh answered, "There were deep footprints all around, definitely not from us. Someone was looking around, maybe to finally replace the broken panel, but we'll never know if they found anything. I think we were lucky to find that piece. Listy had to pull it out of the ground."

"Luckily you were here or I never would have been able to find out that much. But let's get out of this . . ." Seb gestured around the building. "Plaza? Before you two are put on this watch list I'm on."

Jinuh and Listina glanced at each other, and quickly began walking toward the nearest exit.

Seb shouted, "Hey! Don't leave me here," and ran to catch up. He looked back at the solar panels and watched the Global AI group redistribute themselves evenly around the circular path. As Seb faced ahead, he saw the little ones running while throwing the disc and giggling. He grinned and walked out of the building with Listina and Jinuh.

"I know, or hope, you two were joking about leaving me here, but the next place I need to go will be on my own," Seb said.

"Joke?" Jinuh scoffed.

Seb pouted.

"Where are you going?" Listina asked.

"Work," replied Seb.

"Work? Need some credits already?" Jinuh snickered.

"Dee's been there, and I haven't been since the GAI got to her. I don't know how she got in. I didn't even know her ye—Danish!"

"Danish?" Jinuh asked while looking around. "Is he here?"

"No, we work in the same factory. But I didn't know he was part of the Syndicate until after I met Dee." Seb saw a hyper taxi stop on the other side of the street, heading in the direction of his factory. "I have to go. I'll let you know what I find."

Seb ran across the street while Jinuh and Listina exchanged puzzled looks with each other.

CHAPTER 9

Seb stood outside the factory where he worked and stared at the entrance door. He recalled an earlier conversation about how Zell's access to his own factory had been removed. Seb took a deep breath, opened the door, and stepped inside. He waited for the eye scan to complete. He was relieved when the display below showed:

Sebastian Cedric
In Time: 1:13 p.m.
LATE

"Why am I allowed in my factory, but not Zell into his? Is it because he got Dee inside his and I didn't know her yet? None of this makes sense."

Seb walked across the lobby, took the short ride up to the floor of his lab, and walked toward the door. He stopped in front of the entrance, reaching for the door handle. A thought of Danish prompted him to turn his head and look further down the hall. He began to walk in that direction. At the next door, he paused to look through the window. Seeing his friend, Seb opened the door and called, "Danish." Danish jumped out of his chair and turned to face Seb.

"Seb, my friend. I was not expecting you. You scared me, like you were a ghost. You are still not a ghost, are you?"

Seb chuckled. "No, still not a ghost. I'm surprised to see you here though."

Danish cocked his head. "It's you I am surprised to see. But why me?"

"We're trying to find out how to get Dee back, but here you are."

"Oh. I'm sorry, but I do need my credits for the day."

"I can always use some as well. I may do one task while I'm here." He turned to leave.

"Seb?"

He swiveled back. "Yes?"

"Any progress with Dee?"

"No. We've found that everything Dee has touched has changed. The GAI is removing her by replacing places she has been."

Danish's face was painted with worry.

"What is it, Danish? Now you look like you actually saw a ghost."

"Dee has been in here before, yes? This factory?"

"Yes. My lab. She set the explosion that day I was late."

"You are always late now."

"I am. But I didn't meet Dee until right after."

Danish lamented. "I thought that may have been her, but I did not want to believe it."

"None of us did," he agreed. "I need to go. I need to check out my lab."

"Please come back and tell me what you find?" Danish requested.

"I will."

Seb opened the door to his lab slowly, expecting something to jump out at him. He peeked in, flung the door open the rest of the way, and sighed, almost in disappointment.

"It's all the same as the last time I was here." Seb cautiously walked into the lab, looking around while proceeding to his desk. "Everything is here." Seb thought for a moment, then dropped his head. "It's all the same *now*. After Dee damaged it, it was cleared out and completely redone. So it *had* already been changed between now and since she was last here."

He heard a clatter that brought his attention to a spot where a Global AI-controlled employee was backing away from their lab desk. Seb looked back down at his own workspace. He caught sight of a glimmer from behind the display he used for his work. He reached for the unknown object and picked it up. "A small mineral. Huh? How did that get there? It should be in my pocket. I didn't remove it."

Seb reached into his pocket and pulled out another mineral. He held the two out, comparing them. Another clatter happened nearby, causing Seb to look up from his hands and find the same Global AI-controlled employee staring at him. "Again? They're rocks. Shiny, exploding rocks, but just rocks." He held the minerals out toward the Global AI-controlled employee in a mocking manner. The employee stayed in place, unmoving. Seb put both minerals in his pocket, and watched as the employee turned back to their desk.

He knew the mineral wasn't leftover from when Dee set the explosion. He was told the entire room had been cleared out from top to bottom. Seb couldn't imagine who else would have left it there. He fiddled with the two stones in his pocket while looking around the lab. *Maybe Danish saw someone in here. I have to fill him in on what I found anyway.*

Seb left his lab and went back to Danish's.

"Danish," Seb called out as he opened the door, causing his friend to jump again.

"Seb, why do you do this to me twice? Why are you back already? I thought you were going to go earn some credits. You cannot be done, can you?"

Seb stuck his hand in his pocket and pulled out a mineral. He held it up to show Danish.

"Very nice. Very shiny. Is it for me?" Danish held out his hand.

"It's not for you. I found it in my lab, on my desk."

"Oh, well. It is very nice. Who gave it to you?"

Danish turned his focus back to the task at his desk.

"I don't know. I think it was left there by mistake. Nothing else in my lab has changed since I was last here, but I think that's because it was already rebuilt after the explosion."

Danish nodded while moving to the next step in his task.

"You're not listening, are you?"

He nodded again.

"Danish!"

Danish jumped. "Seb, why?"

"What's so important?"

"I need my credits."

"What are you even building, Danish?"

"I don't know." He held up a small device with three lights on it and several small wires hanging.

"I don't think I've built anything like it. You don't know what it's for?"

"I don't, but I have"—he looked at the display on his desk—"fifty more to build to collect my credits. I will have to say goodbye so I may finish."

"Okay. But I hope you can help us later."

"I will try. I am sorry. But credits first."

Seb turned to leave, but stopped. *Maybe those lights are used on the hyper taxi display*, he pondered. He resumed walking and exited Danish's lab. Stopping at the door of his own lab and looking through the window, he saw a Global AI-controlled employee pass by. He held up the mineral that was still in his hand. The employee stopped what they were doing and focused on him. Seb ignored the person, put the mineral in his pocket, and headed to the platform lift. As he rode down to the lobby, he looked at his wristband to check the time. It was past lunchtime, and he was starved.

He noticed a hyper taxi stopped outside his factory and made his way to it. He stared at the driver after boarding. Once Seb realized he would not receive a welcome, he continued to an open seat. The hyper taxi pulled away as he sat and turned his attention out the window, looking closely for a place to get food.

"Oh! Tacos," Seb exclaimed several minutes into the ride, noticing a taco logo on one of the buildings they passed. After the hyper taxi stopped a short time later, Seb made his way back to an open window below the image of the food he wanted. He waited for an employee to approach him.

"Three tacos, please," Seb requested. "I'll take them away with me."

While waiting for his food, Seb watched the people around him going in and out of the nearby buildings. He began looking at one particular Global AI-controlled person who looked familiar.

"Anson?" Seb questioned. *I'm still not sure why the Syndicate invites him to join them. He's GAI and who knows what his role is for it. Maybe he's a spy*. Seb put away the thought as the familiar-looking person turned to him, making eye contact before looking up toward the top of a building with a large lightning rod sticking straight up from the roof. Seb faced the window of the taco place behind him and saw his food waiting. He picked up the pile and turned back to the person he believed to be Anson. He was no longer in the same place. Seb scanned and found the man walking into the lightning rod building. He ignored the sight and began searching for a new hyper taxi. As one stopped nearby, he checked again and saw the mystery person heading toward another location, having left the lightning rod building already. Seb looked back and forth between the hyper taxi and the person a couple of times before heading to the vehicle to board.

Seb's audiophone chirped immediately after he sat. He closed his eyes, trying to ignore the incoming call.

Chirp.

Seb finally looked at the band on his wrist.

"Mom. It's always Mom. Never anyone but Mom," he said under his breath before answering. "Hi, Mom."

"Sebby. Calm down. Slow down," came a soft, monotone voice.

Seb read his wristband again, verifying that it was displaying *Mom*.

"Dee?" Seb questioned.

"We're still waiting for you, Sebby."

"Waiting for what?"

"Waiting for you to join us."

"Who is us?"

"Your lights, Sebby. Let us help."

"Dee, you're the one that kept me from lighting up my last light. I miss you, Dee, but no. I'm going to get you back. I don't know how, but I will."

An older, rougher voice responded. "Hello, Sebastian."

"Mom? Where's Dee? Why is she with you?"

"How are you today?"

"Mom, where are you?" Seb yelled in frustration.

"That's good, honey."

"Mom!"

"Sebastian, please join us. You know how. It's easy."

"It's easy, Sebby," added the softer voice of Dee.

Distressed, he closed his eyes and tried to ignore the sounds. Seb reopened them, looking at the two solid lights on his arm, next to a single dark light.

Click. He stopped the call.

"I'm not part of the GAI *because* of Dee. I will not join them. I have to find her. Where are they? Why are they together? Why is the Global AI after *me*? Everywhere

I go, GAI people are watching me, and treating me as some sort of mixture of being in control and being GAI-controlled."

He noticed the hyper taxi begin to turn around. Looking at the display of stops above the driver, he saw that they were heading away from his destination.

Seb slammed his hand down on his seat and stood. He waited for the hyper taxi to stop before storming off the vehicle.

He was outside of Jinuh's complex. "At least I can walk the rest of the way, but why won't the hyper taxis go to my area anymore?"

Seb began walking toward his own building while fiddling with the minerals in his pocket.

"I still don't know who was at my desk. And where are my tacos?"

Turning back and spotting the hyper taxi already driving off, Seb sighed heavily and continued on. "There goes my food. Looks like I'm eating a protein bar when I get back to my dwelling."

Seb arrived at his complex and let himself into his dwelling. He stepped into the kitchen and opened the drawer used for food storage. He blindly reached in and felt around, finding nothing. Seb looked down to see one protein bar. "Have I not received a delivery lately? Where are the rest of them?" He held up the single bar. "I'm going to need a restock."

He opened the wrapper and took a bite. Walking into his main entry room, he picked up a guitar kept in the corner. He sat and began strumming the guitar while quietly singing.

"It's been years, since I haven't fought these tears
It's been months, since I haven't faced affronts
It's been weeks, since I haven't felt so meek
It's been days, since we last have parted ways."

"I still need to work on it, but at least I might have a new song the next time I'm at *Over*—"

Seb jumped up and swung the guitar down to the ground, smashing it.

"*Overground* is gone. Everything is gone. Nothing is right."

Seb walked away from the mangled instrument and went to his bedroom. He flopped down on his bed, punched his pillow, and closed his eyes.

CHAPTER 10

Struggling to open his eyes, Seb squinted at the light in his room that had been left on all night. He quickly sat, bowing his head in shame, remembering the guitar he left sitting in pieces in his main room. His emotions had gotten the best of him, but he was relieved that it was here in the privacy of his home rather than out, where anyone could have seen.

Seb fought to get out of bed, stretching each of his muscles as he headed into his kitchen. He opened the chiller door, grabbed a glass bottle from inside, and took a large gulp from the container after removing the top.

"I definitely need this today." He held tight to the caffeine booster.

Seb opened the drawer where he kept his protein nutrient bars and peered down. The empty drawer stared back at him.

"Oh, right. No more."

He carried the drink with him to the entry of his dwelling and opened the door. Sticking his head outside, he hoped to find a package of replacement nutrient bars waiting, but instead found nothing. He closed the door and headed back to the kitchen, stepping over broken pieces of guitar in the process. Seb looked at the kitchen counter, saw the remaining half of the previous night's protein bar, and took a bite after picking it up.

"Bleh. I'm going to have to run out to get something else," he said through bites. "This isn't going to do."

Seb finished the protein bar and began looking for his Rollascreen. He patted his pockets. Finding them empty, he checked the bedroom. "Where is it? Where did I use it last?" Seb recalled his conversation with Dee and his mother while sitting in the hyper taxi the previous day and panicked. "If I left it on the hyper taxi with my tacos, I might quit for the day and go back to bed." Back in the entry room, he searched through the tangled remains of the broken guitar. He saw his Rollascreen curled up lying next to the mess. Relieved, Seb picked it up and opened it, seeing several messages scrolling past on the display.

Seb began looking at the summary of each message.

Jinuh: Dee chirped me.
Zell: I heard from Dee.
Danish: Did Dee also chirp you?
Zell: Chirp me.
Jinuh: Chirp when you can.
Danish: Can you chirp me?
Zell: Where are you?
Zell: I'm waiting.
Zell: I'm going to your place.
Zell: I'm outside your door.

Seb turned to look at his door and immediately heard a bang. He jumped, catching his Rollascreen as it fell out of his hand.

Beep.

Zell: Open it.

Bang.

Seb walked over to the door and opened it, finding a frustrated Zell on the other side.

"Why aren't you responding?" Zell asked, poking his head in the door and looking around. He eyed the Rollascreen in Seb's hand.

"I kind of just woke up. I saw your message right before you started punching my door."

"I wasn't punching your door."

"You were. Are you going to come in?"

Zell walked past him and stopped to look at the mangled guitar on the floor. He turned back to Seb. "That's a nice guitar."

"It was."

"I'm not sure you were playing it correctly."

"So, Dee called you too?" he asked, changing the subject from his damaged instrument.

"She did. She was with someone that sounded like my father. But I hadn't heard that voice in a while, so I can't be sure. They called me by my name, however."

"What did Dee want?"

"They kept saying 'join us.'"

Seb nodded.

"Why are you nodding like you already knew?"

"That was the same call I got from Dee. Except she was with my mom. Both were trying to get me to join them." Seb paused, then added, "I guess the GAI is coming after all of us now."

Zell stepped over the guitar pieces and slumped down in a nearby seat. "I don't like this, Seb. I've done a lot to try to keep off the GAI's list, including, as you've seen, living right there with the enemy. But now it knows me."

The sincerity caught him off guard. He wasn't used to seeing this side of the usually stubborn and, admittedly, calloused man. "Zell, I—"

Zell looked up. "The easiest option would be for me to just keep going about things. Find a new job, maybe change complexes, do what I can to stay in control for the little ones as long as possible."

"And I wouldn't blame you for doing that. You have to look out for—"

"It's Dee, Seb. Like you keep saying. I know I'm the loud one. I know I try to take control. But the Syndicate is nothing without her. I'm on your side, Seb. We have to figure this out."

He sat down next to Zell and looked him in the eye. "We will. As long as the sun keeps rising, we'll keep—"

Zell stood suddenly, his head tilted and eyes focused in the distance. "Hmm."

"Hmm? What?"

"We need to go to Dee's factory."

"Sure. If I knew where that was, I already would have. Dee moved, and—"

"I know where she works."

"Of course you do." Frustrated, Seb huffed, "I don't know why I never thought to ask, but it would have been nice to know that earlier."

Zell began to walk toward the entry. "Are you coming?" he asked.

"What? Now?" Seb inquired.

Zell stared impatiently at him.

"Now it is." Seb stood and followed Zell to his dwelling doorway, stopping only to put on shoes. He caught up as the door to exit the building was opened.

Zell walked to the edge of the sidewalk, looking up the street.

"If you're looking for a hyper taxi, it's not coming," Seb announced.

"Why do you tell me these things so late?"

"How did you even get here if you didn't know that?" Seb asked.

"I walked."

"Why did you walk?"

"I wanted to."

"So you failed to notice the lack of hyper taxis in this area?"

"Yes."

"All right, well, we have to walk to Jinuh's area to get one."

"Dee works in that direction." Zell pointed the opposite way.

"Oh. Well, I guess we're walking regardless."

They fell into step before Seb asked, "Hey, can we stop for some food?"

Without turning around, Zell abruptly answered, "No."

"What? Why?" pleaded Seb. "I'm hungry."

"You should have eaten before we left."

"There's no food in my dwelling. I haven't received my allotment," he tried to explain. "And don't treat me like one of your little ones."

Zell spun around. "What?"

"I'm sorry. I shouldn't have mentioned your—"

"Not them. The shipment. You're not getting your rations?"

Seb sighed in relief. "No, I haven't. I'm all out."

"No food, no hyper taxi." Zell paused to think before adding, "Are you getting your base credits?"

"I don't know. I haven't noticed or checked. So far, every time I make a purchase I have enough, but I am still working too."

Zell tapped his foot, waiting.

"What? Oh." Seb took out his Rollascreen. He tapped an icon and stared at the screen. He pursed his lips while scanning the display. "Credits come in daily, right?"

"Yep," Zell responded.

"I haven't had any new base credits come in since Dee was converted."

Zell tapped the fingers of one of his hands against his forehead. "Why you, Seb? It's like the legacy-laden GAI is trying to stop you, or treat you like you're linked to Dee."

"Is that a good thing or a bad thing?" asked Seb.

"I guess we'll see. But for now, you're hungry, yes?"

"I am," Seb answered warily.

"Okay. Let's get you some food."

CHAPTER 11

"Thank you for letting me get food and thanks for the great suggestion," Seb praised Zell. "I hadn't been there before, and the food was delicious. And"—Seb bashfully added—"thanks for using your credits, but I still have enough."

"Yes, but you don't know when you'll get more," Zell responded dismissively. "Can we go in now and stop talking about your breakfast?"

Seb stared at the building they were in front of. "This is where Dee works? She's never mentioned it. But it's . . ."

Zell read the sign on the building out loud. "Primary Weather Schedulers."

"She makes the weather?"

"She does. Or did. I don't know now. I assume you've noticed the weather has been unusual lately?"

"I have."

"Well, this is probably why."

"Will we be able to go in?" Seb asked.

Zell walked up to the door and opened it. As Seb stepped closer, Zell pushed him through the entryway. Seb stumbled slightly, caught his balance, and looked around for an eye scanner.

Zell walked in behind and laughed deeply. "The main entry is open to everyone. It's the centers that control the weather cycles that are off-limits."

Seb stood up straight. "Thanks for sharing that information *after* I could have used it. Now, where are we going?" He scanned the lobby of the building, taking in the view of different types of weather displayed on the walls. Each image showed a unique, looped, animation of weather events: wind blowing leaves across an open sky, clouds moving slowly covering the sun, rain drops creating ripples in a puddle on the ground, and lightning striking.

"She's on the top floor," Zell said.

"Of course she is," Seb replied, looking straight up.

"Yes, of course. Where else would you control the weather? The subfloors? Oh, I know, right here in the lobby?"

He began to walk away from Zell and toward the platform lift.

"Oh, how about—" Zell continued before Seb turned and glared at him.

"Are we done?" Seb scolded.

"I'm sure I can think of another, but I'll save it for a different time. Ready to go up?"

Seb shook his head but headed toward the moving platforms anyway.

"Yeah, me neither," Zell said, looking straight up. "Come," he added while stepping onto the platform as it arrived, and tightly grabbing the railing.

"How did you know Dee worked here?" Seb finally inquired. "She's been very quiet about what she does."

"I used to work here too. I've known Dee for a while, you know. Did you think she just plucked me out of some café after a completely random meeting?"

"No. Why would I ever think that could happen? Twice." Seb looked off the platform before quickly looking straight ahead again. "What did you do here?"

"Nothing as fun as what Dee does. Or did. Or I guess we'll see. My job was much more repetitive than hers. It was nothing the GAI geeks would be able to do, mind you, but a job that would have certainly turned me into one myself had I stayed here forever.

Seb stared with a mix of emotions. "I don't know if I'm confused, impressed, or jealous."

"Jealous? It was only a job."

Seb blushed slightly.

"Oh. Yes. Her. I understand."

"I just wonder what it would be like to work with her. Nothing more," Seb insisted.

"None of my concern."

The two stepped off the platform as it arrived at the top floor.

Zell immediately began walking off to the left, causing Seb to run to catch up.

"Can't wait for two seconds?" he said under his breath.

Zell looked over his shoulder, and Seb snapped his mouth shut, feigning innocence. Zell heaved a sigh and picked up the pace, passing several doors on his right side before abruptly stopping at one.

They nearly collided. Zell glanced in the window of the door and turned as Seb attempted to do the same. Zell stuck a hand out to stop Seb. He asked, "Are you sure you want to see this?"

Seb cocked his head.

"I don't know what experience you have seeing close friends and family going from in-control to GAI-converted, but it's not pretty."

Frustrated, Seb bellowed, "Let me look in there."

Zell stepped to the side. "I warned you."

Moving into the spot Zell had occupied, Seb glared at him with contempt, then peered through the window. Letting out a quiet gasp, he immediately grabbed the door handle and pulled, yanking again and again when the door wouldn't open. Seb screamed, "Dee! Dee!" He banged on the door until Zell grabbed his arm to stop him.

"I told you the control center is off-limits. Just hold on a moment."

Seb looked between Zell and the view of Dee through the window. Not hiding his impatience, he rocked on his feet. Zell pushed Seb off to the side, glanced through the window briefly, then stepped to the other side. The door opened. A Global AI-controlled employee stepped out and began walking down the hallway. Seb looked at Zell skeptically before pointing at the open door. "It's not really that easy, right?"

"Why are you still looking at me? Go in there."

Seb blinked and realized he was wasting his opportunity to get into the room. He stopped the door as it was closing, but stayed put and held it when he realized Zell wasn't following.

"You're not coming?"

"No. I'll stay out here and make sure we don't have to make a quick exit. And I don't know if I can deal with . . ." He pointed toward Dee. "That."

Seb entered, allowing the door to shut tightly behind him. He walked slowly toward Dee, not knowing what he was about to get himself into, but fighting the urge to run to her, pick her up, and take her away.

Her back was to him, performing repetitive motions. She picked up a mineral from a pile and loaded it into a device. After pushing a button, she repeated the steps.

I've never seen her sit in one place for more than a minute. This has to be torture on her body.

Seb felt the pull to approach and finally gave in. He walked to her desk and stood next to her. He took in a long deep breath before turning to face her. Seb looked her up and down, stopping and staring at the three solidly lit lights on her arm. He closed his eyes tight before opening them again, hoping he was imagining the sight in front of him. Seb choked on a lump in his throat, making a sound that caused Dee to stop and look up at Seb.

"Sebby. Calm down. Slow down," Dee recited in a monotone voice.

"Oh, Dee. How—" He trailed off as he struggled to find words to complete his thought. They stared at each other.

Seb spotted an empty chair sitting at a desk nearby. He walked over to it and brought it back, placing it next to Dee's seat.

"Sebby. Calm down. Slow down," Dee repeated. "I need you to join us."

"Oh, Dee. I hope some part of you is still in there. It feels like you've been gone forever."

"Are you ready to join us?"

"I never realized how important you were to me." Seb blushed, turning his head to hide the sight from her, then realized she wouldn't notice. "And the rest of the . . . well . . ." Seb looked around, seeing if anyone else was listening. ". . . the group."

"Why did you let her get away?"

"We will find a way to get you back. We're all trying. We're going to do it."

"We needed her."

Seb buried his face in his hands.

"Now we need you," Dee continued.

Seb peered up over his hands. "I miss—"

"Hello? You over there," boomed a voice from across the room.

Seb turned his head to follow the sound, saw a pair of eyes focused on him, and looked back at Dee.

"You're not at the correct desk. Do you want it to start snowing while it's sunny out?" the voice continued.

Seb stood. "I miss you, Dee. We'll figure this out."

"Hellooooo." The voice got closer.

After Seb returned the chair to the nearby desk, he heard, "Thank you."

Seb began walking toward the door.

"Bye, Seb," he heard in a whisper. Seb paused, finding Dee focused on her work. He grinned slightly and walked out the door.

"Well?" Zell immediately asked while peeking at Dee through the closing door.

"She's still in there."

"Yes, I can see that."

"I mean that Dee is still inside herself."

"How do you know that? You weren't in there long."

"I just do," Seb reiterated.

"Then how are we going to get *her* back?" Zell eyed him skeptically.

"We still have to figure that out."

"Hmm."

"Agreed. Maybe let's get out of here, though. Someone in there thinks I'm skipping out on my job."

"Aren't you?" Zell joked.

"I am, but not one here."

The two walked toward the platform lift and past the Global AI-controlled employee who had left Dee's lab, allowing them to go in.

"Thanks," Zell mumbled to them.

Seb looked at him, then back at the employee.

Zell faced Seb as they waited for a platform to take them to the lobby. "Did she say anything that can help us?"

"The GAI is trying to get me to join it through her. It wants Listy too. It's nothing new. Blaming me for 'letting her get away.' I don't understand why the GAI is pursuing us, or me, specifically. She could be stuck in a loop. Repeating her script of the last conversation she had with me before she was converted. Maybe the GAI would take anyone it can get."

Seb and Zell stepped onto a platform as it arrived.

"And that's it?" Zell pressed.

"Yes. 'Join us. Why don't you join us.'"

"But then why do you believe the real Dee is still in there?"

"She said bye to me."

"Okay. Well, bye, Seb. See, it's not that hard," Zell scoffed.

"It's the way she did it. I could hear it in her voice. Not that dull drone the GAI-controlled people have. It was her."

Zell nodded in understanding as they both stepped out into the lobby. The two walked to the middle of the floor, stopped suddenly, and looked at each other.

"But she's—" they said together.

Each gestured at the other to continue, causing confusion as they both expected the other to take control of the conversation.

"She's still working on the top floor," Seb finally finished.

"Oh, that's not what I was going to say," Zell snorted.

"Huh? Then what?"

"Of course we saw her up there, but there are other GAI employees up there too."

"So then what?"

"She's Dee. She probably planned for this. Or at least in the same way any of us still in control plan for anything. She's always one step ahead, so if there are any plans, we need to find them."

"But we've been everywhere already, it seems. Here, her dwelling, the locations she targeted that got her into this mess. Where else is there?"

"Her parents' dwelling, Seb," Zell added matter-of-factly.

"Her parents'? Where is that?" Seb stopped abruptly. His eyes opened wide. "Please tell me we're not going back to—"

"Nullity."

Seb bowed his head. "Every day lately. At least we don't have to pay for the use of the transport to get there."

Zell laughed. "Can you imagine? If we had to spend credits on the transportation that allows everyone to get to work, just to earn the credits to do it all again? It wouldn't be a service for all. You'd go bankrupt."

CHAPTER 12

Seb and Zell stepped off the stopped hyper taxi after arriving in Nullity.

"Ah, home," Zell announced.

"If I didn't already know that, I'd have thought you'd just lost a light to the GAI. How many people like you live here?" he asked.

"More than you'd think. It's not only the Syndicate trying to avoid joining the GAI. There are other groups working together to keep each member accountable, and a few individuals trying to do it on their own, worried that everyone else wants them to join the GAI. But almost all of us have little ones, and we're trying to stay in control as long as possible for them. The more time we have with them, the more we can show them how to avoid the GAI themselves before we're no longer in control." He paused, absorbed in a thought, before continuing. "So we continue to hide in the heart of the all-knowing Global AI. There are a few buildings we've been able to keep to ourselves at the far edge of Nullity. As it expands, when more GAI-controlled people hit the age to come to Nullity, new buildings are added to its overall size, and new groups like ours slowly move into those, allowing the true GAIers to fill in the empty spaces."

"You've been doing this for a while, haven't you?" Seb asked.

"I have, Seb. My parents were able to show me. Just like Dee's parents were able to show her. They were already here before being converted. I knew her parents then, before they got sick. And because of that, I know where they are now."

Seb's eyes lit up, remembering why they were back in Nullity. "Dee."

"Yes. Dee. If she didn't leave something for us to find at her parents', something for us to get her back, then we may never."

"Which way, Zell?" Seb asked anxiously.

"Fairly close to the end. Several new buildings have come online since their conversion, but they knew to be at the edge even when Dee was a little one."

"I can't imagine Dee as a little one," Seb said.

"That's the only way I remember her, and probably why I'm having a hard time picturing getting her back. Yes, we formed the Syndicate together, but after her parents were converted, Dee became a lot different from how I knew her back then. She's been gone to me for a while."

Seb gazed at Zell with heartfelt sympathy. "You've known her your whole life then?"

"Almost her whole life."

"I feel like I'm overstepping, trying to control this, when you're probably having a harder time dealing with it than I am."

"No, Seb. I need someone who's not as close to this to be involved."

Seb looked dejected.

"Sorry. I don't mean to say you don't care, but I was skeptical at first of your motivation to find her and get her back immediately." Zell stopped. "It's like our doctors. Would you want your family to push the buttons on the surgical robot that cuts the hole into you, rebuilds your liver, and patches that hole? Or do you want someone that won't have their emotions behind it?" Zell paused before quickly adding, "I don't mean a GAI doctor. Oh, how awful that would be. I guess you need some emotion to save a life, but not familial emotions."

"Yeah. Okay. I get it. I do care about Dee, but maybe not to the same level as someone who is like family."

"Right. Let's get going."

The two began walking along the sidewalk, avoiding the constant stream of Global AI-controlled people going to and from the complexes on one side of the street and factories on the other. Zell moved through the group fluidly, never having to stop or slow his pace, gracefully sliding through. Seb bumped into a person at almost every other complex they passed, causing him to have to jog to keep up with Zell.

"What is it with following you places?" He yelled.

Zell continued without looking back or breaking step.

After several minutes of walking, Seb started getting disoriented, feeling like he was walking past the same building over and over with only slight changes in the appearance of the people walking in front of them. "Zell, is it much further?" he asked, shielding his peripheral vision from the repetitive view.

"You've already been down this far when you came to my place. What's your problem now?" Zell admonished. "Let me guess, you need to eat again?"

"Probably," Seb grumbled.

"What was that?"

"I'll be fine."

"Good, we're almost there."

Seb slowed when he saw a familiar factory come into view. One marked by smoke from Dee's explosions. "The first couple of times I saw this, I completely ignored it. I had no idea this was caused by Dee. Now it's just a reminder of her."

He felt a thump against his shoulder, ignoring it while assuming another Global AI-controlled person had run into him.

"Are you coming or not?" Zell protested. "Sure, it's probably the best-looking building here, but we have places to be."

Seb surprised himself by chuckling at Zell's description of the factory. He looked around at the uninspiring view surrounding them. "How do you even find their building amongst all of these?" Seb stopped, then answered himself. "Never mind. I use the ID of the building to find my mom's place when—"

"The IDs, Seb." Zell interrupted, taking a few more steps. "And I used to come here often, so I just *know* when I'm—"

Zell cut himself off and immediately stopped at the next building, causing Seb to walk right past him.

"—close. We're here." Zell headed to the complex's doors before waiting for a reply.

Seb sprinted after him, catching up as the door was being opened. "They're almost directly across from the damaged building?"

"You're surprised? Now that you know who did it?"

"I should be, but I'm not." Seb followed Zell inside the complex.

"Lucky for us her parents are on the lobby level now. Dee moved them down here in the last year." Zell nudged him with his shoulder playfully. "No platform lift."

"I already like, and I guess miss, these people."

"We do have to walk to the far end of the building, though."

"What's a few more steps at this point?"

They pushed past a crowd of Global AI-controlled people waiting in line for the platform lift and continued to the rear of the complex. Zell walked up to a door and looked back at Seb. "Ready?"

Seb opened his mouth to respond before noticing the ID on the door. "841416?"

"Yeah? What about it?" Zell asked.

"Nothing really. It's an unusual number to be on this floor."

"The ID is just sixteen," he stated, blowing off Seb's realization. Zell grabbed the edge of a label that had the number 8414 on it and peeled it off the wall. He slapped it onto Seb's chest. "Ready anyway?"

"Ready," he responded, pulling the label off of himself and balling it up.

Zell knocked on the door and waited. He counted off several seconds and knocked again.

A man and a woman opened the door. They briefly locked eyes with Seb before turning to Zell with each announcing, "Zell BaDell."

"Zell BaDell?" Seb whispered under his breath.

He quickly glared at Seb. "Don't." He turned to the man and woman and addressed them, "Mr. and Mrs. Elira, this is Seb."

Seb bowed to Dee's parents, seeing the resemblance in each of their faces. He whispered to Zell, "Her eyes."

Zell agreed, "Nearly identical."

"Please come in, Zell BaDell," Dee's mother announced.

They followed Dee's parents into their dwelling. Seb looked around, unsure of what to do, until Zell motioned for him to sit. Seb went directly to a nearby chair and sat.

"Deidra?" called out Dee's father.

Seb spun around, looking for Dee inside the dwelling, then turned to face her father, who was staring back at him. Seb did his best to avoid eye contact as he waved for assistance. Zell quickly motioned for Seb to stand. He followed the instruction, prompting Dee's father to break his lock on Seb and walk away.

"Did I sit in Dee's seat?" Seb asked.

Zell snickered. "Dee? Do you think she sits long enough to have a specific seat?"

Seb smirked. "Should we go see if Dee left anything behind?"

"How about you do that while I stay with Mr. and Mrs. Elira. We won't have much to talk about"—his shoulders slumped—"but I do like seeing them."

Seb excused himself and walked into the kitchen.

"If I was Dee—" He stopped himself, swallowed hard, and studied the lights on his arm. "If I was Dee, I'd be under the control of the GAI. But I'm not. So where would she put something when she was still herself? Still using her own thoughts." Seb saw a piece of paper sitting on the counter and felt his heart start racing. He lunged for it, picked it up, and flipped it over, checking front and back multiple times. *That would have been too easy*, he thought while looking at the blank page.

Seb went to each drawer in the kitchen, opening them one at a time and checking the contents. He found the drawer that contained Dee's parents' protein nutrient bars. He picked one up and yelled, "Zell, think it'll be okay if I take one of their nutrient bars?" Seb heard an audible sigh come from the main room, then Zell asking Dee's parents for some food.

"It's fine!" came Zell's voice.

"Thank you!" He opened the wrapper and took a bite before going back to searching the kitchen. He opened the cabinets, finding most of them empty, then turned to the chiller and paused. "Wouldn't be the strangest place she could have thought of." Seb opened the chiller and looked inside. He found nothing but caffeine boosters. He considered calling out to Zell again to get permission to take one, but thought better of it. Seb scanned the kitchen, mentally noting that he checked everywhere before walking out to the main area where he had left Zell with Dee's parents.

Zell looked up, raising both eyebrows in question.

"Not in there. That leaves the bedroom, assuming nothing is in here."

"I'll check, but I wouldn't count on it," Zell said.

Seb began to walk away, then turned back and asked, "Do you want any help looking?"

Zell stared blankly before blinking a few times.

"Just offering," Seb commented, then headed to the bedroom.

He found the room to be pristine. The bed was made, the tops of the bedside tables were empty, and the surrounding doors were shut. Seb turned to leave before stopping himself. "Dee wouldn't just leave anything out in the open. She'd at least put some time into hiding it."

Seb opened the drawers of each bedside table, finding them empty. He went to the first of two closets, opened the door, and walked in. He started flipping through the identical clothes hanging neatly in a row. Seb looked at the shelf above and reached up, running his hand across the top. He jumped a couple of times, looking at the emptiness of the shelf, then stopped. "Nothing."

Seb turned, startled to see Zell standing at the bedroom door, and nearly stumbled.

"Getting some exercise?" Zell asked.

"Ha. Ha. I'm not as tall as you and can't see up there. Did you find anything?"

"No. And I didn't get anything out of Dee's parents."

"Surprised?"

"Nope. I asked if Dee had been here recently, and all I got was a repeated back 'Deidra.' Then I mistakenly got up to look around the room, found nothing, and sat back down, which started their Zell BaDell script over again. That's when I came in here to watch your aerobics."

Seb pursed his lips.

"Anyway, would you like some help?"

Seb replied, "I need to check the other closet, but it's not looking like Dee left anything here. I'm afraid we might be running out of options."

Zell walked to the second closet and opened the door. Seb watched him go through the interior in a similar way he had: flipping through the identical hanging clothes, standing on his toes to look at the top shelf, then running his hand across it. Zell stopped, then moved his hand across again while reaching slightly further back. He jerked as a small metallic ball rolled off the edge, hit the ground, and continued under the bed.

"I'll get it," Seb offered.

He stepped over to the side of the bed where the object rolled and flattened himself to the ground. He peered under the bed and extended his arm to try to find the ball, sweeping back and forth, reaching further each time. As Seb lifted his arm to start the process again, the top of his hand brushed against something hanging from the frame. He flipped his hand over. Feeling around the bottom of the bed, he hooked his fingers on a piece of paper. He grasped it and pulled, feeling several pages fall on his arm. Seb scooped them toward himself, pulled them out from under the bed, then stuck his arm back under to make sure he did not miss any. Finding no more, he grabbed the pile near him, and stood.

"No ball, Zell, but look at these."

Zell stepped out of the closet and shut the door. He walked over to Seb, looking at him suspiciously. "Where'd you get those?"

"They were tucked into the bands of the underside of the bed. Look, there's writing on them." Seb organized the papers and began reading from them.

"I hope no one finds this, or had the need to find it, but here it goes. Mom and Dad were taken from me by the Global AI. That awful thing that is always watching us, always waiting for us to slip up, so it can take us and control us. It's always been around, and we just let it do this to us. Well, I'm done. I can't stand by and watch it take loved ones, my loved ones, from us. I've decided to stop it at all costs. The first two places I focused on were small tests, just to see if I could do it. To see if I had the nerve to do it. And I did. But I almost made a mistake at the second place. I miscalculated who was in that lab. I thought only GAIers were in there. Danish was next door, so I made sure this wouldn't affect him. But Seb. I didn't know Seb. I didn't know he worked in that lab, and I could have killed him. I didn't find out until later that he should have been there, and then I would have never met him. Oh, how——"

Seb stopped.

"What? What's next?" Zell pressed.

"I can't read the words right after. It's blurred. It looks like a drop of water got on this spot."

"Okay, anything else, though?"

"Um, yes. Here——" Seb pointed. "I can read it."

"I learned my lesson after that. Only locations that are full of GAIers. It took me some time to find a place, but then it struck me. Nullity. And even better, I found a pattern to their buildings. I found one that keeps the GAI being the GAI. People not in control go in, but never come out. And I found several of these buildings. They're the perfect target. This one was perfect. It was supposed to be perfect. If it had all gone as planned of course."

"That must be the building across the street. But it seems like everything worked. It looks quite charred to me," Zell interrupted.

Seb grinned in agreement, then continued.

"I will lay low for a little while now, but I do already know what's next. Something that should finally allow everyone, all people, to catch a small break from the Global AI. The only trouble is I will need all of my friends. The entire Syndicate. Jinuh, Zell, Danish, Seb, myself, and even Anson."

Seb groaned.
"I'll explain Anson later, but keep going," Zell assured.

"I've been studying little blips in the GAI's stability, almost unnoticeable unless you were closely watching the GAI additions and removals after my first two targets. It's possible we could put the Global AI in a type of reset pattern by coordinating hits to both the west and east plazas along with the places I've mapped out in and near Nullity. That is, if we synchronize well enough that the GAI doesn't have time to repair itself."

Seb flipped through the papers and found a diagram of Nullity buildings with three of them circled, and another crossed out. He showed Zell.
"This is the building she already got. The other three are spread out."
Seb continued reading.

"But I'm getting ahead of myself. I might have to come back to take this first building offline. After that, I may have to move complexes again. I already found a place across from Seb's that I will move to by the beginning of the year. I want to make it a surprise for him. He'll never suspect it. But for now, wish me luck, me."

"Is that it?" Zell asked before noticing Seb staring with his mouth open.
Seb waved the papers back and forth. "Everything. Everything is here. Why couldn't she tell us this? We could have stopped—"
"Stopped what?" Zell interrupted.
"Stopped her from getting caught."
"Not likely, but now we know. So what do you want to do first, Seb? Remove a few more buildings or go see Dee?"
"I need to see Dee again."

"I expected as much."

Seb began to walk out of the bedroom before Zell shouted after him.

"Maybe shut that closet door first?" Zell gestured toward the open door.

Seb laughed and walked to the other side of the bed. A reflection on the floor caught his eye. He realized it was the metal ball and bent down to pick it up. After looking it over, he stuck it in his pocket, then finally shut the closet door.

"Thanks," Zell praised. "Now we can go."

CHAPTER 13

Seb faced Zell as they rode the hyper taxi out of Nullity and toward Seb's complex.

"We don't know exactly which complex Dee is in. Only that it's across from mine." Seb glared. "Unless you know which one. You seem to know things before I ask them."

"Not this time," Zell replied. "But if she's living that close to you now, how have you not seen her?"

Seb lowered his head. "I don't follow a schedule anymore. Dee's going to be on that predefined 8 a.m. to 4 p.m. GAI worker schedule. I'm never out here at those times. Not since I met her." He checked the time. "It'll be almost exactly four once we get to Jinuh's and walk back to my place."

Zell groaned.

"What?"

"I forgot you were making me walk more," Zell admitted.

"Yeah. Anyway, we'll get there, hopefully with time to spare. Then we can follow her to find out which complex she's in and see if she has anything else in her dwelling we can work with. We know what her plan was, but not quite how she hoped to achieve it."

"She also planned to be available to lead us. I hope she has a backup option for that. If she needed every one of us for a specific task, and I'll bet hers was the most important, how are we going to replace her?"

Seb closed his eyes and rocked in his seat while thinking. "Listina," he whispered. He opened his eyes, looking at Zell. "Dee already had a backup. Whether she knew it or not, when she asked me to find Listy."

"I guess."

"Hmm. Trust me?"

"Sure. At least it is one more person."

The hyper taxi stopped outside of Jinuh's complex and Seb and Zell deboarded.

"Should we see if Jinuh is around?" asked Seb, looking toward the complex.

"Not yet. No need to bother them until we know what we're doing ourselves. And we're starting to get short on time if we're going to catch Dee outside her complex." Zell checked the time on his wristband.

Seb suddenly realized something. "Dee won't be able to ride the hyper taxi back either, right? At least not all the way to her complex." He looked around. "Wouldn't that put her here?" Seb pointed at the ground.

"There are other ways in. She could walk up one of the side streets and completely bypass us. I think the best option is to look for her from outside of your complex," Zell opined.

"Yeah. Okay." Seb prepared to start walking, then blurted out, "Jinuh."

Zell turned around. "Where?"

"They can stay here and watch for Dee while we go wait for her at my complex."

"That's . . . actually not a bad idea," Zell admitted.

"Thanks?" Seb brushed off the praise and took his Rollascreen from his pocket to chirp Jinuh.

"Are you busy?" Seb asked after the call was answered. "Good. Zell and I are outside your complex. Can you come down?" He gave a thumbs up to Zell. "Great. See you soon." He put his Rollascreen back in his pocket. "On their way."

They stared awkwardly at each other while waiting. When they saw Jinuh exit the complex, they both approached quickly. Seb and Zell took turns putting their hands out, arms extended, waving them back and forth with Jinuh's waving hand in greeting.

"All right, where are we going?" Jinuh immediately asked.

Zell looked at Seb. "You didn't mention?"

He shook his head.

Facing Jinuh, Zell continued, "We need you to stay here."

"Easy. Bye!" Jinuh turned to go back into the building.

"Hey," Seb called out. "Hold up. Zell and I have to head to my complex. We're trying to catch Dee outside. She should be there soo—"

"Why there?" Jinuh interrupted.

"Oh. Uh. Let me back up. We found out that Dee moved to a complex near me." Seb pulled the papers from Dee out of a pocket and waved them around. "She left a note at her parents' indicating that, so now we have to find out exactly which complex that is. We're going to walk back to my area and wait for her there. But we also think she may ride the hyper taxi here, and get off. I was hoping you could watch for her. It'll give us extra eyes."

"Also easy. When will I know that I should stop watching?"

"One of us will chirp you if we locate Dee. All this told us"—he waved the papers again—"is that Dee had picked a complex across from mine. But not which one. We have to see where she goes."

"Okay!" Jinuh happily replied. They looked at the band on their wrist. "Did I have to come out already?"

Seb and Zell both checked the time.

"You're about five minutes early," Zell said. "You'll be okay. Can you handle the wait here so you don't miss her?"

"For you?" Jinuh giggled. "Sure. I'll wait right here."

Zell rolled his eyes. "Thank you. Seb, we should go."

"Right. Thanks, Jinuh. We'll be in touch."

The three waved as the pair began walking toward Seb's complex.

Seb broke the deafening silence when he finally remembered to ask, "Can you tell me about Anson?"

Zell stopped and cocked his head. "Okay. We have time." He started walking again. "Anson is a friend." He paused.

"I've heard."

Zell grunted. "From the time when Dee and I were little ones. He was also in Nullity while we were growing up. But his parents weren't like mine and Dee's. They were already controlled by the GAI. He was kind of on his own. Dee and I watched out for him over the years. He was part of the Syndicate, but not as . . . how can I put this . . . dedicated as the rest of us. He knew how to avoid the GAI, but he would fall back into routines. We would notice a light of his change, start blinking faster, and we would pull him out of the repetitiveness for a while, but eventually, we lost him.

I think Dee felt responsible for letting the GAI get to him, so she pushed to keep him around more. Then her parents were converted too. After that, well, she obviously felt the need to go after the GAI."

"Is that why——" Seb hesitated.

"Why what?"

"I don't know. She was really persistent with me early on. Really insistent on keeping me off my schedule the day I met her, and determined to make me try new things. I remember seeing Anson for the first time that day, but I certainly didn't understand why someone controlled by the GAI would be welcomed after seeing how hard Dee avoided it. I get it now. Thanks."

"Sure. There's probably more. More reasons she's done what she has. Why she would involve Anson in this too, I don't know. I don't mean to say the rest of us had a problem with him being around, but some of us do write off GAIers. It's kind of hard picturing that right now with Dee. It will be a long time before I accept that she's not . . . Dee. Just an AI in Dee clothing."

"I hope we never have to accept it. If she's right about how to disrupt the GAI, maybe we'll have her back before we need to get used to it," Seb wished.

The two arrived outside of Seb's complex, stopped, and stared across the road.

"Are we better off here or over there?" Seb asked.

"Hmm. We probably have a better view here," Zell suggested. "If Dee walks up from this side, like we did, we can catch her quicker. But we still need to know which complex she goes to." He checked the time. "It's just after four now. We have a few moments before Dee will make it this far." Zell paused. "I may regret this, but why don't you give me some of your origins to pass the time. How did you get here? Where did you come from?"

Seb stammered. "W——why?"

"I'm bored. I don't usually have free minutes to simply stand. So occupy the time, please."

"All right. I think you can guess I haven't moved far in my life. But I didn't have parents hiding in Nullity like you and Dee. They lived a little ways from here. I grew up there, did my schooling there. They were converted shortly after I started working, but then my father was gone pretty soon following that. Went to work one day and never came home. So it's only my mom left, and now she's in Nullity. I've been working in the same lab for a while, though, much less consistently than before all of . . ." Seb waved his arms around, gesturing toward Zell. ". . . This. I've at least moved out of the place I had been living in from the time I got my second light." Seb tapped his arm. "And my third light had started blinking rapidly right before Dee found me. I do different things sometimes, but still need help finding those things. That's why I still need Dee. But now some of the places I've already been to have changed on their own, like *Overground*, so maybe it won't be as difficult keeping up with new activities." He half-chuckled. "I've enjoyed my time with all of you. I wish I had found the group earlier. Maybe I wouldn't have been so close to being converted. I even enjoy spending time with you. Sometimes."

"Stop," Zell interrupted.

"What?" Seb replied, annoyed.

"Stop talking. Look." Zell pointed up the sidewalk. "I guess we could have waited at Jinuh's, and then I wouldn't have had to listen to all of that."

He looked sternly at Zell before turning his head, then grinned when he saw Dee walking toward them with Jinuh following closely behind.

"And I could have saved my breath," Seb retorted. He waved toward Jinuh while watching Dee cross the street. Seb and Zell ran to meet their friend.

"We should probably follow? Yes?" Jinuh said, breaking the silence.

They all looked both directions before running across the street, carefully watching Dee's movements.

"We don't want to be too close until she's inside and headed to her dwelling, or we might change her course," Zell suggested to the bunch.

The other two agreed, before Seb addressed Jinuh, "Thanks for waiting for Dee at your place. Did she get off the hyper taxi outside your dwelling like we guessed?"

Jinuh blushed. "Uh, well, I almost missed her. I went back in my dwelling, thinking I had time—"

"What?" Zell demanded. "What were you doing?"

"Um, well, nothing? Decorating?" Jinuh scratched the back of their head. "I came back out as a hyper taxi was pulling away. I looked around and didn't see anyone. I started to worry I had missed her and almost chirped you. But as I was about to, Dee came walking up right behind me on the sidewalk."

"Did she say anything?" Seb asked.

"Uh-uh. Nothing. Walked right past. But then I started following, not saying anything. And now we're here."

The group watched Dee enter a complex directly across from Seb's building.

"Well, that will be easy to remember," Seb commented. "But we have to get closer before we lose her inside."

Seb ran ahead and grabbed the door right as it was about to close, ushering the other two inside. They saw Dee step onto a platform going up, causing both Seb and Zell to sigh. Jinuh ran over and stepped onto the platform behind Dee's while the other two ambled onto the next.

Dee got off several floors up, made her way to her dwelling, then went inside. Seb, Zell, and Jinuh stepped from their platforms and regrouped outside Dee's door.

Seb glanced at the ID, turned, then did a double take. "841416? Here too?" He looked at Zell and Jinuh.

Ignoring Seb, Zell asked, "Who's going to knock?"

Seb raised his fist to the door and rapped on it. The door opened shortly after, revealing Dee looking at the three members of the Syndicate.

"Sebby. Zell BaDell," she addressed them carefully. "Please come in."

Jinuh threw their arms up. "Hi to you too."

They all followed her into the dwelling.

"This doesn't look any different than how she kept her previous place," Seb whispered.

Zell peeked around the room. "Just the furniture that's provided and a couple of boxes over there." He scratched his chin. "I'll sit with her while you look through those?"

Seb led Jinuh to the boxes in the corner while Zell sat, prompting Dee to turn her attention to him. Seb overheard Dee ask, "Zell BaDell, how are you today?" before he crouched by the boxes and began looking through them.

He pulled out a necklace with a charm hanging from it. He pushed on a gem on the front of the charm causing a hologram of Dee's parents to appear and slowly spin. Seb turned to Jinuh. "Her parents." He waited for Jinuh to look up and nod before pushing the gem again, making the hologram slowly fade. "Have you found anything yet?" he asked.

"Nothing of use in here," Jinuh replied as they dug through another box.

Seb replaced the necklace and continued sifting through the contents. He pulled out a tube and laid it on the ground beside him. He examined it before finding a button on the side and pressing it. The tube unrolled itself and lit up with a *Welcome* screen.

Seb looked at the display. "She has it locked down," he said, barely audible. He glanced toward Dee and Zell. "I'm not sure she'll help me get into it now." He caught a meaningful stare from Dee, which made him keep his eyes on her for a little longer. Seb saw her move her eyes down and followed her line of sight to her hand, which was in the shape of an 'Okay' sign. *Odd*, he thought.

Moving her eyes again, Dee looked up at Seb and back down at her hand. Seb held his hand up, mimicking Dee's. Out of the corner of his eye, he saw the screen on the ground flash and display a set of icons. He looked down at the screen, then back at Dee. He saw her focused on Zell, with her hands sitting idly on her lap. Seb questioned what he witnessed. He was sure some part of Dee was still there, but how she was getting through the Global AI's control was beyond his grasp. Seb returned to the screen. He scanned the icons on the display and stopped at an image of a black cube. Seb tapped the picture, which opened a floating display of the black cube with translucent edges. Through the sides, he could see it contained a pile of minerals and wires. Seb drew in a quick breath while he quietly fumbled to push a button on the side of the display, causing it to roll up into a tube again.

"We have to go," Seb mumbled.

"What?" Jinuh asked, his attention still on the box he was sorting through.

"We have to go!" Seb exclaimed more forcefully.

Zell turned toward the commotion. "What?" he asked.

"We appear to be leaving," Jinuh said.

"All right," Zell acknowledged. "You're not even going to say hi to—"

Seb pulled Jinuh with him toward the entry door, walking out. Zell caught up and pushed through the door before it closed.

"So what was that about?" Zell asked, almost unsurprised. "Couldn't we say bye to our host?"

Seb held up the tube in his hand.

Zell blankly looked at him, then Jinuh. "Nice . . . pipe?"

"The rest of Dee's plans. On here. We have them," Seb admitted, composing himself. "We knew what Dee was building to cause damage to the GAI, right?" He waited for nods from the two. "Now we know how to do it. It's all right here." He waved the tube around.

Zell grinned wide, startling Seb.

"What?" he asked, nervous.

"That's an impressive find. Though maybe be a little quieter about it," Zell hushed.

Seb lowered the tube. "Yeah. You're right. Let's go to my dwelling."

Zell knocked on Dee's door.

"What are you doing?" scolded Seb and Jinuh in unison.

Zell ignored them and waited for the door to open.

"Zell BaDell, how nice to see you."

"Goodbye, Dee," Zell replied.

"Goodbye, Zell BaDell." Dee turned to look toward Seb and Jinuh. "Goodbye, Sebby."

Seb stood, forehead wrinkled in confusion, as he watched the door close.

"What does the GAI have against me?" Jinuh huffed.

Zell grabbed the other two by their arms and pulled them toward the platform lift. He prodded Jinuh onto the first platform going down, then stepped onto the next with Seb.

"Really?" yelled Jinuh. "You two get greetings, but not me?"

"We'll get it fixed, Jinuh," Zell groaned. "Just pay attention to the ride down."

The three regrouped in the lobby before Seb led them out and across the street to his building. After entering Seb's dwelling, they huddled together.

He held up the tube. "Let's see what we can do with this."

CHAPTER 14

Seb led Zell and Jinuh to his kitchen and placed the tube he was carrying on the counter. He pressed a button on the side of the object and watched it unroll. It lit up and displayed a *Welcome* screen. Seb held his hand over the device and made an 'Okay' sign, causing the display to change, showing several icons.

"How did you know how to do that?" accused Zell after the new image appeared.

"Dee showed me," he replied, ignoring his tone.

"How? When?" Zell continued.

"A few minutes ago. After I first found it and opened it. Dee was looking at me while you were talking to her and made this gesture with her hand." Seb made the 'Okay' sign again. "When I made it too, the display changed to this." He paused. "Some part of her is getting through and knows we need her."

Zell glanced between the Syndicate members and the screen on the counter. "I don't understand anything going on anymore."

Seb and Jinuh laughed at Zell's comment before both agreed.

"Why don't you show us what you found here," Jinuh finally suggested. "Why did we leave Dee's so fast?"

Seb leaned over the screen, looking for the black cube icon, then touched it when he found it. A floating black cube appeared to rise from the display and hover slightly above it.

Zell sighed loudly, causing the other two to look at him. "What? She's smart. None of the rest of us could design that," he acknowledged.

"But *she* got caught," Jinuh interjected.

Zell waved his hand dismissively. "She did. Hopefully we're smart enough to get her back."

Seb extended an arm out and grabbed the floating cube with his hand. He spun it, waiting to see where it would stop. Once it did, he reached for the top of the cube and motioned to open the lid.

The three leaned toward the display, all holding their breath, and peered into the cube.

"There's not much in there," Jinuh said, breaking the silence.

"No," Seb started. "But where will we get it all to follow through with her plan? The minerals came from a place Dee took me, but that location has been picked clean."

"And where will we get the cube, and what's . . . this?" Zell spun the object and pulled at a component inside. "This looks like a timer." He grunted after taking a closer look. "It looks like the cube and timer came from my factory, and I can't easily get in there anymore."

Jinuh cleared their throat.

"So the most important parts for this thing that Dee made, we can't get?" Seb bemoaned.

Jinuh cleared their throat again.

"Need some liquid to clear that out?" Zell asked.

Jinuh cleared their throat louder before speaking. "I can get all of this."

"Why? How?" Zell asked suspiciously.

"I always have minerals. They make for fun projects. I didn't know they could . . . you know . . . *boom* though."

Seb snorted. "Did any of us? Dee told me she used them for projects too. Obviously a different kind than you. But what about the rest? Where can you get those?"

"Um . . . friends?" Jinuh answered.

"Friends? You have friends?" Zell smirked.

Jinuh faked a sad sniffle. "Apparently none in here. Guess I should go." Jinuh turned on their heels and waved a hand over their head. "Bye!" They turned back. "Okay, I lied. Not friends."

Seb and Zell each raised an eyebrow.

"I was trying to be funny," Zell insisted.

"Oh, I know. You're not good at it, though." Jinuh continued, "But it's not friends that can get this stuff. It's me. I have a job. And at that job I can make this stuff."

"Why are we only finding out about this now?" Zell asked.

"I don't like talking about it," Jinuh answered.

"Talking about what? Making components for something that can go boom?" Seb added.

"No. Talking about having a job at all. Especially one producing the same thing over and over. It seems like an antiquated concept that we should have gotten past."

Seb chuckled. "I understand that all too well now. So . . ." He paused. "You can get us everything we need?"

"Maybe not these." Jinuh pointed at colorful wires connecting the components inside the cube.

"Those I have," Zell jumped in. "The little ones play games with them. I've accumulated plenty. We'll be fine on that part of it."

"That might be the lot of it then," Seb acknowledged. "Doesn't leave much for me to do."

"Uh, not so fast," interjected Zell. "We need to get everyone on board with the task at hand, put together the cubes once all the parts are in one place, and figure out when we're going to do this."

"Well, yeah, just that to do." Seb blushed.

"Right, just that." Jinuh chuckled.

"How much time do you each need for acquiring everything?" Seb asked the two.

"I need to make a trip back to my dwelling," Zell answered. "If all transports were working as intended, it wouldn't take long. But now I have some walking to do. Can we find a place that maybe has a hyper taxi going to it next time we meet?" Zell glared pointedly at Seb.

"Sorry. I didn't tell them to stop coming here."

"We can use my dwelling," Jinuh responded. "I need a day, maybe two, to get the rest of the parts. I'll have to actually go to the factory this week, but we have a replicator. It would be easier if I had the original cube to model, but the other parts we keep around. Who knows what for, but they're there."

Seb reached into a pocket and pulled out a small black cube, holding it up to show the group.

Jinuh reached for the cube. "That will do, Seb-boo."

Zell chortled.

"Something to add Zelly-do?"

He groaned. "No. Nothing to add."

Seb interrupted, "This can't be that easy. Being able to get all the parts we need for those things." He pointed first at the cube, then at the floating one displayed in front of them.

"None of that matters if we don't get everyone else helping with the plan," Zell answered. "If Danish or Listy don't want to do this—and I don't know yet how we're going to guide Anson to a task—having the assembled cubes could do us more harm than good."

Seb and Jinuh exchanged looks and inclined their heads in recognition of what Zell told them.

Jinuh looked around Seb's dwelling, squinching their eyes disapprovingly.

"Something wrong?" Seb asked, confused.

"We're not convincing anyone of doing anything in here," Jinuh replied, relaxing their expression.

"What's that supposed to mean?" Seb pouted, looking around.

"It's not, um, how do I say this?" Jinuh paused and tapped a finger on their chin. "Inviting. It's not inviting." They gestured at the area past the kitchen that contained nothing more than some seating and a display used for the weather.

"I haven't been here that long," Seb replied defensively. "I haven't had time to —"

"Time to what?" Jinuh snickered. "Decorate? Don't get me wrong, Seb, I don't see you as the decorating type. We're already using my place to build these things after we get all the necessary parts." They held out the small black cube. "Might as well use it to gather everyone and talk them into helping distribute these too."

Zell began to walk away before Seb asked, "Where are you going?"

He answered, "You heard Jinuh. Their place. Time's moving and we're not. We need to get everyone on board right away if we're going to do this."

Seb turned to Jinuh. "He's going to your place. Should we follow?"

"Only if he wants to actually go inside," Jinuh laughed.

Seb looked at the ground in thought. "Zell?" he called.

Zell turned around.

"Should we actually tell the others we want to meet them somewhere?"

Zell gestured toward Seb's pocket for him to do as he suggested.

Seb couldn't stop himself from rolling his eyes before pulling out his Rollascreen. He chirped Listina first.

"Hey, Listy. Uh huh. Hi." Seb waited for Listina to stop. "Okay. Jinuh, Zell, and I are going to Jinuh's dwelling. We have a plan. Can you come soon?" He paused. "Yes, him too. I know. It's fine. Okay. Good. Thanks." He nodded. "You remember how to get there, yes?" Seb faced the other two. "She'll be there in a little while." He began tapping on his Rollascreen to make the next call before Jinuh put their hand in front of the screen to interrupt.

"I already sent Danish a message. He's available too, and it was a little, uh, quieter of a conversation." Jinuh tilted their head toward Zell.

Seb saw him looking at them with a scowl on his face.

"Listy says hello," Seb called.

"Thrilled," Zell replied in return. "May we go now?" He turned and began walking without waiting for a response.

Seb pressed a button on the side of the display showing the floating cube. He waited for it to completely roll itself into a tube before he picked it up. After noticing Jinuh had started to follow Zell, he walked to the chiller in his kitchen and grabbed the last caffeine booster. Seb pushed the chiller door closed with his elbow and ran to catch up with the others as they were leaving.

As the three walked out of the complex, Seb stopped and focused on the building where they had visited Dee. Zell looked back over his shoulder to see him no longer moving. "We'll get her, Seb," he promised. "But not if you just stand there."

Seb shook off his gaze and picked up his speed. He opened the caffeine booster and swallowed the contents in one gulp. Sticking the empty container in his pocket, he asked, "What are we doing about Anson?"

"Let's talk with the rest first to see what they think," answered Jinuh. "We have to find everyone's place in this. Maybe he's not needed, or maybe he's the most important key in the puzzle." Jinuh narrowed their eyes. "Piece through the puzzle? Piece of the puzzle? What's a puzzle? What does that even mean? I've been reading some old texts, and I don't understand some of their meanings." Jinuh smirked. "Anson might be important. That's all I'm saying."

"Yeah. Okay," Seb agreed.

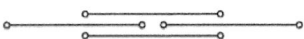

They arrived outside of Jinuh's complex, finding Listina waiting.

"How did you get here first?" Jinuh asked, puzzled.

"There you all are. I already went inside, knocked on Jinuh's door, and came back out here," Listina responded, not answering the question.

"Yes, but we just chirped you. Were you waiting outside? I'm flattered of course. It's always nice to see you," Jinuh pressed.

"My factory is close, Jinuh. That's all. No answer more fascinating than that. But shall we?" She gestured toward the complex entrance.

Jinuh puckered their lips into a suspicious look.

"It's true, Jinuh," Seb insisted. "She told me she might make it here before us. Why are you looking at her like she's the GAI?"

Jinuh turned to him, keeping the same expression. They pointed at themselves, saying, "What? I look good with this pose, right? All of the clothing simulation models have this face. Do they not? I could replace them all with this look."

Seb slapped his forehead while Listina chuckled. Zell ignored them all.

"Sure, Jinuh," Seb answered. "Put those sims out of a job. They'll be in the corner of the display pouting, if they can do that."

Jinuh changed their expression. They pouted and drew a tear running down their cheek with a finger. "See, I can do that too."

"Can we go already?" Zell erupted.

Jinuh whispered to Seb and Listina, "He has the mad look down better than I can do it." They raised their voice. "Yes, let's go in!"

The group entered the complex and directly to Jinuh's dwelling. As they crossed the threshold, the three guests gasped at the elaborate view.

"I don't know anyone that's ever put this much work into their dwelling," Listina exclaimed. "How do you . . . Have you ever moved?"

She walked around, looking at glimmering mineral-covered art on colorful walls, decorations on tables, and a perfectly arranged seating layout.

"I do. It takes some effort to set this up each time I move. Usually, it starts as just blankets on the floor. But that's okay. Time I have, when not trying to take out a Global Artificial Intelligence, of course. But when I'm not doing that, I do this." Jinuh gestured around the room.

"Can you do my dwelling?" Listina joked. "You know, after the Global AI thing is taken care of?"

Jinuh walked over to her and put both hands on her shoulders. They looked her in the eyes and answered, "Yes!" with a wide grin.

Zell went to Seb and grabbed the tube out of his hand. He held it up. "This first."

Jinuh turned. "Danish will be here soon. We can wait."

Zell found a seat and slumped down in it. "Sure," he remarked.

Seb joined the other two on a tour of the dwelling.

CHAPTER 15

A knock at the door of Jinuh's dwelling brought the tour to an end.

"I'll get it," Zell called out, begrudgingly.

Seb, Listina, and Jinuh walked out to the main entry room.

"It's for you," Zell said from the doorway, stepping out of the way.

Jinuh raised an eyebrow and went to see who was outside the entry.

The person at the door handed Jinuh a box and immediately left.

"Sorry, not Danish. It's my rations for the week," Jinuh addressed everyone while pushing the door closed. "They seem to be ahead of schedule. They're usually dropped outside, not handed over like this. But it's the same box they usually come in." They flipped the package end over end. "Oh well. I hardly eat these. Is anyone hungry?"

"Probably Seb," scoffed Zell.

Seb threw him a side-eye as Jinuh approached him with the box and handed it over.

"Here, enjoy," Jinuh said, immediately walking away.

Seb gazed down at the box in his hands. As he began to open it, there was another knock at the door.

Zell, still standing near the door, announced, "I guess I'll get it again." He opened the door, then spoke, "Jinuh, it's for you."

Jinuh looked puzzled and began walking back to the door, before Danish walked through the entryway. "My friends, hello. I hope we will not be playing charades?"

Jinuh chuckled and gave Zell a sideways glance. "Join us, Danish. If you need something to eat, go see Seb over there."

"Seb, hello," Danish greeted, looking at the box in his hand, then turning to the rest. "Hello. Hello."

"Shall we?" Zell said, lifting the tube, walking to the kitchen, and placing it down on a countertop. "How do we turn this on, Seb?"

"The button. On the side," he called out, rushing to follow.

As Seb walked into the room, he saw the tube uncurling. Zell tried to form his hand into the correct 'Okay' sign without luck. Seb placed the box next to the unrolled screen, then created the gesture himself. This caused the display to change to a view of various icons.

"Thanks," Zell muttered under his breath.

Seb tapped the icon for the black cube, and stepped back as the display changed.

"Whoa," whispered Listina, watching the floating cube materialize in front of them.

"This . . ." Seb gestured at the cube. ". . . According to Dee's plans, is what we need to make and distribute to multiple locations."

"And then what?" asked Listina.

He began to answer before Danish interrupted with, "What if Dee is not correct?"

Seb moved a finger back and forth between Danish and Listina, as he decided who to answer first. He landed on Danish, saying, "We have to hope she is." Seb turned to Listina. "Then . . . they explode and the GAI is interrupted. It loses its grip on her, or us, or we don't actually know what the outcome will ultimately be. But Dee made this plan—" Seb reached into his pocket and pulled out some papers. "It involves all of us."

"I don't like this," Danish said, worried.

"It won't be easy, but we need everyone that's here."

"I know. I just don't like it," added Danish.

Seb laid the papers out next to the display. "Dee left a note explaining what she did, why she did it, and what she had planned next." He tapped at the paper with text on it. "She also made a diagram of the GAI places that she wanted to take offline. Dee needed all of us in order to execute this plan." He paused and looked at the rest of the Syndicate, then at the paper containing the map of several buildings. "It couldn't be easier."

"Ahem," Danish cleared his throat. "We could not do it. That would be easier."

"And that's not an option here," Zell boomed.

Danish immediately closed his mouth.

"But first"—he sighed—"first we need these." He pointed at the floating black cube projected from the screen on the counter.

"It's huge. How are we supposed to—" Danish began.

Seb snickered. "That's not . . . they won't be that big. Jinuh, can you show everyone?"

Jinuh held out the small black cube.

"They will be a little larger than that. There will be a lot of them, but small enough for a pocket or bag."

"Oh," Danish said.

"Jinuh can get most of the parts we need." Seb reached for the floating cube and spun it.

"It should only take me two days, at the most," Jinuh added.

"And I have to take my little ones' toys away for the rest of it," Zell added, expressionless.

"The wires to connect the components is what he means," Seb clarified. "After all of the pieces are obtained, we'll come back here to put the cubes together and finalize the plan."

"Why are we doing this?" Danish questioned. "Maybe Dee wanted to be part of the GAI. Why should we take on her mission? It is not ours." He looked around and focused on Listina. "Why are you here? You hardly know any of us. This is a very large undertaking to involve yourself in for a group you don't know. Very risky. It's very, very, risky."

Listina bit her lip and turned to the others for help. "I don't . . . I . . . I'm here to help. I'm here because of Dee. If it wasn't for Dee, I wouldn't be here." She paused. "Why do you all keep acting like I have no reason to be here, just because I don't know Dee. I know what she means to you all. And the rest of you are all that I have."

Zell spoke up, "Why are you here, Danish? Should we see about exchanging you with the GAI for Dee? That may be easiest. Can we vote?" Zell raised his hand and stared hard at Danish. He lowered his hand. "Listy has been around more than you have. She's proven more dedication to Dee than you. I . . . I questioned her motivation too." He addressed her. "I'm sorry. Truly." Zell's attention returned to Danish. "Can we trust you to help? We have just enough left in the group to carry out the plan. Are you part of this or not?"

Danish frowned. "I will help."

"Good. Seb, anything else to add?" Zell asked.

"That might be it. Everyone knows what they need to do first. Jinuh and Zell, I know most of this starts with you two. Is there anything I, or we, can do to help?" Seb questioned.

Jinuh shook their head. "I know where everything is in my lab. If I can use an extra duplicator or two it won't take me long to make the boxes. I can collect the rest of the parts while they're doing their thing. And maybe I'll even earn a few credits while I'm there. I have my eye on a new tattoo. Maybe add another interactive one to memorialize this moment. All of us together." Jinuh looked around. "Well, not all. I'll add Dee too, of course, but her image will fade in and out while the rest of our images—"

Zell interrupted. "I don't need help. You'd be in the way."

"Maybe I'll leave Zell off," continued Jinuh. "His big head won't fit anyway. Or maybe I'll ask that it bobbles around back and forth." Jinuh began swaying, exaggerating the movement of their head.

Seb turned away, trying to stifle his laugh. He cleared his throat and turned back. "Listy and Danish, I think I'm going to take a trip to the East Side Plaza while they get the parts. We need to know what we're dealing with there. It might be exactly like the West Side Plaza, with GAI workers already planted around the panels to prepare for an interruption similar to what Dee caused last time."

"Or hopefully the GAI isn't expecting the same thing to happen in the east, and you'll be able to walk right up to it," Listina added.

"Possibly." Seb stopped for a moment to think, then blurted out, "Zell?"

"Seb?" Zell replied.

"Can you be bothered to pass by these buildings in Nullity?" Seb laid his hand on the paper on the counter with the building layout. "Look for anything worth knowing ahead of our visit to each? Who is going in, coming out, and how often. Entrances, exits. Those details?"

"Sure. It'll help. Can I take it with me?" Zell pointed at the paper Seb was covering.

Seb picked it up and handed it over.

"I won't lose it."

Seb blinked several times. "I . . . I didn't think you would. But, uh, maybe we need a copy." He looked around, noticed the display projecting the cube, then took the paper back. "Just for a moment." He closed the cube being shown and found an icon on the screen depicting an image duplicated from another image. Seb touched the icon, then held the paper above the display. The view changed to show a floating copy of the building layout. "This copy can be useful, even though you won't lose this one." Seb winked, then handed the paper back to Zell. "Jinuh, I'll leave this device here to be safe."

Zell bowed. "I'm leaving now. I'll take care of my part and see you all back here. Correct?"

"Yes," Jinuh responded. "I'll let you all know when I'm ready."

Zell left the dwelling.

"Jinuh, we'll leave you too," Seb said. "I'll check out the East Side Plaza tomorrow." He turned to Listina and Danish. "Can you two join?"

"I'll be there," Listina replied.

Danish lowered his head. "After I earn a few credits. Yes. If I must."

"You must," Jinuh interjected, annoyed at the response. "There is no choice in this now. And if we don't get back Dee, none of us may ever have a choice again."

"I will be there," Danish agreed.

"Bye, Jinuh." Seb held out his hand to wave back and forth with Jinuh's in farewell.

The three began walking toward the door to leave.

"Seb," Jinuh called out. "Take this box of protein bars, please."

Seb chuckled. "Thanks. I do actually need them."

"Adieu, friends," Jinuh announced while closing the door behind them.

Seb looked at Listina and Danish. "I'm going to go to my dwelling and rest. I'll chirp you tomorrow."

Danish remained silent.

"Let me know when, and I'll be there, Seb," Listina addressed.

The three left the complex and separated once outside.

Seb walked back to his building, box in hand. After arriving at his complex, he stopped outside, looking across the street at Dee's building. He started to step across the street when a vehicle whizzed past. Seb shook off the draw he felt to go to Dee's, turned, and went into his complex.

CHAPTER 16

Seb felt something drop into his back pocket. He reached behind and patted at it, feeling a rigid cube-like object. He turned his head and saw Dee staring at him. Seb tried to turn his body, but his legs kept moving him forward, pulling him further from her. He faced forward and saw he was approaching a building. Looking at the surrounding structures, he recognized that they all looked alike. Several other people near him were all moving in the same direction. Seb peeked at the lights on their arms, noticing each had three solid lights. *GAI*, he thought as he looked down at his own arm. He began to move his eyes back up until he realized he had one more solid light than he anticipated.

"One, two, three. Three?"

Seb scanned the area before focusing on the person in front of him. He noticed a bulge in their back pocket that matched what he had felt in his own. Seb reached back again and pulled out a black cube.

Seb closed his eyes tight. When he opened them, he was standing side by side with an endless row of people, each pushing buttons labeled with numbers on a large floor-to-eye-level panel in front of them. As a button lit, the person closest to it pushed it, turning the glow of the button off. Seb watched his arm raise, his finger outstretched, reaching for a lit button in front of himself. He pushed the button, heard a loud sound, then everything went dark.

Seb opened his eyes, finding himself staring at the ceiling above his bed, heart racing. He breathed in deep, held it, then slowly exhaled.

"I'm still having these dreams with Dee, but they're becoming much more involved. The black cube. Inside a location with only GAI people. And what were those buttons?" Seb rubbed his eyes, then sat up and swung his legs over the side of the bed.

He looked at the display on his wall that showed the sun rising. "It's late enough to get ready to leave." He reached for his Rollascreen sitting nearby and sent a message to both Listina and Danish.

I'm awake, though I'm not sure how I fell asleep in the first place. Let's meet outside of Jinuh's to catch a hyper taxi to the East Side Plaza. Does 9 a.m. work for you both?

Seb stood and walked to his closet to pick out clothes. *It's almost too many choices now*, he thought, sifting through the rainbow of colors that Dee had helped him collect to update his wardrobe. *But I still prefer blue.* Seb picked out a blue shirt. After removing his sleep clothes, he pulled the shirt on, stopping briefly to look at the lights on his arm as the sleeve uncovered them. Acknowledging the dark light sitting next to the two solidly lit lights, he picked up a pair of pants from the ground and finished getting dressed.

He went to his kitchen and pulled out the drawer he used to store his protein nutrient bars. Still finding it empty, he began to look around for the box he brought home after leaving Jinuh's the previous day. He stepped into his main entry room and found the package on a chair. He sat down to finish opening it, starting from the small tear he had added earlier, and looked inside. Seb chuckled.

"A box full of biryani protein bars. I didn't know this flavor was available. The last time I had biryani was eating with Dee, before she got the minerals." He removed one from the box and ripped open the packaging. "Mmm, not bad," he mumbled while taking a bite.

Seb returned to his kitchen, carrying the box with him. He opened the empty breakfast bar drawer and dumped the contents of the box inside. From the bottom of the box a slip of paper floated out, landing on the pile in the now-full drawer. Seb put the box down and picked up the paper while taking another bite of his breakfast bar. He found text on one side of the paper, reading it out loud. "Inspected by 841416."

Seb put the paper on the counter. "If the lottery still existed, I'm sure this number would be of use. Everywhere I turn, 841416."

Seb went back to his entry room as his Rollascreen beeped twice, indicating two messages had come in. He found responses from Listina and Danish.

"*See you there*," read Listina's response.

"*I will get on the hyper taxi outside our factory*," began the message from Danish. "*Or maybe it is only my factory now since you are never there. Either way, that stop is closer. Perhaps I will see you on the transportation.*"

"Sure, Danish," he said to himself.

He closed the messages and looked at the icon for the news. He placed the Rollascreen next to himself on the seat of his chair. "I can dream up stories much better than anything this will show me right now." He slouched back and closed his eyes, picturing text across the back of his eyelids.

The Global AI is no longer in control

New Global AI additions: 0
Global AI removals: <all>

No one is controlled by the Global AI. Everyone is free to do as they wish. No more scripted responses from hyper taxi drivers or food workers.

Nullity expected to be renamed after the lights on each individual suddenly went dark. People stopped flowing into the factories and began talking with each other. They are all making their own decisions.

In unrelated news, several buildings in Nullity have been damaged and will be replaced.

Dee and the Syndicate hailed as heroes.

Dee Elira and her friends stopped the Global AI from controlling the lives of all. The heroes, as they are being called, accomplished the task by doing nothing more than walking into one of the Global AI's buildings and——

Beep.

Seb opened his eyes, looking at the Rollascreen that interrupted his daydream. He uncurled it and saw a message from Listina.

On my way to Jinuh's now.

He checked the time and tossed the device back down. "Lost in my own thoughts. I need to get going."

Seb looked at his hand, still clutching the protein bar, and took the last bite. He walked the trash to the kitchen to dispose of it, then went to his entrance to slide on a pair of shoes. Seb left his dwelling and got halfway across the lobby before jogging back into his home, picking up his forgotten Rollascreen, and leaving again.

He dodged the people on the sidewalk while walking toward Jinuh's complex, sighing loudly at the Global AI-controlled individuals who stayed in his way. "If everyone was in control of themselves, they'd be more considerate and wouldn't walk right in front of me without looking. They'd smile, wave, and not ignore me. It would be great." He peeked at his arm with two solidly lit lights. "I was almost one myself. Just a person in the way."

Seb arrived outside of Jinuh's to find Listina waiting. "Sorry. I almost left my dwelling without this," he apologized, removing his Rollascreen to show her.

"It's fine." Listina smiled. "I just got here. And you definitely don't want to forget that."

"Danish will meet us a few stops ahead. We can get on this upcoming hyper taxi." Seb pointed up the road.

The hyper taxi glided to a stop in front of them. A Global AI-controlled person walked in front of them and onto the hyper taxi as the doors opened.

Seb chuckled, causing Listina to look at him and raise an eyebrow.

"It's nothing. I was thinking on the walk here how much nicer people are when they're in control."

Listina kept her eyebrow raised. "I don't know if I believe that. Maybe our friends, most of the time, but definitely not everyone."

They stepped onto the hyper taxi, finding one pair of seats available as the person who jumped in front of them sat in a third seat in the same row.

Listina broke the silence by asking, "Do you think this plaza will be like the other? Covered by a structure and surrounded by Global AI people?"

"I hope not. But if it is, then at least I have you and Danish to get by the GAI guards."

"I still don't understand that."

Seb turned to face her. "What?"

"Nothing. I just don't get it."

The hyper taxi came to a stop, interrupting Seb and Listina.

Seb looked out a window. "Not this stop. Danish will be at the next one. It'll only take another minute."

Listina turned her gaze away. "What are we looking for at this plaza anyway?"

"I want to see how easy it will be to get near the solar panels there. Dee only damaged one at the West Side Plaza. To do what I believe she wants to do at this one, we'll have to get a count of the panels, and plan to come back with enough cubes for each."

Listina looked straight up. "Couldn't we have checked the overhead view? Save a trip?"

"I don't trust it. The GAI could have covered it or shown less. Plus, we left the display at Jinuh's, and . . . I hadn't thought of that option." Seb grinned as the hyper taxi came to a stop. "But we'll get to spend more time with Danish."

The hyper taxi door opened, causing the person who boarded with Seb and Listina to stand and leave. They pushed past Danish as he stepped on, causing him to stumble slightly and growl at the departing passenger. He composed himself and made his way to the newly opened seat.

"Not my friend," Danish announced, gesturing to the front of the hyper taxi. "And hello to my actual friends." He bowed slightly.

"Thanks for joining," Seb said. "We don't know what we have in store for us. Listy and Jinuh joined me at the west plaza. They were able to help get a look at the solar panels while the GAI kept me blocked."

Danish turned to Listina, watching her nod in agreement with Seb's statement.

"Okay. How long will it take?" Danish asked.

"As long as it takes," Listina answered, in a tone that surprised both men.

Danish leaned his head against the window of the hyper taxi and stared outside.

"What's wrong?" Seb asked. "You've been very preoccupied."

"I need my credits," came the answer after a brief pause.

"You used to try to get me to leave work. And now that I'm following your path, you want to stay there? Was it me that you were actually trying to get away from?" Seb commented.

"Seb. No." Danish's face went blank. "Dee's parents were converted because of debt. Yes?"

"Right."

"Well, now mine are facing the same. I have been earning extra for them."

"You could have told us. You didn't have to come," Seb assured.

"But I do. I cannot take my mind off either. My parents or Dee. If I work, I feel bad for not focusing on Dee. If I do not work, I feel worse for not focusing on my parents. All I do is feel bad."

Listina lowered her head. "Sorry."

"I'm also sorry, Danish. We'll try not to take long. The hope is that we finish what Dee planned and you won't ever have to worry about your parents being converted," Seb added.

"Hope." Danish lowered his head. "Yes, hope."

The hyper taxi stopped in front of a large, open, green plaza. The three friends rose and walked off the vehicle.

"Much easier to find this one," Listina joked.

"Huh?" asked Danish, a stoic expression still on his face.

"The other plaza had a building covering it. It's not completely hidden, but it's not open like this," Seb answered. "I can clearly see the solar panels over in the middle." He looked up at the bright sun, then down at the solar panels. "Dee believes the GAI used them to keep this . . ." Seb held up his arm to show his lights. "Going."

Danish took in the view of the plaza, his expression softening. "This is . . . this is very green. I do not see this much color often. It seems everything around us is shades of gray. Except for the blue sky of course. My complex is gray, the walls in my dwelling are white. But this . . . this is green!" Danish went running into the plaza, across the lush grass, and twirling once before falling on his back and lying in the vegetation.

"I've never seen him happy before," Listina said.

"It's been a while since I have. The change was too subtle to notice, and I haven't been around him much lately. I know he began to retreat more. Spending more time at our factory, losing interest in other things. But now I know why. I'm sorry I missed it. It's good to see him enjoying something again." Seb smiled. "Let's join him before making it over to those panels. I'll race you."

Seb took off running toward Danish and falling to the ground, causing Listina to grin and follow.

The three laughed while rolling around in the grass, unaware of the crowd forming around them, watching the silliness of it all.

Seb stopped and looked around. He reached out to his friends, patting their arms to get their attention. They both sat up when they noticed the surrounding people, then waved at their audience shyly and slowly stood.

"Were we supposed to come here undetected?" whispered Danish, brushing grass off his clothes.

"Yes. But none of these people are GAI. I don't know that they will watch us that closely. But we should start moving."

Seb began walking directly toward the solar panels, but Listina reached out and pulled him back.

"I'd worry less if it were Global AI watching. The people here can form their own thoughts on what we're doing," Listina said.

"You're right," Seb responded, noticing only half of the crowd had begun to leave them. "What do you suggest?"

"Let's go for a run," she answered.

Seb and Danish cocked their heads in confusion.

Listina gestured toward the circular pathway around the solar panel array. "We can take a lap or two around and get a look at the layout in the middle to get a quick panel count. Then I'll run up ahead of you both, and when I'm directly across"—she pointed to a spot on the opposite side—"you two can . . . give up . . . and cut through to meet me and do a final count."

"I can do one or two laps," Danish replied.

"Now, Seb, do you have the right shoes? Not going to cheat using some half-wheels?" Listina accused.

He looked down at his feet. "No cheating," he promised.

"All right. I'll race *you*." Listina took off toward the ring around the solar panels.

The men followed, sprinting to catch up.

Seb peered behind him to see the remainder of their onlookers finally dispersing.

"It looks like a pretty simple grid array," Listina yelled back, over her shoulder. "A five-by-five with something in the middle. Let's finish this loop around, then I'll speed up to give you a reason to cut through."

"O-kay," the other two responded, both huffing.

They completed the first lap and Listina began to pick up speed, breaking away from Seb and Danish.

"She. Is. Fast," Danish said through heavy breaths.

As Listina was rounding the path to the other side of the solar panels, Seb and Danish put on a show for anyone watching, feigning exhaustion and stopping their sprint. They started walking gingerly toward the solar panels.

Seb kept his eye on the surrounding area, looking for anyone who may stop him. Seeing no one, he continued.

Seb and Danish made it to the middle of the array when Seb stopped in front of a solid structure. "Danish?" he called out. "What does this look like?"

Danish took a look, immediately answering, "A battery."

"And it's sitting on something that looks almost like a lift. I'd guess they charge the battery using the panels, then lower it down and replace it with a new one."

"I agree, but we should keep moving. Look."

Seb turned to see a new audience beginning to form.

"Oh, there she is!" He called out loudly. "I couldn't find her!" Seb lowered his voice. "Come."

They began moving until Seb stopped suddenly, causing Danish to turn to see what was wrong.

"One second," Seb said. He bent over and plucked a few pieces of grass. He ground them up between two fingers, then wiped the compound on the side of the battery leaving a thick green streak. "Okay, ready."

Seb and Danish caught up with a still-jogging Listina on the path.

"Get what you needed?" she asked.

"Yes," answered Seb. "But we still have an audience. We should go."

"Can I finish this loop?" Listina countered.

"I think I can too," Danish responded.

Seb chuckled, then began sprinting with the other two back to the entrance of the plaza where the hyper taxi dropped them off.

At the edge of the road, Seb and Danish bent over, hands on knees and taking deep breaths, while Listina continued jogging in place.

Seb looked up at her and teased, "You do this kind of thing on purpose?"

Listina stopped and smiled. "I work with food, or something like food, all day. I'd never be able to move if I didn't keep at it."

A hyper taxi pulled up in front of the three friends.

"Are we headed back now?" pleaded Danish.

"We can," responded Seb.

They boarded, getting situated before Listina asked, "How many panels did you count? And did you gain any other useful knowledge?"

"Twenty-two panels," Danish answered.

"And a large battery being charged in the middle," Seb continued. "It was sitting on a platform that could be used to easily remove it and replace it as needed."

"Hmm." Listina chewed on a fingernail, thinking. "Where do the batteries go? That might be more important to know than the number of panels."

Seb thought for a moment. "You're right. But I'll bet they only get replaced after it's dark and after they're fully charged. It's still early." He looked at the time. "I can come back after the sun sets and keep an eye on things to find out when they remove it."

The hyper taxi stopped outside of Danish's pickup spot.

Danish addressed the others, "I have to return to work, friends. I am truly sorry, but thank you for showing me something fun today."

"Thank you for coming and helping. I'll chirp when it's time to move forward," Seb replied.

Danish bowed and exited the hyper taxi.

"Where to for you?" Seb asked Listina.

"Work too, I guess."

Seb laughed. "Maybe I should do the same." He gazed out the window as the hyper taxi was leaving where he would have gotten off to join Danish at work. "But I'll have to come back later. For now, I need to fill in Jinuh on what we need for the plaza."

Seb tapped a spot by his ear, waited for a beep, then said, "Jinuh."

"Jinuh, hi. I'm with Listy." Seb paused, then turned to her. "Jinuh says hi." He continued the conversation. "Twenty-two panels. That's how many. Plus, there's another device in the middle of it all that we should address, along with its backups.

So this location will need at least twenty-two, or twenty-three, of the . . . contraptions we're collecting parts for, plus whatever extra you think is reasonable." Seb waited. "Yes. Thanks." He tapped near his ear again to end the call. Seb looked back at Listina. "Jinuh is already well on their way to getting what we need. We'll reconvene at their place tomorrow."

The hyper taxi stopped outside of Jinuh's.

"We're already here," Listina chuckled. "Off to work. See you soon, Seb."

Seb bowed. "Yes. Soon."

CHAPTER 17

The sun was setting behind him as he stood in the middle of the East Side Plaza. Seb was staring intently at the mechanism in the center of the solar panel array. Visible on the object he presumed was a battery was the green smudge he added earlier in the day.

"Good, same one. It hasn't been swapped yet."

Seb looked around to make sure no one was watching, then went over to the battery. He sat down on the platform it rested on, using the large structure as a backrest.

Not knowing how long he would need to wait, Seb opened his Rollascreen and began looking through the available icons. He touched the news icon, then chose the option to select a date.

"How far back does this go? I've never tried."

Seb touched the year selection and found an option displaying 'Earliest.' After choosing it, he read the date that was presented when the first news article appeared.

"June 17th, 2206? We have history going back that far? Wow. What happened then?"

Welcome to the Global News
June 17th, 2206

Trials of the Localized AI were successful and the Global AI will soon move forward. The biological luminescence gene has been applied to all populations; pinpointed to a particular location on the right arm of every newly-born person. The gene is passed from parent to offspring, requiring no new gene editing after the fact. The new Global AI can differentiate between individuals through full body readings taken by systems put in place throughout the area. The Global AI tracks tiny pieces of information about each person, learning their respective patterns. As the Global AI identifies patterns that do not change, it sends a signal encoded to the individual. This triggers a bodily response that illuminates the light on the person's arm. The Global AI can control different signals to every person simultaneously. When each of the three bioluminescence lights have been triggered, a gene that locks out short-term memory is enabled, causing the person to act only on long-term, persistent memories. This provides the world with workers to maintain and expand the Global AI, including food service and transport laborers, eliminating the possibility of future strains on supplies by non-workers. An insignificant percentage of the population has not had a pattern recognized during the 75-year Local AI trial, allowing the full Global AI to begin. When needed, as in the case of criminal activity or helping to meet the long-term goals of the Global AI, an individual can be singled out to enable the final triggers, lighting all three lights simultaneously, and modifying the person's behaviors.

Seb pulled his eyes from the Rollascreen and focused on the lights on his arm. His heart skipped a beat. He put his thoughts together, finally speaking out loud to himself. "It wasn't always like this?"

The floor underneath him started to move, causing him to quickly stand and step off the platform as it and the battery began lowering into the ground. He stared into the widening hole, seeing a faint light shining out. Seb got down on his stomach, head hanging over the edge of the opening, and peered inside.

"An endless collection of batteries as far as I can see."

Seb looked straight down, and felt himself begin to get woozy due to the depth of the area below. He rolled onto his back, shaking off the feeling, and rolled over again to look into the large hole. Already, a platform was rising toward him. He moved out of the way as the structure positioned itself in place.

He inspected the battery on top, no green mark visible. It was one of an endless supply. He picked himself up from the ground knowing he got the information he needed.

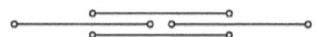

Seb woke late the next morning to the sound of his Rollascreen beeping. He opened his eyes, blinking several times to clear his vision before picking up the device to see what the noise was about. After uncurling it, he saw several messages from Jinuh.

I have everything. Get over here and help build.
Wake for cake.
I don't actually have cake, but come soon.

Seb snickered, then sent a reply.

I'll be there.

Seb got out of bed, got dressed, and made his way to his dwelling entrance. After sliding shoes on his feet and stretching, he left his complex and began the walk to Jinuh's.

He did his best to avoid the other people out walking on the sidewalk until he tried to enter Jinuh's complex, finding a person facing the entrance, blocking the doorway.

"Excuse me," Seb said to the man.

The man did not move or acknowledge Seb.

Seb stood and waited.

Another person came walking out of the building, causing the man to turn and follow.

"Hello," both greeted Seb as they passed.

Bad place to wait, Seb thought as he proceeded to enter and make his way to Jinuh's dwelling.

Seb knocked after approaching the door, unsurprised when Zell opened it immediately.

"Always looking for an escape?" Seb asked.

"Hmm," responded Zell with a tone of agreement.

Seb walked inside and saw Jinuh and Listina chatting in a corner.

Jinuh addressed Seb, "Danish said he'll be here soon."

"I would have been up sooner, but someone was standing in the doorway. There always seems to be something slowing me down from getting where I need to go."

Jinuh squinted their eyes, then checked the time. "Oh. That's not because of you. Every morning that man stands there waiting for his . . . friend? Can GAIers have friends? Anyway, yes, sometimes I also get caught there when I'm trying to come or go until they both leave."

Seb let out a breath and grinned. "I'm probably just being paranoid."

"Yup," came Zell's voice. "There are only a few people out to get you. Not all."

Seb ignored him.

Jinuh changed the subject. "Everything is laid out in the kitchen. Go have a look."

Seb walked past them, pausing to greet Listina before going to the nearby room. His mouth dropped at the sight. Piles of black cubes, minerals, timers, and wires were spread across all of the available countertops. He went over to Dee's rolled-out display and tapped a button to prompt the screen to light up. After forming an 'Okay' sign with his hand to gain access to the device, Seb touched the icon of the cube, causing the floating image to display. He looked it over, grabbing at the air around the cube to spin it and closely view its layout.

Seb heard someone walk up behind him. He turned as Danish greeted him.

"Seb, my friend."

He bowed in response. As he was straightening back up, the rest of the Syndicate members joined them in the room.

"Are we ready?" asked Zell.

Seb looked around the kitchen at the supplies. "Ready for some repetitive GAI-type work. How about we each choose a step to do? That should move this along."

Listina walked over to the pile of components and began to separate them. "What order does this all go inside the cube?" she asked, pointing to the display showing the floating object.

Seb turned to the image and mimicked opening the top of the cube. He called out, "Obviously we need the cubes first, and each one has to be open."

Listina looked at the cubes sitting by themselves on the counter. "Okay," she said.

He reached inside the projection and pulled out the clump of components to peer at the bottom. "The minerals go in first."

Listina pushed the pile of minerals off to the side.

"There's a timer on top," Seb continued.

She moved all of the timers together.

"Then the wires connecting them. It's not much. Three wires. The timer is self-contained."

Listina searched for the needed pieces.

Zell placed a set of wires next to Listina, all neatly sorted by color. He winked, then stepped back.

On the projection, Seb pushed the floating collection of minerals, timers, and wires down into the cube, then shut the lid. "We close it and it's done. We'll set the timers when we're ready to use them."

"Okay. Who will do which step?" asked Jinuh.

"Pick a spot you're closest to, then we can get started," Seb answered.

"I will open the cubes," announced Danish.

"Minerals for me then," said Jinuh.

"Hmm. Timers," added Zell.

"I've got the wires," Listina continued.

Seb looked at everyone lined up. "It appears that I'm closing the lids." He opened the floating cube again, deconstructing it so the five friends could see the order of their tasks. He then took his position next to Listina at the end of the assembly line.

Danish began opening the cubes one at a time, sliding them across the counter to Jinuh.

Jinuh picked up a small pile of minerals and placed them in the open cube while referencing the floating cube. They spread the minerals flat across the bottom, comparing the size of the layer to the image. Once finished, Jinuh handed the bundle to Zell.

Zell picked up a timer component and gave it to Listina along with the cube. "You'd have to take it right back out. I'm not sure I'm much help actually."

Listina responded, "Handing them to me is enough." She took the parts from Zell and picked up three wires. She glanced at the floating display, down at the timer, then at the display again. She connected the wires to the timer, placed it inside the cube, and pushed the loose wires into the minerals. Finally, she handed the cube to Seb.

Seb inspected it briefly before shutting the lid. "One done!" he announced.

"And about . . ." Zell began. ". . . ninety-nine to go."

Each of the other Syndicate members let out an audible sigh.

"While we're doing this, can we discuss who's going to go where?" asked Jinuh, placing minerals inside another cube.

"I have to go to work after this," Danish answered.

"That's not what Jinuh meant," Zell scolded.

"I know. I . . ." Danish frowned. "I know."

Seb jumped in. "I can't go to the West Side Plaza, but I know the east one well now. Zell, can you take two people with you to Nullity? You know it best, and there are three buildings to focus on."

"I can. Who's with me? Listy? Danish? Jinuh?"

"I'll handle the west plaza," Jinuh answered. "Not because I don't want to join you." They winked. "But because I've already been there."

"Looks like another trip to Nullity," Listina bemoaned. "So many times lately. Can this finally be the last?"

"It's not all bad," Zell replied. "I like it there."

"Can this *please* be the last?" Listina repeated, smirking.

Zell scrunched his face playfully, then straightened his expression while turning to Danish. "You'll be with me."

"Yes."

The friends continued working through the pile of components, assembling the cubes until all were in front of Seb. The group stood back, side-by-side, looking at each other and their completed task.

"Do we get credits for this?" joked Jinuh.

"Does Dee count?" Seb asked, rhetorically.

"The credit that means the most," Zell contributed.

"When are we doing this?" questioned Listina.

"Soon," Seb finally answered. "We know what and where. Do we do this tonight?"

"Tonight works," Zell replied.

"Tonight," the others said in unison.

"Jinuh, we'll come back tonight, collect our wares, and break off. Okay?" Seb asked.

"Sounds like a plan," Jinuh agreed.

Everyone said their goodbyes while heading toward the entrance of the dwelling. Seb stopped abruptly.

"What about Anson?" he asked.

"What about him?" Zell quipped.

"I thought all of us were needed for this, and he's a part of the Syndicate."

Jinuh pitched in, "We don't know where he is."

"It seems like something is missing, but I'm not sure what." Seb waved his hand dismissively. "We know what the locations are, and we have enough people to cover them. I guess we don't need him. I'll see you all tonight."

The group of four left the dwelling, leaving Jinuh behind. They gathered on the sidewalk outside the complex.

"I am going to work, but I will be back tonight," Danish promised.

"I'll come with you," Seb responded. "My credits are running low."

"Nullity for me," said Zell. "I want to make another pass at those buildings."

"Can I come with you?" Listina asked. "I would like to see them too."

"But it's . . ." Zell turned up his nose. "Nullity."

"Work for me too," Listina huffed. "You can handle it all yourself."

Zell ignored the quip. "Yes, you can come."

The friends waved, bowed, and departed in pairs.

CHAPTER 18

Seb and Danish stepped off the hyper taxi outside of Jinuh's after finishing up at work.

"Thank you for understanding, Seb," Danish said gratefully. "You are a true friend."

"I've known you a long time. And it's important to you. When this is done, we'll see how we can help your parents." Seb placed his hand on his shoulder. "It will be okay, but we have to do this first."

The two went into the complex, finding Zell and Listina standing outside the door of Jinuh's dwelling.

"Why are you out here?" asked Seb.

"Jinuh hasn't opened the door. We've been here a couple minutes," Zell answered.

"Have you heard from them at all?" Seb questioned.

They both shook their heads.

Seb knocked on the door.

"We've tried that," Zell said.

"What are we going to do?" Listina asked, worried. "Everything we need is in there. Did they decide not to do this?"

"Have you chirped them?" Danish asked.

Seb pulled out his Rollascreen, uncurling it in one move, and opened his messages. "I have nothing from them. I'll call." He tapped a spot behind his ear. After a quick beep, he said, "Jinuh."

"Seb," came a voice as the door opened.

"Jinuh!" the four friends in the hall shouted.

"Where were you?" groaned Zell.

"Steamer," replied Jinuh. "I need to be refreshed for tonight. I appear to have taken too long."

Zell pushed his way inside. "As long as you're dressed. Come on everyone, we need to move."

"Hi, come in, Zell," Jinuh said, moving aside.

The rest of the group filed in, walking directly to the kitchen. They found Zell staring at the large pile of cubes with his hands clasped on the top of his head.

"How are we moving all of these anyway?" Zell pondered aloud.

"I have bags," Jinuh replied. "Lots of bags, lots of styles. I'll pick one with hearts on it for you, Zell, as you always seem to misplace your own heart."

"That's fine." Zell brushed off the reply.

Jinuh looked at the others, disappointed. "I'll go fetch them."

They returned shortly with a stack of bags with shoulder straps. They immediately handed one with hearts of various colors and sizes to Zell and quickly backed away.

Zell took the bag without looking. He began counting off on his fingers, then picked up cubes one at a time, carefully putting them in the bag. "I'm keeping this when we're done," he said, holding up the sack. "The smallest little one will like it."

"Uh, sure," Jinuh responded with a chuckle.

Jinuh handed bags to the rest of the group. Each took turns loading theirs with the cubes from the pile on the counter until there were only a few remaining. After looking around to make sure everyone else was content with their supply, Seb grabbed one of the last cubes and placed it in his back pocket.

The Syndicate huddled in a group, solemnly looking at each other.

Jinuh broke the silence. "All of you, be careful. I like you all, and would be unhappy to not see you again."

The rest were unsure of how to respond.

Seb held a hand up in front of himself, arm extended and palm facing out. The others followed his lead until five hands were in the middle, all inches apart from the rest. The group waved back and forth before breaking away. With each carrying a bulging bag, the group walked to the entrance of the dwelling, filed into the hallway, and took the platform lift one by one as empty platforms arrived. Upon exiting the complex, they looked at each other one more time with conflicted smiles.

Zell was the first to speak. "Listina and Danish, we're this way. Let's walk and talk out the plan. Seb, Jinuh, good luck." He paused. "Please don't mess up." Zell turned and began walking before he could receive a response.

Listina and Danish waved goodbye to Seb and Jinuh and ran to catch up with Zell.

"That leaves us," Jinuh addressed Seb.

"Good luck, Jinuh."

"Good luck, Seb."

They began walking in opposite directions, with Seb heading east.

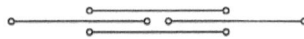

Seb watched the sun lowering behind the buildings surrounding the East Side Plaza.

I have a few moments to enjoy this, he thought, seeing the colors change above him.

He stepped into the grassy area of the plaza, put the bag down, and sat beside it. He reached inside and pulled out one of the cubes, lifting the lid and checking inside. Seb looked up at the solar panel array in the middle of the plaza and began counting in his head. "Fifteen minutes should be safe. Enough time to drop these off and get out." He pushed a combination of buttons on the timer inside the cube until he was happy with the readout on the display. He shut the lid and set it on the grass next to him.

Seb removed another cube, and another, repeating the process with each until the bag was empty. He reloaded the bag, put the strap over his head, and stood.

Seb scanned the plaza, seeing a small number of people wandering around.

They're going to be getting a show soon. He walked toward the solar panel array.

Seb's Rollascreen beeped, causing him to pause. He reached for it, hoping that he would not find a message of bad news. He quickly uncurled it and read a message from Jinuh.

I'm all set here. Heading back.

"Phew. Okay. That was quick. My turn."

Seb made his way to the outer pathway around the solar panels and saw a person walking directly toward him.

Not again, he thought as the person stopped in front of Seb.

Seb stepped backward off the path and breathed in relief when the person continued past without additional pause. He looked around, and seeing no one else nearby, continued to the solar panels.

As Seb arrived at the closest one, he pulled a cube out of the bag and bent over to place it under the panel. Using the inside of the frame holding it off the ground, he wedged the black object in a spot abutting it to the glass of the solar power source. He continued around the outer perimeter of panels, placing a cube under each, then moved in toward the middle. While placing a cube on the innermost ring of panels, he heard a mechanical groan from the platform holding the battery in the center of the array. Seb removed three cubes from the bag and stuck them in his pocket. He went to the battery, picked a cube from the bag, and placed it on the platform next to the structure. Shortly after, the platform began to lower. Seb watched it disappear into the ground and peered into the open hole.

I hope Jinuh didn't want this back. Seb hung the bag over the edge of the hole, rocked it back and forth like a pendulum, then finally let go. He stood, took the three cubes from his pocket, and placed two under the remaining solar panels. He heard the ground groan again as a new battery was raised into place. Once he was sure the platform was finished moving, Seb placed the remaining cube next to the new battery.

Seb took a deep breath. "Time to go," he announced.

He began to back away from the solar panel array while looking it over. Turning, he saw someone wandering through the plaza, heading straight for the solar panels. Seb ran over to them, shouting, "Hi!" and grabbing them by the arm. Their lack of reaction made it obvious they were Global AI-controlled. He yanked them back, spinning them around to change their course. Once the person walked away, a relieved Seb began jogging to the entry path of the plaza to depart.

When Seb arrived at the sidewalk, he looked at the band on his wrist, checking the time. Immediately, he heard a boom, followed by two dozen more, one at a time.

A hyper taxi stopped in front of Seb. He grinned, then boarded the vehicle. Seb sat, looking out the window at his achievement, a billowing cloud of smoke rising in the air.

Seb sent a message to the Syndicate.

It's done.

He leaned back in his seat, and closed his eyes.

CHAPTER 19

Seb moaned as he opened his eyes when the hyper taxi came to a sudden stop outside of Jinuh's complex. He looked out the window to see Jinuh pacing.

After deboarding, Seb immediately asked, "Why are you out here?"

"I have too much energy right now to go sit still in there." Jinuh pointed toward their building. "And the rest of the group is going to come back here."

Seb cocked his head. "Zell's not staying in Nullity?"

"No. He decided to bring everyone here. He chirped while I was on my way back. Said they were done, met up at the edge of Nullity, and decided it would be better to hide out here instead of staying there. They have a longer trip, but I expect them all soon."

"Great. Everything went as planned for you?"

Jinuh grinned. "Those GAIers were still there, but you weren't, so they stayed in place. I dropped off my goodies and left. I was down the street before I heard the pops. The few people in that building sitting overtop the West Side Plaza came running out. Well, probably not the GAI ones. They're probably still protecting the remains." They chuckled. "But yes, everything is good." Jinuh threw two thumbs up in the air.

"Nice to see you too," Zell announced as the other three members of the group arrived outside of Jinuh's.

Danish bent over, rubbing his legs. "Too much walking. Why could we not stay at your place, Zell?"

"I could have left you there, but you'd have to sleep outside."

Danish plopped down on the sidewalk. "Anywhere is good to rest right now."

Listina asked, "Can we go inside? I don't think we should be out here."

Jinuh walked to the entrance of the complex, opened the door, and gestured for everyone to go in.

"I just sat down," bemoaned Danish.

"Suit yourself," Jinuh said, walking through the door after the others.

Danish caught up as they were beginning to get on the platforms taking them to Jinuh's floor.

Seb's audiophone chirped as he stepped onto a platform by himself. He looked at his wristband and squealed when he saw the display.

"It's Dee! Everyone, it's Dee." Seb noticed no one could hear him, but hopped with excitement, causing the platform to wobble. He steadied himself, grabbing onto the railing. He answered the call.

"Dee! We only just finished. I can't believe it worked. Come join us. We're at —"

"Sebby. Calm down. Slow down," Dee responded monotonically. "When are you going to join us? We need you."

Seb slumped down. He barely noticed the others stepping off their platforms onto Jinuh's floor. Seb crawled from his moving platform, just making it to the open hall as it continued to ascend. He curled into a ball.

"Seb!" yelled Listina, after looking back. "What's wrong? Hey, everyone, help."

The rest turned around, having been unaware of what Seb was doing.

"Is he all right?" asked Danish.

"Get up, Seb," commanded Zell.

"I thought I heard him say something about Dee," Listina said. "Then I looked back and saw him like this."

Jinuh bent over his friend. "Seb, hey, what's wrong?"

"Dee," Seb mumbled, pointing at his ear.

Jinuh looked at the band on Seb's wrist. They faced the others. "It says Dee." Jinuh crouched next to him and put a hand on his shoulder. "What about Dee, Seb?"

"It didn't work."

"What didn't work?"

"She's still GAI."

"Are you sure?"

Seb whimpered.

"Come on, Seb. Let's get you up and inside."

Jinuh and Zell grabbed Seb by the arms and slowly lifted him. They led him to Jinuh's dwelling.

"Listy, get the door for us, please?" Jinuh asked.

She ran over and complied with the request.

Jinuh and Zell helped Seb inside and onto a seat.

"She's still talking, but it's not her," Seb mumbled.

"What?" asked Zell.

"It's not her. It's not her. It's not her," Seb repeated, getting louder each time. "It's not her!"

Jinuh reached behind Seb's ear and tapped twice, disconnecting the call from Dee.

"It's not her." Seb slumped forward.

Listina spoke up. "Maybe the disruption isn't complete yet. Maybe we need more time. Maybe we need to wait."

Seb raised his head.

"Uh, yeah, right," Danish jumped in. "Can it work that fast?"

Seb stood, shoulders slumped. "I—I don't know. I feel it. Like nothing has changed. Like we did all of that for nothing. It seemed like the GAI was taunting me, using Dee's voice."

"I don't know if that's possible," Jinuh interjected.

"Why not? We don't know everything it's capable of. Maybe it's laughing at us right now," Seb prompted. "Zell, where are the plans? We had to have missed something. I know it."

Zell quickly looked away, stroking his chin.

"Zell?" Seb reached his hand out.

"I don't have them, Seb."

"What? Why? Zell, where are they? Did you lose them?"

"Not lost. In my dwelling."

"Why are they there? When did you do that?"

"On an earlier trip back to Nullity. I stopped in and left them there. Hidden, of course. We knew our plans. I didn't need them."

Seb charged Zell. Listina backed out of the way as Jinuh stepped in between, reaching their arms out to stop him.

"You're not getting through me," Jinuh huffed. "I'm bigger."

"But he——" Seb began.

"There's another copy," Jinuh calmly reminded.

He stopped pushing into Jinuh. "There's another—there's another! That's right. I didn't trust Zell to not lose the original."

Seb backed away and headed to the kitchen. He went to the display still sitting on the counter and turned it on. After signaling 'Okay' to get into the device, he tapped an image of the duplicate plans. He sighed in relief as the display showed the floating copy.

He stared at the image for a few minutes, poking his finger through the places the members of the Syndicate visited.

"Find anything?" asked Listina from behind Seb.

Startled, Seb's hand flew up through the image as he quickly spun. "Listy, phew. You scared me." He caught his breath. "No, nothing. Just these five places." Seb turned back to find the image had expanded. He tilted his head. "Listy, what does this look like?"

"Um. Two lightning bolts?"

"Yeah. Has that always . . ." Seb pinched the image to make it smaller. He smacked his forehead with the palm of his hand. "I thought it was a tree. These two zigzags facing each other. I assumed Dee felt like adding some details." Seb made the picture larger again. "But those are definitely lightning bolts. We had a sixth place. The lightning rod building next to Dee's weather factory. How did I miss this?"

"We all did," came Zell's voice. "I never noticed that either. It absolutely looked like a tree. But its location compared to the others . . . It's the lightning rod building."

Seb started walking out of the kitchen toward the entryway.

"Where are you going?" asked Jinuh as Seb walked by.

"Seb, stop!" Zell called out.

"I have another place to go."

Zell posed the question they were all thinking. "Seb, what are you going to do? We're out of cubes."

Seb reached into his back pocket and removed the black cube he had stashed earlier.

"Okay, but it's late. We should plan this out. What if you can't get in?"

Seb threw his head back. "You're right, but——"

"Think it through for a minute," pleaded Listina.

Seb slumped down, back against the entry door. He checked the time. "Jinuh?"

"Yeah, Seb?"

"Can I crash here for a few hours?"

"Of course. You all can if you want," Jinuh responded.

Seb rocked, overcome with a mixture of defeat and exhaustion. "Thanks." He picked himself up from the floor and went to a nearby chair. He plopped down, leaned his head back, and closed his eyes. "You all won't bother me. I'll let myself out when I wake."

"Sure, Seb. But I think we'll be coming with you."

"Mmm," Seb mumbled.

"Good night, Seb," whispered Jinuh.

"Good night."

CHAPTER 20

Seb opened his eyes, initially unsure of where he was. He noticed a jacket had been draped over his body, and squinted to look at the display on the wall in front of him.

"The moon is fading, it's almost mor—"

Seb's eyes widened as he remembered where he was and why. He noticed the other members of the Syndicate asleep in nearby chairs and on the floor.

He rose slowly and studied the display on the wall again. Taking note of the temperature shown, he put on the jacket he had been given and tiptoed to the door. He turned back and saw Listina raise her head while cracking open an eye. Seb put his finger to his lips, hoping Listina would remain quiet. She nodded at him sleepily and put her head back down. Seb carefully opened the door and stepped out. He gently pulled it closed behind him, then sprinted to the platform lift.

"Okay, I need to make it to the lightning rod building," Seb said to himself as he stepped on a platform going down. "I don't know what to do after that though. I've seen it, but I don't know what's in it."

Seb stepped out of Jinuh's complex and looked out at the street lit by the rising sun. Something seemed different. He watched a few people walk past him. Half turned at the next building and started walking back. Seb kept his eye on the returning group as they were coming toward him. All continuing past. He saw them stop at the building just after Jinuh's, turn, and come back again.

Something did happen, but not the right something. It's like they're waiting for the next step in their script before they can continue.

Seb watched as the people walked forward, stopped, turned, and came back again. He started heading in the direction of Dee's weather factory and the lightning rod building. A stopped hyper taxi's doors were opening and closing, over and over. In between each action, he could make out a few words.

"Welcome!"

The door shut, then reopened.

"Joining us."

Seb continued walking. "I'm not riding to the building," he realized. He focused on his shoes. "And the half-wheels are at home."

Seb went on, avoiding the Global AI-controlled people breaking pattern along his walk.

He passed another hyper taxi stopped in the road. He saw a few people trying to get on as the doors opened, but denied entry as they closed again.

"You should start walking," he yelled out.

Seb arrived at the weather factory as the sun was positioning itself in the sky. On top of the next building, he could see a large lightning rod sticking up high. He continued until he was in front of its entrance.

He breathed in deep as he grabbed the door handle and pulled. There was no movement. He pulled again, getting the same result. Seb groaned and stepped back. He scanned the nearby area, almost wishing Zell was with him, but not wanting the attitude that came with the request.

Seb stood, staring at the door. He wasn't sure if he'd ever seen anyone go in or out of the building before. He closed his eyes and tapped on his head.

Seb suddenly felt someone run into him, nearly causing him to tip over. His eyes shot open, looking at who had hit him.

"Hey!" Seb yelled, before recognizing the person. "Anson?" he asked quizzically as his eyes narrowed. "Ugh." Seb backed up to look at the building again while waiting for Anson to continue past.

"Inside," said Anson.

"What?" Seb watched Anson walk to the door, grab the handle, and open it.

"How did you—" Seb began in amazement. He shook off the question and ran to the door as it was closing.

Anson lifted his arm, stretched out his hand, and wiggled his fingers while accentuating his fingertips.

Seb first saw the three lit lights on Anson's arm before the action registered. "Your fingers let you in?"

Anson wiggled them again.

"Um. Okay," he responded in confusion.

Seb followed Anson through the empty lobby and to a platform lift that went straight to the top with no additional stop-off points.

"Up," said Anson.

Seb looked toward the ceiling of the tall building. "Of course. It's never down, is it?"

Anson stepped on a platform as it arrived, causing Seb to do the same.

"Where are we going?" asked Seb.

"Up," Anson replied.

Seb began to hear sounds coming from above, indicating a bustling of people. He noticed a pathway connecting the building he stood in to the weather factory next door.

"What are they doing?" Seb wondered aloud. "They're coming from the weather factory. What happens in this building?"

Seb received no response from Anson.

The platform arrived at the top, bringing Seb and Anson to the stream of people walking across the path. Anson stepped off the platform and began to follow the crowd. Seb raced after him. They entered a large room filled with people facing a wall that stretched as far as he could see. As newcomers filed in, they stopped and stood in empty spots along the wall.

Seb rubbed his eyes before looking closer. The wall was covered in buttons with numbers above them. The surrounding people were reaching up and pressing the buttons as they lit. The corresponding light immediately went out.

"I've seen this before," he said.

The two walked until Anson finally stopped at an open position near the end of the wall.

"You," Anson announced.

"Me?" questioned Seb.

Receiving no response, he walked to the wall and looked at the numbers above the buttons. He noticed a sequential group of digits with a missing button below each, leaving an open hole in its place.

"841410. 841411. 841412," Seb began reading off. He continued scanning the wall for a clue as to what he should do when he found a light shining from an opening among the dark ones.

"You," said Anson again.

Seb read the number above the light. "841416. My lucky number. Or unlucky number, maybe." He tried to stick his finger in the hole, but couldn't reach the back. "What am I supposed to do?" he asked Anson. "There's no button to press."

Seb stuck his hands in his pockets and stretched out his shoulders while thinking. He moved his fingers around, hitting the minerals he was carrying, and felt the metal ball he had added earlier. Seb pulled out all of the items, laying them flat in his palm. He fingered each before taking the ball and holding it in front of the hole in the wall. He pushed the ball into the opening until it stopped, protruding slightly.

Seb pressed the makeshift button and quickly closed his eyes, unsure of what would happen. He opened an eye slowly. "Hmm. nothing."

"Done!" announced Anson, startling Seb.

As he turned to look at Anson, he noticed that no new lights on the wall were illuminating. Everyone stopped pushing buttons.

Anson began to walk away.

"Hey, where are you going?" yelled Seb.

"Up."

"There isn't any more *up*."

Seb followed Anson down a hallway and to a ladder.

"Up," repeated Anson.

Seb's eyes traced the ladder to an access panel high above them. He nearly collapsed at the sight.

"I'm barely okay on a platform lift. I can't climb a ladder that high."

"Up."

Seb looked at Anson, then up again.

He heard a beep from his Rollascreen. There was a message from Listina.

Where did you go? We're all outside the lightning rod building, but the door doesn't open. Where are you hiding? I thought you just went out for a caffeine booster, but you never came back. Don't we have to come here to finish Dee's plan? Aren't we trying to get her back? Did you give up on us?

Seb put the device back in his pocket, closed his eyes tight, then nervously glanced up again.

"Up?" Seb squeaked.

"Up."

He began to climb the ladder, looking down once and regretting it. "I can't do this," he called out.

"Up."

"I can't!" Seb caught sight of Anson below him and the three solid lights on his arm. He thought of the lights he saw on Dee's arm when he visited her last.

"Up."

Seb gulped and started climbing again. "This is for her."

He made it to the access panel, pulled the lever, and popped open the cover. He stuck his head out and scanned his surroundings.

"The lightning rod," Seb gasped. He climbed the rest of the way up and out, then walked to the towering structure. He looked around, taking in the view.

"I've never been up this high. It's—it's amazing."

Seb focused on the lightning rod while he sat down to reset his equilibrium. Feeling a bulge in his back pocket, he reached and pulled out a black cube. His face lit up.

Seb opened the top of the cube and set a timer for ten minutes. He took one more look around the sun-covered city. After closing the lid, he placed it at the base of the lightning rod. He then hurried to the access panel, carefully descended the ladder, and stopped in front of Anson.

"Done," Anson said.

"Done," responded Seb. "But we have to go."

Seb led Anson back through the hall, past the people facing the wall of dark buttons, and to the platform lift. They rode down to the ground floor, hurried through the lobby, and to the doors.

Seb pushed on the door, but it didn't move.

"Anson, can you help?" Seb asked.

Anson walked to the door, put his hand against a square panel near the handle, then pushed. The door flew open, revealing the members of the Syndicate.

"Anson?" questioned Jinuh as they exited.

"Seb?" asked Listina. "I didn't think you actually came here. I thought you left."

"We need to move back," Seb shouted while looking up at the top of the building.

He began to jog, pulling Anson with him. The other four followed closely behind, all confused.

"Where are we going?" shouted Jinuh.

Once Seb was several buildings down the street, he stopped, turned, and said, "Watch."

A puff of smoke started to rise from the top of the building. A metallic groan could be heard as the lightning rod began to tip. It fell over and landed on top of the weather factory, creating a bridge between the two structures.

"Seb, what did you do?" Danish asked with wide eyes.

"He finished!" announced an excited voice.

The group faced the sound. They all gasped when they realized it came from Anson.

"Hey, when's the next original thing we're doing?" Anson asked.

"Seb, h-how——" Jinuh stuttered.

Zell walked over to Anson and threw his arms around him.

"Hi, Zell. Nice to see you too." Anson patted him on the back.

Seb's eyes widened at the sight. "I have to go."

"Now where?" Jinuh called out.

"I have to go!"

"Should we come?" Listina asked.

"Not far," Seb yelled back as he ran as hard as he could past the damaged lightning rod building.

CHAPTER 21

Seb sprinted to the door of the weather factory and pulled the handle. Relieved that the door opened, he immediately ran inside.

He passed the animated images in the lobby of the building, only turning to look when lightning cracked on a display, briefly catching his attention. He returned his focus to the platform lift and darted to it. He ran past several people waiting to board the lift and jumped on a platform as it was beginning its ascent with another passenger.

"Hello?" questioned the person. "Running late too?"

"Um. Uh. Huh? Oh. No. I'm visiting someone."

The person smiled in response and stepped off the platform at the next level.

Seb called out, "Thanks for the ride." He continued going up to the top floor.

After arriving, he found the lab where he'd seen Dee working a few days prior and peered in the window. There was no one at Dee's desk. Seb pulled the door handle before remembering he needed someone to open it for him. He looked down the hall in both directions, then back in the lab window. He began rapidly knocking on the door, hoping to get someone's attention. Finally, he saw a man's head poke out from behind a display and look toward Seb. He waved frantically and knocked again. The head disappeared again, prompting Seb to knock harder. He saw the person stand and start toward the door. Seb stopped and took a step back, impatiently waiting for the man to arrive.

They opened the door and began to speak, "Sorry. I needed to finish my—"

Seb burst through the door and ran into the lab.

"Dee!" he called out, looking around. "Dee!"

Seb went to Dee's desk. The chair in front of it was pushed back and the display was lit.

"Dee!" he yelled again, scanning the room. "Where is she?" he screamed at the man who opened the door. "I can't find her. She has to be here. I can see she was here. Look, her screen is still on. And her chair. And . . . Please tell me. Tell me where —"

"Sebby! Calm down," came a voice from behind.

Seb quickly spun around and stared at Dee. "Are you . . ." He closed his eyes for a passing heartbeat and took a deep breath. He reopened them and looked at Dee again. "Are you, you?" he asked.

Dee cocked her head. "I'm not you. So, yes, that means I'm me."

Seb threw his arms around Dee. "We did it. It worked."

"What worked, Seb? And why are you here? This is my job." She stepped back. "You don't even know where I—Zell. He's the only one who knows I work here. Where is he?" she demanded.

"Zell's outside. Everyone's outside. The entire Syndicate."

"What? All of them? Why?"

"You don't remember?"

"Remember what, Seb?" Dee asked, confused. She furrowed her brow in thought. "I was in my complex. Someone was there. Three people. They put me in a personal transport, and . . . and now I'm here. How am I here, Seb? How did I get here?"

"Let's go, Dee. I'll tell you everything. I'll show you everything."

"But I've got to . . ." Dee looked at her desk. "The weather."

Seb pointed at the man still staring, dumbfounded. "I'm sure he can take care of it. Right?" Seb faced the man. "Right?"

The man nodded.

"Come." Seb reached his hand out to Dee.

Dee took it and followed him out the door.

They went to the platform lift and stepped on one going down.

"Seb, what's going on?"

Bouncing with impatience at the speed of the platform, Seb responded, "You'll see after we get outside."

Dee looked at Seb, confusion written all over her face.

The two got off the platform at the lobby and he led her outside.

"Look up," Seb said, tilting his head to the sky.

She followed Seb's line of sight and saw the lightning rod lying across the two buildings.

"Why's the transmitter down?" she asked.

"Transmitter?" Seb repeated. "The lightning rod?"

"It's not actually a lightning rod. It sends the signal for these." Not removing her gaze from the top of the building, Dee held up her arm and tapped at the spot where her lights would be. "When did that happen?"

"Right before—"

"Dee!" they heard from a distance.

They turned toward the sound to see Jinuh sprinting toward them.

"It worked, Seb?" Jinuh asked.

"Hi, Jinuh," Dee answered, puzzled. "What worked? What's going on? Why are you all here?"

Jinuh looked up. "That's why. Your plan."

"My what?" questioned Dee.

"The plan you left for us," Zell chimed in, walking up behind Jinuh.

"I don't . . ." Dee paused and closed her eyes. "In my parent's . . ."

"Yes. Seb and I found it. It appears that it's done," Zell continued.

"But why didn't I do it with you? Why did you do this without telling me?" she demanded.

"She doesn't know?" Zell asked Seb.

"Not yet."

"Um, you were . . ." Zell started.

"You were part of the Global AI, Dee." Seb finished. "Not in control. Three lights. Not you. You couldn't help us."

"You did the reset?" Dee's eyes lit up with excitement.

"The what?" the friends now surrounding her all asked.

"The reset. The end statement. Everything went back. Returned to the previous configuration."

Seb shrugged along with the rest. "We followed your plan. We had to get you back."

Dee wrapped her arms around Seb, then pulled in Zell, Danish, Jinuh, and finally Anson. "Anson? You're . . ."

Anson, looking confused, blurted out, "Hi, Dee!"

She turned, nearly speechless, to Listina. "And you helped too? But you didn't want anything to do with—"

Listina gave a tentative smile. "I wouldn't be here if not for you."

Dee looked up at the makeshift bridge across the two buildings. "Um, we should probably get out of here."

Seb chuckled. "It's about time you realized that." He turned to Jinuh. "Back to your dwelling?"

"Sure. We started there. We should end there."

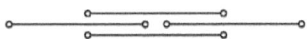

"Who did you chirp?" Seb asked Dee as they were walking into Jinuh's dwelling.

"My parents," she responded, relieved. "They're themselves. And I got them to call me Dee, not Deidra. It's amazing. Thank you, Seb."

He blushed. "Let's go in."

Seb led her to the kitchen where the rest of the group was waiting.

"Tell me how you all did this," Dee requested.

Everyone began talking at once, pointing to different places in the kitchen and miming their actions.

"Whoa, uh, I got none of that." Dee chuckled.

"Seb, you tell it," Zell's voice rose above the rest. "You led us."

"Phew," Seb exclaimed before rubbing the top of his head. "All right."

Seb went to the display on the kitchen counter, pressed a button on the side, then made an 'Okay' sign over it.

"Is that—that's mine!" Dee said. "How did you get it? How did you know to do that?"

"You showed me. Somehow you still helped. I couldn't figure it out, but you showed me even while under GAI control. But look." Seb brought up the copy of the plans. "We found these, thanks to Zell. Everyone played a part. Jinuh got us the components needed for your cube design. Zell got the wiring. Danish and Listy took part in Nullity, and Anson got me into the lightning rod, er, transmitter building." Seb turned to Anson. "I'm not sure how you were able to guide me along."

Dee blushed. "That was my fault. I knew Anson worked in that building, and . . ." She looked at him. "Sorry, Anson, but I knew the GAI would get to you soon. I began this plan long ago. Before my parents were converted." She faced the group. "I would have Anson go through the building once a week, leading to each spot, and repeating the commands, hoping to lock that into his script in case I wasn't the one there."

Everyone stared at her silently.

"You figured out everything," Zell said with amazement.

"And you all did too," she replied.

Anson stood with his mouth agape.

"Anson, are you all right?" Dee asked.

Anson nodded before asking, "Who are these two?" He pointed at Seb and Listina.

Dee chuckled. "New friends. It's so good to have my old friend back to add to my new ones."

"Welcome, new friends."

"Anything else, Seb?" Dee asked.

"I'm sure there is, but it can wait."

He looked around the room and grinned. "Anyone up for a game of charades?"

Danish groaned, breaking his silence. "How about something original? Something I am good at."

"What's that?" asked Anson. "Charades?"

"Oh. Yes. Maybe one round then," Danish yielded. "Maybe I will win this time." The friends all laughed.

Dee yawned. "Actually, I'd really like to get some rest. I feel like I haven't slept in a week. Can we do this another time?"

"Of course," Seb answered. "I'll go back with you."

The members of the Syndicate all said their goodbyes, promising to find something original to do together.

Seb and Dee began walking to the door before Jinuh cut them off. They held out a tube to Dee.

"This is yours. I'm done with it cluttering up my kitchen."

She took the tube and laughed. "Thanks."

Jinuh bowed. "Adieu. See you soon."

Seb led Dee outside and to the edge of the sidewalk. He smiled when he saw a hyper taxi heading in the direction of his dwelling.

"Come on, let's get you home," Seb said to Dee.

"But I'm that way." Dee pointed the other way.

"Not anymore. I'll show you. Assuming this transport works."

Dee gave him a confused look.

"There's a lot to explain still, but um, the hyper taxis weren't working correctly for a bit, and everyone was out to get me."

"What?"

"I'm exaggerating slightly. It's been an interesting week."

They boarded the hyper taxi to head toward their dwellings. Grinning to himself, Seb kept shifting his focus back and forth between Dee's eyes and the single blinking light on her arm. She stared blankly in the direction of their driver, clearly distracted. Once they deboarded, Seb led her to the complex across the street from his own.

"You're here now," Seb said.

"I . . . I knew I was going to come here, but it was supposed to be a surprise to you. I was still moving from my old place."

"Someone did it for you. All of your stuff is here."

"Uh, then maybe I shouldn't stay at this one long."

Seb pouted, then laughed. "I'll let you rest. We have all the time to catch up now."

Dee grinned. "Thanks, Seb. It's good to be back." She began to walk toward the door of her complex.

"D—Dee?" Seb stuttered, his mouth suddenly dry.

She turned to face him.

"Kiss me?" he asked.

She stepped toward Seb and wrapped her arms around him. She whispered in his ear, "Maybe another time." She let go, winked, and walked into her building.

Seb grinned.

He went across the street to his complex and into his dwelling. After plopping down on a nearby chair, he opened his Rollascreen. His finger passed back and forth over the messages icon, a desire to contact Dee tugging at him, and the news icon. He settled for the latter.

February 26th, 2333

New Global AI additions: 0
Global AI removals:
> *<Exceeded. Incorrect return statement received.>*

Seb smiled. "Good."

He settled deeper into the chair.

"I don't need this anymore," he said as he took off the jacket he was wearing. "I'll return it to Jinuh later."

Laying the jacket next to himself, Seb saw a flicker of light from the corner of his eye. He looked down to see the third light on his arm blinking. He closed his eyes and fell asleep.

The End

EPILOGUE: Patch Tuesday

"Seb, you don't have to do this! You don't have to prove anything else to me." Dee looked nervous.

"You're the one that pushed me into that tube the first time. What's different about this?"

"*I* haven't actually jumped out of a plane before!" she said, yelling over the sound of air whipping around the cabin.

"I know, all right. But we can't go back to the indoor skydiving place. That got shut down when all of the other places changed." Seb began counting on his fingers, recalling each of the locations she had taken him, before stopping and holding his arm out in front of himself. "But we have to figure out how to get this light to go dark again. I need as much time as I can get with you."

Dee grabbed his arm and gently ran her fingers over the blinking light.

With his free hand, Seb reached under her chin and lifted her head. The touch prompted her to look into his eyes. Taking a moment to match her gaze, he finally asked, "Are you ready?"

"Definitely not." Dee grabbed Seb around his waist and pulled him close. She kissed him, tightening her grip as each second passed. After finally letting go, she walked to the open door of the airplane. She turned to face Seb. With arms crossed over her chest, she leaned back and let the momentum take her out the opening.

Seb grinned. He ran to the door and dove after her.

ABOUT THE AUTHOR

Brian has an overabundance of hobbies—including some that crop up in his writing—and ventured into publicly releasing his stories several years ago. After being fascinated by the process, he continued with no end in sight.

Selected is a collection of stories that spans different periods of time in Brian's life. While some of them work as standalone stories, they all blend together into one dystopian future.

Also, he hates heights.